EL PANTERA

No-one said it would be easy

Gabriel Lee

Kmaccab Publishing

ISBN-13:9798447589370

Cover design by: Gabriel Lee
Library of Congress Control Number: 2018675309
Printed in the United States of America

I dedicate this book to the Police Officers, Worldwide, who continually attempt to maintain law and order in increasing difficult and dangerous circumstances.

I would like to thank my friend and ex colleague, Steve Howe, for his excellent insight into the methods used to conceal drugs on ships and the underwater search methods used by British and other police forces.

Also many thanks to my friends Maria Harris and Alan Pearson who have helped throughout the writing of this book.

CONTENTS

INTRODUCTION

Steve Bond was a Detective Sergeant in the Newcastle upon Tyne Crime Team. He was sent to Panama, to liaise with the NCA (National Crime Agency) officers based in Panama, to investigate the murder of Filipe Lopez, a young man from the town. It started a series of events that culminated with the police in the UK, Panama, USA and Venezuela working together, combating a serial killer, a Columbian drugs cartel and large-scale drug dealing.

Steve developed a relationship during the investigation and also a desire to work in different countries after his Latin American experiences.

Following the Newcastle Crime Team's closure, he began working as a Liaison Officer with the NCA. He was due to be posted to a Latin American country, when something happened which shocked Steve immensely, his posting was changed to Madrid, Spain.

After a short time in Spain, working with his friend and ex colleague, Sarah, from Newcastle Crime Team, a chance meeting started their investigation into the Organised Crime Teams who were operating in the Costa's. Working with the Guardia Civil and Policia Nacional they began the operation known as the 'Devil's Crossroads.'

The operation was a huge success for those involved, dismantling three OCG's, however, it had only a small impact on the constant wave of people, drugs, and weapons entering Spain illegally.

There was little time to enjoy this success however, as whilst back in Newcastle upon Tyne, celebrating with his old colleagues, a phone call from someone unexpected, ensured there was more work to be done and big decisions to be made.

No-one said it would be easy.

FORWARD

Thursday 30th March 2017

Steve and Sarah had left the office in the Embassy in Madrid and had walked the short distance to The Covent Garden pub. They were welcomed by the staff, who knew them so well, as they walked through the open doors into the bar area. They took a seat in a small section where three tables had been reserved. It was a bright afternoon and the sunshine and warmth flooded through the open doorway. Steve again checked his wristwatch as the first two pints of Stella Artois were carried to the table and placed on beer mats by one of the bar staff. They sat facing the open doorway.

Their second pint had been placed on the table when they heard them, before they saw them. "Hey man, it just looks like a proper pub. Billy, do you want an Estrella, boss what do you want?" Alan walked through the doorway blocking the sunlight.

They stayed in their seats in the segregated corner, watching and smiling as Alan walked to the bar, he only had eyes for the beer pumps. Facing one of the barmaids, he tried, slowly, "Hola, have you, any Estrella or San Miguel, por favor?" He heard the laughter coming from the corner and looked in that direction. "Whoa!" he shouted and walked quickly towards Sarah and Steve who were now out of their seats. He went to Sarah first, obviously, he gave her a tight hug, cuddle, and a kiss on her cheek, then a big handshake and buddy hug with Steve. "How man, this is great, do they sell nowt Spanish like?" They were all laughing as Billy entered the bar pulling two flight bags and the boss followed carrying his document bag and pulling his flight bag.

They all embraced each other then took the seats around the tables, they were promptly attended to by the bar staff. The boss, Detective Superintendent Colin Tinkler, had travelled to take part in the debrief of Operation Devil's Crossroads. Alan and Billy had hoped to be involved in the debrief but had not been included on the required list. They had taken some time off and by chance, had booked the same flight as the boss and by chance, Sarah had managed to obtain match tickets for Real Madrid against Alaves on the Sunday afternoon. Alan and Billy were stopping in the accommodation used by Steve, who would share with Sarah for the weekend. The boss was on expenses and had his hotel and flight paid for; the conversation flowed about everything, apart from the operation, that was for tomorrow. The two lads were excited and determined to enjoy themselves, the pints of Stella were coming very regularly. Steve, Sarah, and the boss were more conservative in their drinks, they needed to be sober in the morning.

It was 5:20pm when the last of the seats at the tables would be filled. Leon entered and joined the group, his widening smile showed he was happy to be back with them, especially Steve and Sarah. He hugged Sarah and gave her kisses on each cheek.

"Hiya candy features, are you still keeping Lauren happy?" She gave him a smile and a wink.

"I try my best, she seems happy." the grin widened.

Leon threw a light punch into the right ribs of Steve, who gave a little wince and they both laughed and hugged, their small reunion was now complete.

Friday 31st March

Sarah had collected the paper documents that were required to be circulated to those present at the debrief, they were placed in the document case, along with the tablet that would be used for visual displays. The debrief was being held at the Guardia Civil headquarters on Calle Alcalá. Sergento Primero Ivan Fidel Sanchez would lead the debrief, the Senior officer in charge would be Brigada Cuéllar. The British officers attending along with Sarah would be the Senior Liaison officer Bert Ingham, Steve, Leon, Rajid Badia from NCA, and Detective Superintendent Tinkler. Policia Nacional officers would also be present.

At 11:00am they were all present in their seats in the conference room, having already exchanged pleasantries over coffee or cold drinks in the reception area. Ivan had taken the chance to kiss Sarah on both cheeks and give her a small hug whilst smiling towards Steve, who had returned the smile and both men shook hands warmly.

Brigada Cuéllar was wearing his dress uniform, an exemplar of immaculate appearance. He opened the debrief by extending a warm greeting to all of those present, then expressed his pride and gratitude to all the officers, who had contributed in the excellent result obtained by those involved in Operation Devil's Crossroads. He was stood on a raised platform next to Ivan and Sarah who were sat at a table with the computer and tablets. He paused and then indicating the two officers continued, "I cannot speak highly enough of the tireless work, constant liaison and communication these two officers performed throughout the entire operation, to maintain everyone with up-to-date intelligence and information, wherever, in Spain or England." He took two rolls of paper wrapped in red ribbon from a box at the side of the table and indicated for Sarah and Ivan to stand. He then handed one roll to Ivan, shook his hand then saluted him. Those seated, stood in unison and applauded. Ivan stepped back as the Brigada stepped towards Sarah, he handed her the roll, shook her hand gently, kissed her on both cheeks then stood back and gave her a salute. Ivan was leading the applause for Sarah with those present, as her cheeks flushed tears of happiness and embarrassment began to fall down her cheeks. The presentation had been filmed and photographed. Sarah for once was lost for words, for a short time anyway.

The Brigada took his seat in the front row facing the two, now embarrassed presenters. Ivan regained his composure and started the debrief. He commenced by giving an update on the Spanish arrests, all of the persons were still in custody and the evidence files were mostly completed. Kevin Wilson was now housed in the Malaga Penitentiary, having been moved from the hospital wing. The girls Anwuli, Nneka, Sade and Isioma were still in safe care and being looked after, they had indicated during welfare discussions that they wanted to return to Nigeria. The deaths of the Montenegrin clan at the villa had been closed with no new evidence forthcoming. He then gave some surprising information. Sarah was already smiling, as she knew and had known for a few days, 'Trigger' whose name was Colin Ball, was to be released with no further action on his next appearance at court. The prosecution had accepted, (had been persuaded by CITCO, the Intelligence Centre against Terrorism and Organised Crime) that he was coerced into his actions through fear and intimidation of his family, Ball was not aware of this. Steve was also smiling when he pointed his finger at Sarah and shook his head.

Sarah took over, she updated the audience that those arrested in East Lancashire and those connected with the collection and deliveries from the Birtley locations were still in custody. James Arrowsmith had subsequently been arrested when attempting to leave the country in Hull and was also in custody, the CPS were confident of convictions. The Albanian was still in custody awaiting trial for the murder of Mawson; the girls rescued from the house in Gateshead had been taken to an illegal immigration centre awaiting their applications to be heard. The police officer who shot and killed the armed Albanian, was still suspended from duty; Ivan was shaking his head in disbelief.

The boss, Superintendent Tinkler, added his thanks to everyone who took part in the operation as did Bert Ingham and Rajid Badia.

They all returned to the reception area where non-alcoholic drinks and snacks were available. Ivan and Sarah received plenty of good wishes and gentle pats on their shoulders, this was always a good time to develop relations and friendships after a successful completion to a difficult operation. Slowly, the officers started to drift away to return to their offices, home, or in the case of the UK group, The Covent Garden.

Sunday 1st April

It was a late Sunday morning breakfast in Steve's apartment. The boss had left early from his hotel for his flight back to Newcastle, nobody was sure where Leon was, Steve hadn't bothered ringing him but had sent a message 'Breakfast at mine 11.30'. Sarah had showered and was dressing for breakfast, grey sweatshirt and black training bottoms. Alan and Billy were out for a walk to help clear their heads, while Steve was preparing the breakfast.

It had been a fun weekend. They took the tourist bus which Steve and Sarah had never been on, they saw so much which was new, so many different tapas bars in different squares, it had been non-stop, fun, laughs and drinks. The door opened with Alan, Billy and Leon walking in together much to Steve's surprise. They were followed a minute later by Sarah who brought some fresh orange juice and a large pot of fresh coffee. Steve had heated up some local supermarket tortilla, cooked a mixture of tomatoes, red peppers, onions, mushrooms and ham, and fried some eggs. There was also fresh warm bread and butter on the table, "Help yourself guys."

After breakfast had been eaten and cleared away, Sarah, Alan, and Billy got dressed for the match day experience. At least it was warm and sunny and they had plenty of time for the 3:15pm kick off. Leon and Steve arranged to meet up with them after the game. Sarah was wearing her white Real shirt and the scarf was tied around her wrist. Billy had brought his Sunderland shirt but at the last minute decided not to wear it, both lads deciding they would buy a Real shirt at the club shop, they decided to leave early to do some shopping.

The apartment was quiet, which was unusual for Steve and Leon until Leon broke the ice, “Okay, I’m not hearing anything. What is it you want to say?”

Steve shrugged it off, “What do you mean? What makes you think I want to say anything?”

Leon pointed his finger towards Steve, “You have something on your mind, something is bothering you.”

“What gives you that idea, where does that come from?”

“We’re never quiet. In the short time we have been working together, mates together, fight partners together, there has never been silence.” He paused, but there was no reply from Steve.

“What is it mate, what’s up?” He was looking straight at the face of Steve. He knew how Steve could look in different moods, it was in his training, but this was different. He stayed silent and waited.

Steve spoke slowly, “I’ve had a phone call from Maria. You know, the murderer from Panama.”

Without showing emotion, he was looking at Steve, “Yes, I know of Maria, how did she get your number?”

Steve was thinking before his reply, he knew there was no need to say keep this quiet, “A friend of Jessica’s, and mine I suppose.” There was silence again.

Leon asked, “And?”

“She wanted to meet.”

Leon reacted in surprise, looking directly at Steve, “The murderer, who is an escaped prisoner, who is probably responsible, no, is responsible for the murder of Jessica, wants to meet you? What did you say?"

"I told her it would be a bad idea."

Leon's mouth opened in shock, "What the fuck did you say that for?"

"I wouldn't be able to control my anger, I'd, I'd, want to kill her."

"You have to ring her back, get in touch with her. Me and you, we can sort this out."

Steve was shaking his head, "I don't want to involve anyone, not a mate anyway."

"Okay, okay," Leon held his hand up for Steve to be quiet, "I think I can understand that, what I can't understand is why she would want to meet you. She must know that the least you would do, would be to lock her up. That's proper life in jail, why the fuck would she do that?"

"She told me she knew who killed Jessica, that it was the same guy who killed Greg Simons the cop in L.A. I think I told you about him."

Leon, "You do know how much time we have spent together? We know more about each other than we do ourselves. Who is it then?"

"I don't know, I started asking questions and she went off the phone."

"Sometimes you're a better bad guy than old bill, what did you start asking questions for?"

"Look," Steve paused for thought, "I wasn't happy about it but she did say she would tell me where this guy was and what was happening."

Leon was being sympathetic, "Again, I can understand losing your rag. Imagine, a big-time criminal, informing on murderers and drug dealers, what's new in that? It's what we live for. Seriously here, can you get back in touch? We don't have to tell anyone about it, not yet, maybe not at all, just make some inroads, find out what she has or wants? She must want something. She can't get immunity, disappear maybe, did she say what she wanted?"

"Just revenge. She says she liked Jessica which I believe, that's why Jessica went to Panama, she says she tried to stop the gunman. But honestly, I'm scared about Sarah."

"Why Sarah? Is she threatened, what has she got to do with it?"

Steve was thinking hard, "How would she react if I did anything unlawful or went after the killer of Jessica for revenge?"

"Okay, okay, I can again understand that but it's simple, don't tell her. What would be unlawful if we are acting in self-defence, protecting ourselves?"

Steve "I never said you would be involved in anything, that's nowt, whatever I do is down to me, what I decide, my decision. You are not invited."

"Sorry mate, but I am involved now. You are doing nothing without me, you make the decisions but they better be better than the one to end the call. Get back in touch, I'll have your back 100 percent, I'm in. Just make inroads, like I say, then call in the locals wherever that may be and if they don't come, we have a decision to make, don't we?" Leon held out his right hand.

Steve took hold of his hand, they shook hands and embraced. He stood back from Leon, "I will make the call, I promise, but not for a few weeks. If she calls me meanwhile, I will talk to her. Thanks for that mate."

CHAPTER 1

Tuesday 25th April

The afternoon sun was shining down in the suburb of Barcelona. Steve was with Raul, an officer from Mossos d' Esquadera, the Catalan Police force. They were sat on high stools looking out of a vacant office window on the fourth floor, looking down onto the front door of the 'Xtreme Fitness Centre'. They both had binoculars hanging from around their necks resting on their chests and were also monitoring the screen which was showing the same picture from the installed camera. Steve checked his watch it was now 14:17, they had both been there for over six hours.

Raul was looking through his binoculars. "I think that is him walking past the Caixa bank towards the gym, grey hoodie and shorts, Barca baseball cap, carrying a dark sports holdall."

Steve immediately zoomed in with the camera onto the figure, "Yes, looks like him, can't get a clear look at his face."

Raul, immediately informed the arrest team who were parked nearby to go on standby but first the identity needed to be confirmed.

The subject of the observation was Michael Patterson from Middlesbrough in England, one of the top 100 on the NCA wanted list. He was wanted in connection with the importation of 60 kilos of cocaine and the murder of a gangland rival in Hartlepool. He had escaped custody by assaulting the guards in the dock of Teesside Crown Court, then running out of the court building and had been driven away from the court in a waiting car. He had been 'on the run' for over three years, which meant he was now thirty. His associates, including the driver of the car, had been convicted and were now serving long custodial sentences in prisons in the North of England.

Steve zoomed the camera in on the darkened glass entrance door which served as a mirror, as Patterson turned his back on Raul and Steve. He was looking directly at the door. "I think that's him." Steve said looking at the reflection. The shorts drawing the conclusion that he certainly wasn't Spanish.

"Si, si, si," Raúl replied. "Arrest team to phase two."

Two minutes had passed when Edgar, one of the officers involved, was seen to enter the gym carrying his holdall. The arrest team moved closer, closing in on the escape routes from the gym door. The fact that Edgar had not come back out of the gym within a short time, made the identification. At 16:04, Edgar exited the gym and placed a baseball cap on his head with the peak down his neck. Patterson would be behind him exiting the gym shortly.

They saw the signal, Raul gave the update, "Stand by, stand by, Edgar has confirmed Patterson. He should be leaving the gym soon, phase three, repeat phase three."

The team closed in on the door, workmen in overalls, a young couple with a pram, a man pushing a shopping trolley. The outer cordon was also set, belt and braces as Steve would often say. Other officers were sat in their unmarked cars very close to the gym. Edgar had entered a nearby fruit shop which was displaying their fruit on the street pavement.

The door opened, Patterson was full face on to the view of the camera and binoculars, again a further positive identification. Raul, "Subject is out, out, of the door and turned right towards Caixa bank walking on the pavement."

Patterson was looking at his mobile phone as he walked towards the two workmen, "Strike, strike" Raul gave the command.

The two officers took hold of Patterson. He was startled and shocked into action; the holdall and mobile phone were dropped immediately, he used his head and butted the officer who had hold of his right arm fully in the face, crunching his forehead into the officers' nose and cheek bones. The blow made him release his grip and fall immediately onto the ground. Patterson then used his ample strength to swing the officer holding onto his left arm backwards against the wall then instantly started thumping him hard in the head, throat, and body. The other officers were running the short distance to the assistance of their colleague. The female officer drew her firearm and pointed it at Patterson who held onto the injured officer, continuing his assault until he was released and then threw him into the road and started to run bent low behind the parked cars out of the line of fire. He ran about six metres when Edgar tackled him front on, knocking him backwards. They crashed into the fruit stalls sending the boxes of fresh water melons, mangoes, apples, peaches, and strawberries down the pavement and rolling into the road. Edgar was on top of the struggling Patterson as the female officer arrived and stood above them both, her Glock pistol pointing into the face of Patterson, who stared back into the officer's face with rage and anger. In her best English she spoke to Patterson, "Make one more wrong move English arsehole and you will be a dead English arsehole." Patterson knew the threat was real and slowly nodded. He closed his eyes knowing his time had come and a lot of time was coming his way, he stopped resisting Edgar. The other officers then took hold of him and rolled him onto his stomach, after pulling his arms around his back they placed handcuffs very tightly on his large wrists.

The arrest vehicle pulled up next to the scene, Patterson was placed into the back of the vehicle with four officers and immediately taken from the scene.

Two of the officers needed treatment for the injuries inflicted by Patterson. The officer he had head butted was concussed and already had heavy swelling around both of his eyes, it was obvious by the shape of his nose that it was broken badly. The second officer was having trouble breathing after the blows to his throat, his left eye was swollen and bloodshot, there was a trickle of blood coming from his left ear, and his ribs were very sore from several vicious blows. They were both taken to the nearest hospital. Patterson's mobile phone was recovered from under a car and placed in an exhibit bag. The holdall was examined, the sweaty gym wear was moved to one side and revealed a large hunting knife in a protective leather pouch. The holdall and its contents were placed in a large paper forensic bag.

Raul and Steve cleared the equipment from the room they had used and returned to the Mossos station. Bert Ingham, the Senior British Liaison Officer, was waiting for the arrival of the team and the prisoner; he would deal with the European arrest warrant and organise the return of Patterson to face British justice. There was a short debrief where Bert thanked Raul and his team for their magnificent effort in arresting a known murderer and extremely violent escapee. Steve was going to join the team later in Barcelona before returning to Madrid by train in the morning. He collected his personal mobile phone and document holder from his allocated desk, after switching on his mobile and waiting for the activation, there were a few emails, a couple of WhatsApp messages from Sarah, and a missed call from an unknown number. A message from an unknown sender which read, 'please answer my call, message Gloria, I will call'

Sarah was in the NCA training school on a two-week suitability assessment for her to do undercover work, her ability, physically and mentally, would be severely tested. She had finished her two-day introduction to the course and from midnight tonight she would not be able to contact anyone. She was going dark, the first test of many. Steve had completed the course and knew of the stresses, the problems, and difficulties that Sarah would be faced with in the coming two weeks, with a further eight weeks should she prove successful in her assessment period. Sarah would be an excellent undercover officer, Steve was sure of that, but he wanted her to fail. It's a tough world and he didn't want her subjected to what he had been through, or worse.

He made a call and after a short delay Sarah answered, "Hiya, you took your time ringing. I hope you got him."

"Of course, was it ever in doubt? Big fight in the end but they eventually got him down."

"I missed it! Were you in the fight again or are you still protecting your ribs?"

"No, I wasn't involved. Just a watching brief letting Mossos do what Mossos do. Big lad though, bigger than when he left England. You could tell he's been going to the gym a lot. Lot of muscle, still, it doesn't beat an angry Mossos policewoman with a Glock in your face."

"Gan on, girl power man, that's great."

Steve asked, "So how are you doing on the course? Put you off yet?"

"No, not yet. They're telling us what I can do, what I cannot do. Apparently, I'm not supposed to take my knickers off and gan shagging. I thought I'd stopped doing that," she paused, "I think it was, ehm, last year." There was a silence, "You're supposed to laugh at that Steve."

Steve gave a laugh, "You're crazy enough to do it, the job I mean, not the shagging. You will be tested and tested hard but I'm telling you it will be a hell of a lot harder when you do it for real."

Sarah was twisting her face; Steve knew she would be. "Oh aye, really hard, drinking cocktails and singing karaoke in Benidorm and telling a few porkies. That was really tough, even I did that without the training."

Steve was more direct. "What about going into OCG's, getting body searched? They're wanting something from you before they do a deal, tempting you, or forcing you, when you're on your own with no back up, or putting you on your back. Are you going to stop them? You want the deal but how far do you go down the line, when do you stop, when do you know what's right and wrong, if you know it's wrong, do you carry on, who would know?"

Sarah interrupted, "Hold on Steve, I've got trainers here, I don't want a lecture from you. What's up with you? Give me a chance to find out if I'm any good. I've never heard you say owt like that man, if you don't want me to do it just say. It won't matter like, cos, I'm doing the course. If you do anything, speak to anybody to get me failed, I'll, I'll..."

"Sarah I'm sorry, I really am, I'm sure you will be okay, I was just highlighting a few problems that will come if you do UC work."

"Okay, do you know what's right and wrong and have never carried on? You better not answer that, cos I know you will be lying. Have you got a problem with me, other than doing this course, cos if you have, I want to know?"

"Sarah, I have no problem with you, I was just thinking last night, if we both do the work, we mightn't see each other for weeks, months or maybe longer. Where we would be working, could be anywhere in the world and they're not short jobs." Steve thought that sounded plausible as a good answer.

"Steve, I know what you're saying, it's not like we haven't spoken about it since the course was advertised. We've talked loads about the problems, more so for the women I agree, but it's something I want to try. I've worked in offices for so long, I'm intelligent, I'm good at languages, I know what intelligence is needed, I've done the organising bit. I know it will be scary at times, possibly, I know I would be working with the nastiest of people, but just let's see if I get through the assessment first and then possibly the course. I know it's going to be tough; they have told us there's less than ten percent get through the assessment, but I'll say this again, I do not want you interfering either in my favour or certainly not against me."

"I definitely will not interfere. Good luck, honest, if it

is what you want to do, good. Okay. When you pass the assessment when do you do the next course?"

"That's better Steve, a positive note at last. Why do you ask, are you planning on going away or is there another job in the offing?"

"No," Steve lied, "I was just wondering how long I would have to miss you in Madrid for."

"Okay, well when I pass on, wait a sec," Sarah opened her diary, "When I pass on Friday 5th May, I will start the course on Sunday evening 21st May for eight weeks. So we should see plenty of each other between courses, then no contact for eight weeks."

"Sarah, I'm sorry about, ehm, sounding off. I just care about you, I don't want you to get hurt, I'm sorry."

"Steve, I'm pleased that's sorted, I know I'm going to miss you, I miss you now, but in just over ten days we will be together cuddling up, having a drink and laughing and other stuff eh."

"Sounds great, look, I'll let you go, concentrate on what you're told, I really hope you pass. You will contact me first? I am missing you as well."

The call ended.

He looked around the empty office to make sure the door was closed then he pressed the buttons sending the message, 'Call me now'.

Two minutes later, the mobile activated to an incoming call. Again, there was no number disclosed, there was a delay when he answered the call, "Hola Steve."

Steve recognised the voice, "Hola Gabriella."

"Please call me Gabi, should we speak in English, or do you prefer Español?"

"Gabi, English will be fine. You do know that this is very difficult for me?"

"Of course I do, but what I know will benefit a lot of people, most of all you and me."

"What will you get out of this, ehm Gabi?"

She laughed, "What can I get? Justice for you, me, Jessica, her family and friends, Gloria, the policeman in the US. I don't want anything, I don't need anything, I have my freedom, for now."

"I must ask, please don't close the call, was the escape from the prison van planned?"

"No. I swear I knew nothing. I had told Jessica and Gloria the truth, I was going to die in prison, that's all I knew. There was this big explosion and gun fire. I was hiding in the cage cell, then another explosion blew off the van door and the guard was killed, I thought they had been sent to kill me because I killed Borja. They opened the cage and pulled me out, my head was dizzy with the explosions, I thought I was dreaming when I saw Jessica coming to rescue me, I was thinking why would she do that, then he raised his rifle and pointed at her. I grabbed at his arm but was pulled away by the other man, I shouted at Jessica, then I saw her get shot and fall behind the wall. That is the truth, honest."

Steve had listened intently, "Jessica was not coming to rescue you, but her friend Gloria who had already been shot."

"Yes, yes, I know this now but not then. Gloria was in a bad way; I have helped her a bit."

Steve, "Yes, she told me. What happened when you were pulled out of the van?"

"I was put on a motorbike for a short distance and then into the back of a van for about thirty minutes. I got out of the van in the jungle, and someone injected me with something, I thought I was dead. I don't know how long later, but I was in a longboat with an engine on a river in the jungle, my head wasn't clear. I was helped to walk to a native type of hut on stilts next to the river. I was there for some time possibly two weeks, I was given food and water."

"Do you know where or why?"

"I didn't, but I do now." Steve waited for the answer, "I don't know where, other than a jungle village on a river a long way from any town, there was no river traffic so it must be near to the head of the river. I believe it was in Colombia"

Steve asked, "What makes you think that?"

"The natives use the poison from the Golden Frog to put on the tip of their arrows and spears when hunting. The frog, I've since checked, is in the Colombian jungle, the tribe are known as Emberá people. These people were milking the frogs for the poison and putting the fluid in small plastic bottles."

Steve was intrigued, "How do you milk a frog?"

Gabi, "Let me explain, I didn't know this, but the villagers showed me and told me about the toxin, it will easily kill a man. " She paused, "I think that is what I injected Borja with."

Steve, "Just continue please."

"Sorry, the frogs are small, two to five centimetres, when there are predators about, birds, spiders, snakes they secrete the toxin onto their skin. The natives had collected many frogs, they were in glass cases. Every so often, I don't know how many times, they would lift a cloth which was between the cases and there was a jungle snake in the next glass case. The frogs would secrete the toxin then the natives would be very careful and sweep it off the frogs backs with a plastic spatula then drain it into the plastic bottles, it was small amounts. The natives told me that one very small amount on the spatula would kill a man."

"Why were they doing that?"

"They were getting paid by the Cartel, the Cartel who rescued me. The MMV, Manolo Martinez Valero Cartel."

"Getting back to the question, why should they rescue you if they think you have killed Borja and caused them so many problems?"

"This may shock you, but, my sister Carmen, she is the lover of Manolo in his hacienda. It shocked me, apparently Manolo did it as a favour for my sister, she is beautiful. I have spoken to her once on the phone, she told me she loved me and was deeply upset about our family, she was doing something for me. I know she doesn't want to be there; she didn't tell me that, but I know."

"When was that?"

"I don't know the day, it was the day I was taken from the jungle, I was drugged again, I thought it was the toxin. I woke up on a small plane and it landed in Haiti, I didn't know where I was. I was told to get out of the plane then they threw a small case to me and took off, there was a lot of money, dollars in the case."

Steve could hear talking outside the door, "There are people coming I have to go, please ring me back in a few days, Saturday or Sunday is better. I believe you."

Steve closed the call.

Wednesday 26th April

The train to Madrid had departed from Sants station in Barcelona on time, Steve had a seat in the first-class coach. He made a call from his personal mobile.

"Good morning Steve, this is a pleasant surprise, how are you?" It was Maddison Roberts, who was now running the business and was a partner with Steve and Josh of 'JOB Security' in Alderley Edge. Steve was a sleeping partner and didn't interfere, it was doing well.

"Good morning to you Maddison, sorry I haven't been in touch lately, I can hear you've not lost your accent yet, are you and Josh both okay?"

"Yes, we are fine, both very busy you will be pleased to hear. Josh is doing very well on the security side of things and I'm about ready to launch the new investigative mobile technology. The NCA and most of the British police are interested, and I've got a stall at the Interpol meeting and a few security events in Europe, so I'm hopeful."

"Sounds very promising, I'm sure it will be a success. Just thinking, are you still doing trials or is it working?"

"It's working, but not in an official capacity, sort of, so I suppose you could say it's being trialled, do you have something in mind?"

"Would it work on a call that was being used without a number?"

"I have been trialling that recently, obviously the recent problems with the new criminal encrypted phones, they are causing major problems but also VPN on messaging. It's difficult, but I'm sure you will remember the set-up Walter had in Panama when you were identifying numbers, well it can be used the other way to identify locations."

"Go on, it sounds complicated."

"Walter used the call from one phone to identify other active mobiles in the area, a series of calls eliminated numbers until it was down to one number as the mobile moved around. In reverse, if the nearby calls are coming from numbers that are not using hidden numbers, you would identify a location where the nearby calls are being made from."

"Does it work Maddison? Do you want to run a trial this weekend?"

"It would probably take a few minutes to run, depending on the distance involved." A thought came into the head of Maddison, putting two and two together, "Would this be a long-distance call possibly, any paperwork involved?"

"I don't know really," he lied "it could be I suppose. There would be no need for paperwork, let's just say I've got an interest in someone's location."

Maddison without hesitation, "Yes, no problems, I will do it myself. Do you have a time period?"

"Yes, Saturday or Sunday afternoon. If it is on Saturday, I can ask for another call on Sunday if that would be helpful."

"I can fit that in, is it your phone, the phone you are using now?"

"Yes, it will be."

"Yes, okay, I will come in at eleven on Saturday and Sunday for a trial run. That's correct, isn't it Steve?"

"Thanks Maddison, I will be in touch."

CHAPTER 2

Saturday 29th April.

It was a warm, sunny day in Madrid, it was already 24 degrees as Steve was running through Parque de la Ventilla. Quite a few locals were out running, walking, and enjoying the sun and the shade of the trees. He had run to the farthest point of the park and was now returning in the direction of his apartment; his dark blue running vest was sticking to his back. Checking his watch, he saw he was doing a good personal time this morning, then checking the time, it was 09: 38. He pushed hard to finish towards the end of the park, he was building his fitness.

Steve had showered and made his breakfast of black coffee, tostada with tomatoes and olive oil. His personal tablet was switched on, it was to the side of his plate; he was researching the Golden Frog and the Emberá people. He ignored the villages that were used by the tribe to attract tourists with their dollars which would be spent on the dancing displays, photographs, and woven multi coloured items made by the women of the tribe. He explored inland, further upstream of the large Chagres River into the forests, the Chepo and Rio Maje had small tribal camps, these were all in Panama. The Rio Atrata ran across the North Colombian mountains. It was close to the Panama border and emptied into the Atlantic Ocean. Thousands of square miles, it would be impossible to pinpoint. Steve was favouring the Rio Atrata, it was in the natural habitat of the Golden Frog. "Why would the

Cartel be collecting so much toxin, they have easy access to firearms, explosives, why this primitive lethal method?" he asked himself. He thought then answered himself, "Silent, easy to conceal, easy to use but you would have to be close to the intended victim." He made notes in his handbook and underlined Atrata. He cleared the table, picking up his mobile he made a call.

"Good morning Maddison."

"Hi Steve, good morning, I've been in a little while and I have your phone linked to the system, just in case you have any private calls to make you don't want me to know about."

"Oh yes, that's highly likely, not. However, hopefully there should be one call incoming I want you to know about. Do I have to do anything?"

"No, just keep the other person on the line, keep her chatting, I mean, keep the other person talking on the line."

"Maddison, you do not know who is calling me, is that clear."

"Very clear, I meant to say person." As she pulled an awkward look on her face, "Sorry about that Steve."

"No problem Maddison, I'm just trying something that might work, possibly for all of our benefit."

"I'm fine, I'm fine with whatever it is, I'm definitely on your side. I don't want to know and don't need to know, but if I can help I will."

"I know you are Maddison; I trust you. I will not get you involved in anything you shouldn't be, I promise. What do I have to do now?"

"Nothing really, just keep your phone charged and in a good reception area and wait for the person to phone. It will automatically activate the search system, hopefully hitting some nearby calls which the system will close in on. I don't know if I should ask this, but it could help if you had a number of a mobile in the same area, it would make it quicker"

"I might be able to get one but not today, it's a better test of the system anyway."

Maddison raised her eyebrows but didn't ask the question, "Yes okay Steve, we just have to wait. I'll call you after the call is finished to let you know the result."

"Thanks, I'll just watch a bit of tv and wait."

The call was ended, it was time to wait again, it felt as if Steve spent most of his time waiting.

It was 3pm on the hour in Madrid, 2pm in Alderley Edge when the mobile started ringing. There was no number displayed, Steve answered the call, Maddison activated the search system.

"Hola." Steve responded.

"Hola Steve, I told you I would call."

"Thank you Gabi for calling back, I've been waiting and I have been thinking since your last call."

"I thought you would, are you attempting to trace this call?"

"No, why would I do that, I want to talk to you."

"Possibly because I'm an escaped murderer and you want to put me back into prison."

Steve answered honestly, with wishful thinking, "Gabi, you are more important and valuable to me when you are a free woman. Panama police will not think that way, so I will not let them know."

"So, we have to trust each other. Me, I have nothing to lose apart from my freedom, which will not last long, I am sure of that. Prison, or preferably a quick death waits for me, how long, who knows."

"I am alone in my apartment, please believe me, that is why I asked you to ring. I have told no-one. This is just us two, unless Gloria is involved." Steve asked.

"Gloria knows some of what I know, and she can be involved if needed, she knows us both but I prefer just you and I."

"Can I ask questions? It might make it easier for me."

"Yes, I have time on my side. You ask questions?"

"What you told me about the frog toxin, do you know why they are collecting the large amounts from the natives?"

Gabi shook her head, "Steve, I have told you what I have

seen. They did not tell me, there were two guards in the village watching me, where was I supposed to run or swim? They didn't have conversation with me, like in the movies. What do you think? They must be planning on a killing spree, I proved to them that the poison worked."

"Okay, I understand."

Gabi spoke first, "Before you ask, I have no idea where, I have also been thinking. Yes, it was in the jungle, I think it was high, the camp was on the west side of the river, the sun was first seen through the trees across the river then moved right, south. The river was moving quite fast, in the time I was there no one, no other natives passed the village. One more thing, there were no women in the village, just the men collecting the toxin, the two guards and me."

"How did you get the call off Carmen?"

"It was amazing, I was sitting in the shade of the hut, one of the guards walked to me and handed me the phone. I put it to my ear, and I knew it was Carmen's voice, she said, 'Hola my beautiful sister, I hope you are being looked after.' She then told me that she was with Manolo in the hacienda, and she had asked him to release me from prison."

"How long was the call?"

"Not long, Manolo was listening, she could not say much, but I knew she did not want to be there. She wanted me to be happy, I was supposed to go somewhere, with the money I was going to get and start again. I did not know I would get so much."

"Why did they inject you before they took you out of the camp?"

Gabi answered surprised, "Why do you think? They did not want me to know where the camp was."

"When did they inject you, not the day but how?"

"We would go with one of the natives to get the fish nets on the evening, I was sat in the canoe, the guard behind me pushed it into my neck, I told you, I thought I was going to die again."

"Then you woke up on the plane?"

"Just about half an hour before we landed in Haiti, it was dark. I got out of the plane walked to a road nearby and into the nearest town."

"Okay, Gabi, you say you can trust me."

"No, I said I wanted to trust you. You could be telling me lies, and there are other police where you are, listening to this call."

"Yes, you can trust me. I can assure you; no one is in my apartment listening to this call."

"Okay, I want to believe you, I think I can."

"You told me you knew the name of the man who killed Jessica."

"Yes, I do, he also killed the American policeman who was looking after Josh."

Maddison had eventually traced the country where the call had originated and was closing on the signal. "Keep it going Steve" she was saying repeatedly to herself.

There was a knock on the door, "You have people in your apartment, I have heard them."

Steve immediately looked at the door, "No Gabi, believe me, I haven't, it will be one of my mates from one of the other apartments, just asking about going for a drink."

The line went dead, Steve threw his mobile down onto the sofa in anger and frustration, he calmed himself and walked to the door. On opening the door, he was face to face with Gabi. He could only see her face; she could have been naked he would not have known. His mouth dropped open as they both looked at each other. Steve had a sudden urge to grab her and hold her tight in a hug, not a restraining hold. He had a quick look both ways down the corridor, then indicated for Gabi to enter his apartment, she slowly walked in looking around the door into the space she could see.

Maddison pinged the unknown phone in the immediate vicinity of Steve's mobile, she didn't swear, "Oh my God, oh my God. What the fuck." The accent hadn't changed but the language had. Picking up her own mobile she went to call

Steve and then stopped herself, she sat down looking at the screen, the other mobile was not moving.

Steve felt awkward in more ways than he could tell, he was wearing a tee shirt and shorts, his leg scars were visible. He was harbouring an escaped prisoner, who was responsible for murdering Felipe, the Pig, Martin Chapman, and Borja Sanchez. International drug dealing on a massive scale, her father had tried to kill him and Jessica, they had killed her father and the actions of her prison escape resulted with Jessica being killed. "Please, sit down, anywhere you want." He now noticed that Gabi was wearing a brightly coloured flower-patterned blouse, tight blue denim jeans and blue converse shoes with a white sole. She was carrying a black leather bag over her left shoulder. Her hair was the same style as the last time he had seen her, dark and wavy below her shoulders, a small amount of makeup on her face, a very close resemblance of Sarah.

Gabi had a look in the rooms of the apartment. Steve had been telling the truth, she looked out of the window down onto the street below, there was no urgent rush of police cars or sirens sounding. She took a seat facing the television and the photograph of Sarah, she asked Steve, "Is this your new friend, she reminds me of someone." She gave Steve a smile, "No photograph of Jessica?" she asked.

Ignoring the question, "How did you know where I was living?"

Gabi shook her head, "Where do you work from, The Embassy? Where do you go with your friends, The Covent Garden? It was so easy to find you, you do not think people are looking for you, so you don't look for them."

Steve picked up his mobile, Gabi looked at him as he switched it off. "I don't want any more interruptions and I certainly don't want anyone knocking on my door." Steve took a seat opposite Gabi. "You know when I said it was difficult for me, that was an understatement, if you know what I mean."

Gabi smiled and nodded.

Steve had a sudden frightening thought, “Have you come here to kill me?”

Gabi had heard similar words before from a British policeman, “No, I have not. I don’t blame you for asking.” she passed her handbag to Steve for examination, he didn’t bother and placed it on the coffee table which made him think.

“I’m sorry, do you want a coffee or a cold drink, a little shocked I have forgot my manners.”

Gabi was relaxing and sat back into the chair, “Do you have a diet Cola?”

Steve was out of his chair, he took two glasses from the cupboard, two ice cubes in each glass and filled them both with diet Cola. Gabi was scanning the room as he was pouring the drinks.

They sat facing each other in silence, the beautiful young woman sat opposite Steve was a killer, he found it hard to believe but he knew she was a killer. He was thinking. “Did you have a plan when you came to my door?” he asked.

Gabi replied, “I haven’t seen your friend, is she working away?”

Steve immediately pointed his index finger into the face of Gabi, “You leave her out of this, she has nothing to do with this, or whatever we have is over.”

She smiled back at him, “What exactly do we have, we are not lovers, not in a relationship? We want the same thing I believe, justice for Jessica, that’s if you still remember Jessica?”

Steve was losing his calm, “Of course I remember Jessica, but I’m trying to move on. I still want justice.” He continued after a brief silence, “Why did you come to Madrid, you could have gone anywhere, called me from anywhere?”

“I wanted to know that I could trust you.”

“Well, that’s a really big risk, walking into the lion’s den, an apartment block full of police officers, to see me? The guy who flattened you and stopped you escaping, who loved Jessica, who was killed in your escape.”

“Well, it has worked so far,” she cupped her hand around

her left ear. "I do trust you and we can go on together from here"

Steve was confused, "What do you mean, go on from here?"

"I have plans, some involve you, and some involve your policia colleagues and some on my own. I am currently safe in this country, I have legal documents, I cause no problems, so, I plan to stay here for a while, no more killing."

"What about cocaine? You haven't given up everything"

Gabi opened her hands out to Steve. "As they say, it's a hard habit to break, but it keeps me in touch with sources."

Steve was curious, "What kind of sources."

"People who tell me everything, they think I am stupid or scared, they don't know me."

Steve nodded his head, "They certainly don't." he paused they were looking at each other, "You can't visit here anymore."

Gabi was smiling, "That's a disappointing statement, when you were looking at me, I thought you wanted to make love with me, I could have been tempted."

Steve laughed as he answered, "I didn't know you could read minds."

"It is one of my many accomplishments, maybe another time. You are right, I will not come back here. If you can promise to stop the searching for my phone number," she waved her finger in the face of Steve, "I will not come here."

"I wouldn't do that." He lied again

"I will phone you, keep that phone number, it could be at any time, when something is happening, it will be worth your while. I do not want money, just trust, friendship would be nice, but for now trust. I am really a nice person. I know you find it hard to believe but if you had been in my position, I hate myself for killing Filipe."

"Do you want to tell me who this guy is who killed Jessica?"

"I will, but in the future, I will keep in touch to make it easy."

"What do you mean, easy?"

"You will know when the time comes. I must go, I have been

in here for too long." She stood up and moved towards Steve, facing each other again in silence, she held her right hand out to Steve. He took hold of her hand it was warm and gentle, "I am so sorry about Jessica, it hurt me as well."

Steve pulled her in close and lightly hugged her, he resisted the urge to kiss her on the cheek, "It was not your fault, I know that." They separated after a few seconds.

Steve opened the door and looked along the corridor, it was clear, Gabi walked along the corridor away from the apartment and never looked back. Steve closed the door and walked to the window, he looked down onto the street below, he never saw her leave the building.

He turned and looked at the photograph of Sarah, he could see Gabi. He was deep in thought, 'What the fuck have I done, how do I explain this, for fucks sake, no-one said it would be easy, but this, this is fucking ridiculous.'

He switched his mobile on, there was a message from Maddison, 'Call me when you can'.

He took another drink of Cola from the fridge and gathered his thoughts, it was difficult, very difficult. He made a call to Maddison. "Hi Maddison, did it work?"

"I thought it had Steve, it was bouncing all over the place, then it centred on Spain and eventually on your mobile vicinity, then the call went dead."

"What would cause that Maddison?" He was lying and thought Maddison knew he was lying.

"I've never seen it happen before," she explained, "It is possible they got similar to crossed lines and sent back to the receiver." Maddison knew that it was impossible but it would give Steve a way out.

"Oh, shame, never mind. I got some information which would be useful, it would have been interesting to know where it was coming from, but there will be no more calls, he told me. It was too dangerous for him, he said. Sorry to spoil your weekend. Thanks for trying Maddison, I'll be in touch soon, good luck with the presentations."

"Thanks Steve, we will keep in touch. Did you get the business credit card, Josh was saying it's never been used?"

"Yes, yes, I did thanks, I might use it on a holiday I'm planning. See you both soon."

The call was closed, he dropped the mobile on the sofa he was sitting on. He bent over and put his head between his hands, "What the fuck have I just done, what am I doing?"

CHAPTER 3

Sunday 30th April

The overnight bag had been packed; Steve checked inside the document holder again to ensure the flight documents were in the zipped pocket. It was 12:16 on the digital display of the microwave in the kitchen as he made himself another coffee. He carried the coffee and placed it on a Union Flag coaster on the coffee table. He sat down on the sofa, then after another thoughtful pause, he pressed the digits on the mobile.

"Good morning mate, or should I say good afternoon?" Leon was in his apartment and was now lying on his bed, a large grey towel was wrapped around his waist, he had just showered.

"I've had another contact."

"That's good news," Leon sat up, "did she have much to say?"

"Yes, but it was awkward."

"We discussed that; we knew it would be awkward. How awkward do you mean?"

"How about, knocking on my door and coming into my apartment awkward."

There was a silence, Steve waited, "Fucking hell mate, there's awkward, in like," Leon paused, "like, someone who's an escaped murderer making a call and you answering it, and," again there was silence for a couple of seconds, Leon was holding his head in thought, "how the fuck did she know where you lived?"

"I've never slept, it was absolutely crazy, listen, I'll tell you how it happened, okay."

Leon spoke first, "No, first, how did she know where you lived?"

"Quite easily really, she followed me from the Embassy, she even saw me go to The Covent Garden then back here. Like she said, I wasn't expecting to be followed so I wasn't looking for anyone."

Leon was shaking his head, "I just, just cannot believe this, this is real scary man. Tell me, I have to know."

"I'll keep it brief. She rang dead on three in the afternoon, she kept asking about trust, if she could trust me, she had life in prison to look forward to if she was arrested. She told me about the escape, she knew nothing about it, she thought they were going to kill her, she was drugged and taken to a village in the jungle somewhere, she doesn't know where. Apparently, the natives were taking toxin off some Golden Frogs and getting paid by the Cartel."

Leon interrupted, "Toxin from a frog, what's that about?"

"Leave it for now, anyway, after a few weeks, she gets a call from her sister, she's shacked up with Manolo, the MMV boss, he apparently loves her. She has persuaded Manolo, to get her out of jail and give her some cash, lots of cash and she is taken by plane to Haiti. She kept on going about trust, trust. I ask her about the guy who killed Jessica, there was a knock on the door, she heard the knock, she told me there were cops in my apartment and closed the call. I was fucking fuming."

"Did she call back?"

"No. I opened the door; she was just stood there in the corridor. There was no-one about so I quickly got her in."

"Holy shit mate, what happened?"

"She had a look around the rooms then relaxed, sat on the sofa and we started talking."

"What was she like?"

"She's really good looking, what is scary is she is so similar to Sarah, long wavy dark hair, same shape face, Sarah is a bit taller, more athletic."

"I meant; how did she react?"

"She was calm, told me she could tell me who killed Jessica but that was for later." There was a silence, "She's living in Spain."

"No way, where?"

"She obviously doesn't trust me that much but will keep in contact. There's something big happening soon, she will tell me when it is."

Leon was thinking, "I take it she is still in the coke trade?"

"Yes." Steve was thinking about Gabi, "I was uncomfortable when she was in the apartment, I must admit I am worried about meeting her again." Steve didn't elaborate on the reasons why.

"Why is that, apart from her being a killer and an escapee?"

"I like her, it's crazy, but I really do, but I know she is a killer. She is so much like Sarah in appearance, I know Sarah wouldn't kill anyone, even Gabi said Sarah looked like her."

"Ooh, Gabi now, is it?"

"Yes, she wants to be called Gabi. Anyway, I was thinking."

Leon interrupted, "I bet this will be good, come on then, what's the plan?"

"I can't really get involved with her, I was there when she was arrested, I know her, even with false documents I would know it was her. There is no way of getting around the fact, that if the truth was known, I would be arrested for harbouring an escapee, murderer and drug trafficker, that's what's fucking awkward."

"That is an accurate assessment mate, so how are you going to handle it?"

"I will introduce you to Gabi, or whatever name she is given, then you can develop a relationship without knowing her background."

Leon was astonished, "You have been telling me she is a cop killer, a serial killer, killing blokes she has sex with, a black widow if you ask me, no fucking way."

"No, no. Honest Leon, would I put you in danger?"

"It certainly sounds like it."

"I'm not asking you to have a relationship with her, you would, I know you would, she is just," Steve stopped himself, "wanting to help us, get the killer of Jessica and Greg Simons."

There was another silence as Steve waited for Leon's response.

"It might work, but how can we get an introduction without the Spanish police being involved. They would dig to find out who she really is, does she look the same as she did in Panama?"

"Yes. Exactly the same, not even coloured her hair or changed the style but there are loads of Latin Americans living and working in Spain now, they blend in with the area. Anyone looking at her would never, ever, imagine, she was a killer. As long as she doesn't come into contact with the Spanish police, criminal wise, fingerprints, DNA, she will be anonymous."

"You've really thought about this, it might work. It keeps you out of it, just got to sort out an introduction. Would she trust me, like me, like, as in enough not to kill me?" He gave a little laugh.

"What really scares me, I know who she would like and trust."

Leon interrupted, "You obviously, but that ain't going to happen."

"Sarah."

"Holy fuck man, what are you saying, you are crazy, you can't do that to Sarah."

"I wouldn't, I was just saying what I know about her, she likes women, good-looking women, and good-looking men."

"She killed Jessica and you would risk Sarah?"

"No. No way. I was just saying she would like Sarah. I don't want Sarah to be involved, she would probably recognise Gabriella, no, she would recognise her, no doubt."

"So, Sarah is working with you on the same stuff and she will not know it's Gabi, Gabriella?"

"We don't keep photos of informants, and she wouldn't if she passes the course and is away for eight weeks."

"What about the two weeks between the courses, what happens if she fails the assessment and works in the office?"

"Leon, stop complicating things, Sarah will pass, she's a natural. I'm hoping so, we both know it's tough, she will." Steve was convincing himself, "I've thought about taking her away for a well-deserved break, we've only had a few days off really, never been on holiday together, I'm going to ask Bert tomorrow. I've got a job to do this week and then it should be okay."

"You have really thought this out haven't you. Okay, she gives you or me, the intelligence, we work on it, get a success with coke etcetera, then she tells you, me, for fucks sake, us, who and where the killer is, what happens then?"

"I get the guy checked out and it gets dealt with."

"What do you mean by that?"

"We tell the police, wherever he is and they deal with it."

Leon was unconvinced, "Oh yeah, really? Then what happens to," Leon was thinking, "Shakira, after she has given us all the information, is she returned to prison?"

"I like that name, good name, I haven't worked out that bit yet."

"Do you think it would work, seriously, think about it. If, 'Shakira', is on the scene of the drug jobs there will be photos, videos, CCTV recordings. If she is spotted, she could get identified, well would if Sarah has a look."

Steve was positive, "Yes, it would work if we, I, go about it in the right way."

Leon started laughing at loud, "It's a bit late for that mate but we can give it a go. You have not spoken to me about this, okay. When it gets sorted, contact is made and you need someone, suggest me, suggest me strongly. I've got nothing in my book for a few weeks so it had better be quick or I could be anywhere."

"Thanks Leon, I've got a plan for a contact arrangement,

which could happen soon. I'm relying on her getting in contact with me, I need her trust to get her contact number, that is a big ask. I'll work on it, I'll be in touch soon, hopefully."

Tuesday 2nd May

After packing his overnight bag, Steve had his breakfast in the hotel and went for a walk along the sea front. The sun was shining down on the Mediterranean and the beaches, some sun worshippers were already laying out their towels for a relaxing day ahead. He had completed the preparations on Monday, the bank holiday, then had a social evening with Ivan in the local bars. He made a call to Bert, "Good morning Bert, did you have an enjoyable bank holiday?"

"Hello Steve, yes I did, quiet though. Is everything sorted for today, any problems?"

"Yes, it's all sorted, just waiting again, it will not be rushed."

"It never gets rushed in Spain, just do what has to be done."

"I will, I'm just walking along the sea front to kill some time. I was wondering if it would be okay for Sarah and I to have some leave from this weekend, we've never been away together, just a week or ten days."

"It should be okay, the crew who are on leave this week for the bank holiday will be back, Sarah will probably need it and you of course. I'll check the schedule, have you got any work planned for the next two weeks?"

"Nothing specific unless something new and urgent comes in, the usual liaison but nothing operational." Steve was lying and felt guilty lying to Bert, the less he knows the better for Bert.

"I should know by this afternoon, is that okay?"

"Thanks Bert, I'll keep you updated."

"Good luck, see you when you get back."

He took a seat in a café overlooking the marina, he checked

his personal phone, nothing. The waiter took his order of sparkling water and a black coffee, he looked at his watch and relaxed.

Later that afternoon he was sat in the departure lounge at the airport, the final passengers were showing their boarding passes, he walked to the desk. He was last in the queue, showing the pass, he followed the line and climbed the steps towards the aircraft front door. He knew his seat number, entering the cabin he walked down three rows, he placed his overnight bag into the overhead locker, he took his aisle seat, 3D. Just two occupants in the row of three seats. The male in the window seat was watching the luggage trailer reversing from the side of the plane, he turned and glanced at the late arrival who had been holding the plane crew from closing the door.

Trigger looked in amazement and surprise at Steve who had his right index finger across his lips and was smiling. He kept his composure, smiling back he nodded and again looked out of the small window, still smiling. The stewards went through the pre-flight safety procedure, then announced the flight time would be 2 hours 50 minutes to East Midlands, the arrival time would be 17:50.

Shortly after take-off, the seat belt signs were switched off, the two shook hands and started a neighbourly passenger conversation.

Steve broke the ice, "Have you been staying anywhere nice?"

Trigger joined in, "Yes. It was full board, loads of staff, some of my friends were staying in the same place."

They were both smiling, "Was it your first time?"

"Yes, but I don't think I want to go back." Trigger continued, "I don't think you would like it for some reason."

"Did your mates like it?"

"They didn't go with me, they came later. I hope they like it they've booked a long stay. I'll miss them."

"I can give you a lift from the airport if you want?"

Trigger was laughing, "Yes, that would be great, that's if it's not out of your way. I was hoping to surprise my wife, she thought I was staying for a while longer."

Steve was shaking his head, "She doesn't know you are coming." He said quietly.

Trigger closed his eyes, his head dropped, his hands were over his face and tears started to roll, he took a handkerchief out of his pocket, he wiped his eyes and looked out of the window to regain his composure. He placed his left hand on the right thigh of Steve, "Thanks mate." was said quietly.

After landing, Steve was one of the first passengers to leave the aircraft, he was fast tracked through passport control, he collected the firm's car that had been designated for him, then waited.

Trigger, to his annoyance had to wait for assistance to get into the terminal, it helped in a way, as the other, more mobile passengers had already left the arrivals hall. He thanked the porter for the wheelchair push and gave him a five Euro note, the only currency he had. He carried his plastic holdall through the terminal, the taxi stopped next to him, a shiny black Audi A5, looking at the driver it was Steve, he threw his bag into the back and sat in the front passenger seat. Steve drove the few miles into Kegworth, Trigger was starving, he wanted fish and chips, they were not going to be eaten inside the prized Audi, Steve parked the car and removed the taxi sign. They each had a large cod and chips, they sat on a bench in the car park, Trigger was savouring the cod, the batter, salty with plenty of vinegar, "real food" he kept saying. Trigger had to be debriefed but that could wait until tomorrow or Thursday, today was celebration time, and as yet no alcohol. He was determined to be sober to enjoy the time when he saw Laura, Chelsea and Frank then he would have a drink, or two. Steve pushed on there was still a three hour drive.

Laura had been told to expect a visit from an agent who would give an update on the court appearance of Trigger, plus a routine welfare check, it was usually on an evening so as not to draw attention. She was watching the news, the kids were in their bedrooms, supposedly going to sleep, "Why is it always bad news nowadays, what's wrong with the world?" She got out of her chair to pour a cold glass of white wine, her only enjoyment these days. She opened the fridge as the doorbell rang, "Shit, he picks his moments." Closing the fridge door, she walked the few paces to the front door, remembering what she had been told, she looked through the spy hole in the solid reinforced door. Laura began to shake and struggled to get the key into the lock, she was shouting, "Chelsea, Frank, come here."

The door was opened, and she threw herself into the open arms of Trigger, nearly knocking him off his balance, they hugged tightly together, crying, smiling, laughing, shaking, they were joined by the two kids who had run down the stairs screaming, "Daddy, daddy." They both grabbed a metal leg each, hugging their daddy who had been gone a long time.

They were still standing in the doorway, "How, how are you here, I'm so, so happy and the kids, aren't you?"

"Yes, yes, yes, are you stopping here daddy?" Chelsea asked.

"Yes, I am, all together again."

Frank asked, "Can we go back to Spain now daddy?"

"Maybe in a little while, lets enjoy it here first."

"Laura again asked, "How did you do it, how are you here?"

Trigger moved to the side of the door, pointing to the car, "That man, he did it." He waved to Steve who got out of the car.

Laura saw Steve, she ran down the garden path and hugged him, "Thank you, thank you, thank you. You fucking bastard, why did you not tell me. I owe you and Sarah a massive apology, I'm really sorry Steve. Come on, let's get in the house, I'll try and get the kids to bed and the three of us can have a drink, something to celebrate at last."

Wednesday 3rd May

Laura was still sleeping, it had been a late night, Chelsea and Frank were awake but playing in their own bedrooms. Steve was sat at a table outside in the garden looking out over the North Sea. Trigger brought out the tea pot, milk, sugar, two large mugs and a packet of ginger snap biscuits on a tray. "I like it here, should have stopped, I just wanted a better life for her and the kids."

"In the words of Ragnar Lothbrok, 'Don't waste time looking back, you're not going that way'."

Trigger was impressed, "That's good that, since when have you started quoting politicians, you were a thick Geordie when I first knew you, mind sometimes, I think you still are, some of the shite you come out with."

"He's not a politician, he's a Viking."

Trigger was taking the piss, as he would say, "A Viking, a real fucking Viking said that."

"No man, he's not real, well sort of real but, did you not watch The Vikings, you can get it on box set."

"See what I mean, he's a fucking actor, not real. You should have told me when I was in my cell, I could have asked the guards for a Sky card. Sometimes you talk some real shite, I'll ask you again, how the fuck are you old bill?"

They were both laughing again, Trigger was spilling the tea on the table, missing the large mugs, "I'll tell you why you're a good copper, you're a genuine lad, a generous lad, sensitive at times, you generally have your head screwed on but you do say some stupid things. I owe you a lot, all of us do, thanks mate."

"You have to stop thanking me, I was just a part, Sarah, Ivan, the biggest player was someone you don't know, Brigada Cuéllar. You made it possible by saying what you did."

"Well, I thank the lot of them, I did thank Ivan in Malaga, he's another good bloke, I like him. Not looking back but I've lost a lot, I'll just have to start again."

"I know what you have been through, but I know how you can make some cash, maybe quite a bit."

"Is it legal?"

"Of course, kind of. You will have to tell a lie or two"

Trigger was interested, "Does this involve you?"

"Yes, it does, I'll tell you what it is and you can think about it."

"I'm in mate if it involves you, could it involve jail time?"

"For me, yes. For you, no."

"Tell me what you can, if you don't trust me, don't tell me stuff. I'll say fuck all but I'm not doing time."

They both took a drink of their tea, Steve started, "I know someone, who I should not speak to, not a friend. They've contacted me and want to give me information about drugs, as you would imagine, lots of drugs and other stuff. No-one, and I mean no-one, can know who this person is but the information is really good."

"So, you want me to go and speak to this geezer?"

"No, nothing as difficult as that. Listen, you are like a go between, this person tells you stuff then you tell me, except I already know and you don't need to talk to anyone."

"Like I said, sometimes you talk real shit."

"No, no, it's not that. Basically, we're keeping the other person's identity unknown."

"But that's what you're supposed to do, you wouldn't have many grasses if you told the fucking world who they were, would you?"

"The information that the other person gives me, when it leads to seizures of cocaine and arrests, you will get paid handsomely"

Trigger was smiling, "Now you see, talk simple and I understand, I could go for that. So, when do I start talking to the geezer, is it by phone?"

"No." Steve had the conversation planned but it wasn't going the way he had planned it. They both drank some tea, "The story would be, you met someone in prison who mentioned a person who was active in bringing drugs in, he trusted you because you were in for the same thing. He was annoyed that those outside, they were not looking after his family as they promised, so he was a bit loose tongued. He told you the names of those involved, where they were based and some other stuff that I don't know about as yet, I will tell you when I know. I'll start up another operation, like the one you instigated."

"Wait one sec, can I get paid for that then?"

"What, after they've dropped charges and saved you from at least 15 years inside?"

"I see what you mean. Go on then."

"Where was I? Yes, the operation starts and I introduce someone, another police officer, who infiltrates the group and we eventually get the arrests and recovery."

"How can you introduce a UC guy to someone you don't want anyone to know about?"

"You don't have to worry about that. You just have to do that bit that I've told you, a few calls to me, I can start it off after what you've told me this morning about the group."

"I haven't told you anything yet, oh yes, yes, I've got you."

"You call me thick: you Cockney legless dimwit, how the fuck did you run a business?" They started throwing ginger snaps at each other, laughing uncontrollably, that's what friends do.

Trigger raised his arm in the air and shouted "Freedom!", he had never felt this good in years, happiness.

Later that afternoon Steve dropped his bag into the Audi, he hugged and kissed them all, including Trigger. He tried his Arnie impersonation, "I'll be back."

Trigger, "That was shit mate, stick to policing. Really, thanks mate, pass on all our love and thanks to Sarah. I'm in. Keep me updated."

"I will do, enjoy life, it's great here, settle down, look to the future."

He was in the car, he gave one more wave to them all, Trigger was holding his thumb up as he drove off to catch his flight.

CHAPTER 4

Friday 5th May

Gabriella was sitting in her small villa overlooking the Atlantic. It was a dark cloudy morning, the distant thunder could be heard as it was getting closer, the lightning flashes quickly followed with a piercing cracking sound, the shroud of grey falling rain was moving towards her from the horizon. It would not be pleasant on the ocean, even close to shore it would be uncomfortable riding the increasing swell in her small boat. She received a message on the encro phone from her associate Lucas, 'Delivery on schedule'.

She typed her reply, 'When is the slaughter?'

A few seconds passed, 'Monday'.

The news from Lucas brightened up a very dull, boring day. She picked up her 'Steve' mobile and sent a message.

He was in the office talking to Ken, one of the intelligence officers. He could feel his personal phone vibrating next to his right hip, it was a short activation, a message. He finished the conversation and walked back to his desk, he glanced at the wall clock 10:59. He read the message 'need to speak today 12:20'.

It was a bright, warm day in Madrid, Steve had a coffee in a polystyrene cup and a ham salad bocadillo from the local café. He headed to a seat on the park bench and had his lunch while he waited. The call was on time, 12:20. "Hi Gabi."

"Hi, there is an incoming shipment on Monday."

"Is it a large shipment?"

"Yes, well the shipment will be in today but it will be getting slaughtered on Monday."

"Will there be many big players at the slaughter?"

"Yes of course, but I will be there."

"I have no intention of raiding the slaughter, well not yet. Will you meet someone else, a great guy, a big friend of mine. I cannot have anything to do with you in a way."

Gabi interrupted him, "So I have to trust another man, a policeman, undercover man I can guess, look what happened to Filipe when they thought he was an undercover cop."

"Gabi, you killed him if you forgot."

"Yes, yes I did, but if I didn't someone else would have."

"I know you would like him; you can trust him."

"I like your friend, she's nice."

"No way, I can read minds as well, I saw the look, when you were looking at her photograph."

"She reminds me of me, that is good."

"Gabi, no fucking way, you keep well away from her, I have already lost Jessica because of you."

"That was not my fault, I have told you."

Steve was firm in his tone, "You keep away from her. There is only one way to do this without you and me ending up in jail or worse."

"If I meet this man, he will know who I am, it's crazy."

"Listen to me, I'll explain. You do have Spanish I.D. another name, a home somewhere, as long as you do nothing that gets you arrested you will be safe, no fingerprints, no DNA samples. This man will know you by the name you have now, you can trust him. You make an introduction to the other people and you move away, he will look after your interest. The Spanish police will not be aware of you."

"Is he a good-looking man, a fun man?"

"Yes, I promise you will like him, he will like you, do not kill him, he is my friend."

Gabi was laughing for a change, "I promise, I will not kill him. I have told you, I didn't want to kill anyone, well apart from Borja."

"Will you meet him, maybe next week, somewhere you suggest, you will know what he is like then?"

Gabi was thinking, "You could be setting me up to be arrested and sent back to jail."

"Yes, I could be, but I'm not, I'm trying to keep you out of jail. I want to know who killed Jessica and the police officer."

"I will tell you; I think he is coming to Spain. I am hearing things even now."

"When, do you know when?"

"No, not yet, he is coming to ask some questions, he usually gets the answers."

"He's coming to torture I take it, then kill. Do you know who his target is?"

"Me"

"What! Why? I thought Manolo gave you the money and got you out of jail."

"He did, to keep Carmen happy, my sister."

"So why the change?"

"No change, do you think he would be happy with me, I've cost him millions of dollars, I killed Borja? He has kept Carmen happy; he did what she asked, now who cares, she will never hear from me again, she will think I'm living in paradise somewhere. I love her, she loves me. He still loves her, at the moment."

"How do you know this?"

"I have my assets; how do you think I was well looked after in that shitty jail? I made friends, use your imagination, men and women, they still think I'm their friend, they are also afraid of me because I am out of jail, I could say things, I can use a little pleasure or pain in my talks."

"Why has he not come then?"

"He doesn't know where I am, like you, Spain is a big country. When the time is right, I will tell someone and they will tell him where I am. That is when I will tell you, who he is and where he is."

"Fucking hell, this is getting more and more crazy."

"Steve, you say fucking a lot but it is crazy."

"Gabi, I apologise for using the word, I don't usually say it. We both have to trust each other as you keep saying, we could both go to jail if this isn't worked out alright, for all I know, you could be setting me up, so I'm trusting you. I need you to meet this man to get the action moving. I'm not in Spain next week, I will not have this phone with me. Please give me a day and location you will meet him and get to know him."

"I will meet him, okay, I'm thinking," there was a silence, "Okay, Wednesday, in Segovia next to the viaduct, the Bar El Desvan at three."

Steve, "Wait I'm writing that down. Okay, got that, he will recognise you, you look like someone as you said. He's a good-looking man, brown skin."

"Okay, tell him to go in, I will follow, if I do not feel safe, I will leave."

"It will be okay, he will not be followed, I promise. I will tell him. He will explain in more detail what we have planned, to keep us all safe."

"Okay, I will trust you, I will meet him."

The call was closed, Steve made a call to Leon. Leon agreed to travel, he would stay in Steve's apartment and take the train to meet up with Gabi. Steve now started thinking about Sarah, the course she was on and the impending holiday, Sarah would soon know if she had passed the assessment. As he was waiting for her call, he walked back to the office.

His mobile was vibrating in his pocket as he walked into the office, it was a call, he took the mobile from his pocket and sat at his chair. "Well then, tell me?" he asked.

Sarah took a little time to answer, "It was tough, very tough, I'm not going to say it, but you told me."

Steve was impatient, "Sarah it's okay, whatever, what did they say in your assessment?"

"They were concerned about the lack of my police experience, I hadn't worked the streets, my ability to defend myself if attacked."

Steve couldn't wait, "They failed you for those reasons."

"No, there was more," again she paused, then rapidly said "they said I was a natural, intelligent, quick thinking, good with languages and accents, I did it, I got through!" Steve could hear the excitement in her voice. "They told me they would work on my self-defence and that the lack of police experience was a bonus, yabadabadoo bonny lad."

By this time Bert and a couple of Sarah's colleagues were standing close to Steve, watching Steve's expressions and one-sided conversation. Steve looked at Bert and gave him a wink, "Congratulations, that's fantastic, how many passed?"

"Just two, it was tough Steve."

"Aye, they don't pass many, just shows how special you are, Bert and the team want me to pass on their congratulations to you, well done."

"It's great to hear your voice Steve, it feels like ages since I talked to you. Have you been up to much this last ten days?"

He raised his eyebrows, "No, not much, took Trigger home, that was fun."

"I bet the kids were excited."

"Laura didn't know, she nearly knocked him off his feet when she jumped on him, the kids were great."

"That's smashing for him and the family."

"Oh, something else, I've booked us a short holiday."

"Really," Sarah sounded excited, "When, where to, Benidorm, Malaga, Majorca, I don't care, just tell is?"

"We're leaving on Sunday and get back the following Monday."

"Have you sorted it out with Bert, you're a gem, so where are we going?"

"Yes, it's sorted, I hope you like it."

Sarah couldn't wait, "Will you just tell is?"

"Panama." There was a silence for a few seconds, Steve waited.

"That sounds great, are you okay about it?"

"I am, you don't sound too sure."

"Steve, I'm really, really excited and I know I will love it, seeing the things you've seen, the places. Will you meet any of the team you worked with when we go over?"

"I wasn't planning on it, I've booked a great hotel on the beach, we can visit the islands, you will love it there, maybe even stop a night. The city, canal, jungle trip, just have fun."

"Steve, how much is this costing, it can't be cheap?"

"I've paid, my pressie for passing the assessment. It will be a great experience as well, seeing the Latin country, it can add to your new history. We'll get plenty of photos of you on the beach, on a yacht, drinking cocktails."

"Can I give you something for it?"

"I'm expecting you to."

"You cheeky," She stopped herself and laughed. "I should be landing about six if everything goes okay, I'll just get a cab, are we going out for a drink?"

"Waye aye, stupid, we're celebrating. See you when you get here."

Sunday 7th May

They were both finishing packing their suitcases in their apartments, Sarah had done some necessity shopping for new swim wear and holiday clothes, sun protector, flip flops. Steve had his four pairs of swim shorts, two of which he had taken on his first visit to Panama. He took the opportunity to phone Trigger.

"Hi Steve, okay mate?"

"Yes, great Trigger, I know it's early days but how are you, Laura and the kids?"

"Great mate, will be better when they get back to school this week, I'm knackered."

"Making up for lost time, anyway, just to let you know, it's started."

"Oh, yes, right, do I have to do anything?"

"No, just leave it to me but I'm away with Sarah for a week so it will be the week after, but wheels are in motion."

"Thanks for keeping me in the loop as they say. Where are you off to, anywhere nice?"

"I'm taking Sarah to Panama."

"Do you think that's wise, after what went on there?"

"That's the kind of reaction I got from Sarah, but she didn't say the words. Yes, I like the place, despite some of the memories. I suppose I'll find out when I get there, I'll call you when I get back."

Three hours later, Sarah and Steve had boarded the Iberia direct eleven hour flight, from Madrid Barajas airport to Panama Tocumen airport.

It was a year to the day since Filipe had boarded the canal cruise and met Susannah and Maria. So much had happened in one year.

Tuesday 9th May

Leon had taken a taxi from the airport and was sitting on the sofa in Steve's apartment. He was calculating the time in Panama, it was 15:32 on the digital clock, 08.52 in Panama. He made a call and waited for activation, Steve answered, "Hi mate, how's things."

"Great, I'm in your apartment. I'll have a walk out later, how's the holiday going?"

"We're loving it, just chilled out yesterday on the beach, around the pool and stayed in the hotel last night, it's very good."

"Is Sarah enjoying it?"

"She is loving it. We had some champagne on the flight, then a great day topping up her tan yesterday and more today. We're going into Panama City tonight, a few bars, something to eat, show her some sights."

"Good ones I hope"

"Yeah definitely, planning on going to the Pearl Islands on Thursday, we might stop over."

"You aren't doing any recent history stuff then?"

"No, it's a holiday and Sarah is out of the way, you know. I've talked her into going back to Newcastle when we get back, chance to see her parents, as she's going to be on the course a long time. It works all ways. Are you sorted for tomorrow?"

"Just got to get my train tickets. Can I ring you same time on Thursday?"

"You can try, but I might not get a signal, but keep trying, I want to know how it goes. I'm sure it will be okay; she is a killer, so remember do not do anything stupid"

"I know what I'm doing, we both do. Anyway, enjoy the rest of your holiday, give Sarah my love."

CHAPTER 5

Wednesday 10th May

The crowds were looking at the majestic aqueduct that Segovia is famous for. Built at the command of the Roman Emperor Trajan 1900 years ago and still carries water from the Frio River into Segovia. A magnificent structure, Leon looked at the height and length of the stone aqueduct as he walked to his meeting place. Gabi was stood in the crowds, she noticed him from his description given to her by Steve. She waited and watched behind him and around him, she could not see any followers, but she now knew the teams were good. When she was satisfied that he wasn't being followed or watched, she walked to the Bar El Desvan.

The bar was very busy with tourists, the tables were full and the staff were very busy. They both instantly recognised each other so there was no need for any introductions. Leon stood as Gabi walked to the table, they kissed each other on both cheeks then sat opposite each other, as they looked at each other, nothing was said. The waiter stopped as he was passing and took the order from Leon for two glasses of white wine.

Leon spoke first, "Is it okay to speak English, my Spanish is not very good?"

Gabi nodded and smiled.

Leon continued, "I'm not wired, if that's why you're not speaking?"

"No, I just like looking at you."

"Gabi, that I believe is a compliment and I thank you. I think you're a beautiful woman, but we're not going to get much talking done, about what we are supposed to meet for, if we just look at each other."

"Do you have to leave quick for some reason?"

"No, I don't, I have all day, tomorrow too if need be."

Gabi's smile widened, "Then we can get to know each other first, then we can talk, the talk."

The waiter delivered the glasses of wine and continued on with his large round tray full of drinks to other customers.

Leon sipped from the glass, "This is no place to talk, too busy, too noisy."

Gabi raised her glass, "It is a good place to meet," she opened a small bag and placed a ten Euro note under her full glass, "follow me now."

She walked into the bar closely followed by Leon, they walked through the door towards the toilets, down some steps and through an open door into the street behind the bar, she deactivated the alarm on a red Audi S5 hardtop convertible, "Get in, we can go somewhere quieter."

She drove away slowly out of the town then lowered the roof; the music was playing as the Audi sped along the carriageway towards their destination. Leon was impressed as the Audi was driven through the large metal ornate gates of the Parador de Turismo de la Granja de San Lldefeuso, a beautiful building and hotel. The car was parked and the roof raised automatically as they were walking towards the hotel entrance. Gabi led, Leon was close behind, as they walked through the hotel into the magnificent gardens at the rear of the hotel. She walked to a small table and took a seat with a view of the gardens, Leon sat next to her. They were quickly attended to by one of the numerous, immaculately presented staff, who took the order and left immediately.

Leon was liking what he saw, the gardens and Gabi. A usual starter, "Do you come here often?"

"Now, why would you want to know that?"

"It's not a trick question, forget it. I'm not here to track you down, I could have arrested you when we met, Steve could have done. The reason I'm here, is because my mate Steve asked me to meet you. For all intents and purposes, I do not know who you are, I don't know what you have done, you are just another woman."

"I am certainly not just another woman."

Leon looking her in the eyes, "As far as I'm concerned you are just another woman, a good-looking woman, but you are just another woman I have met."

"So, you are wanting to use me?"

"That's what you asked Steve for, to use the information you have about, certain things, so, yes, I am wanting to use you."

"Is that all?"

Leon thought about what he wanted to say without losing any trust. "Gabi, I have never met you before, you are a stunning woman, rich possibly, you have the sign of wealth and you know how to use it, that is my first impression of you. However, I do know that you've killed three men, when allegedly being passionate with them, you've also killed an English police officer. That does not fill me with confidence about being a close friend, if you know what I mean?"

"I know what you say is right, I admitted it to Gloria and Jessica, but I am not a killer. The only friend I have now is Gloria, I do not have friends. I only keep in touch with Gloria by my mobile, I have no love, no warmth in my heart. I don't know you, but I like you, you have a nice smile, you look a warm person, I do trust you, I want you to trust me."

The waiter brought the white wine and an ice bucket on a stand, he opened the bottle and poured a small sample into the glass of Gabi, she waved for him to pour wine in both glasses, he did then draped a white cotton towel around the neck of the bottle, placed the bottle into the ice then left the area of the table. They both raised their glass and clinked them together, Gabi said, "For trust." and looked into the eyes of

Leon.

"For trust" he answered.

Leon then discussed what Steve and he had planned, which would hopefully keep Steve out of the connection. There was the problem about some person not being Steve checking the information from Trigger and tracing it back to Gabi before Leon was introduced.

Gabi was quiet throughout and let Leon make the explanation. She asked, "Where did I meet you?"

Leon was puzzled, "When?"

She repeated the question, "Where did I meet you?"

"At the bar near to the aqueduct."

"And that is the first time you have met me, seen me?"

"Yes."

"How did you know it was me?"

"You looked like someone I know."

"So, you sat next to me because I looked like someone you know?"

"What are you getting at here? Yes, I did, why?"

"We don't need any introduction, we have met ourselves, at a historic famous place and we have had a drink and a relationship is building."

Leon took a drink of his wine and was thinking, "But, how did you know who I was?"

"I didn't, we just got on, I'm sure a man like you, likes to talk with beautiful women, sometimes?"

"Sometimes, I see where you are coming from, tell me if I'm wrong. You and me become, friends, you find out I am a police officer then tell me what you know and I go in and find out, then tell Steve and we do the operation."

"Yes, but I am not involved in the operation, nowhere, I don't want to be, I have only been in to find out and tell you. You can take over from me."

"Yes, that's possible, we need to talk about it a bit more. Just friends?"

Gabi, "Yes, close friends, you can strip search me anytime

you want officer, everywhere."

Leon did not need his day return ticket for the train.

Thursday 11th May

Gabi was driving at a steady 125 kph on the A50 towards Salamanca heading for Pontevedra. Leon was dozing in the passenger seat; it would be a four hour journey. The music was playing U2 'Where the streets have no name." He tried to tell a joke about a U2 sat nav system, where the streets have no name. Gabi didn't understand, it was his last attempt to stay awake.

When he woke up from his sleep, the windscreen wipers were clearing away the steady rain falling from the sullen grey clouds, miserable English weather he thought. They passed a motorway sign, Vigo 130 kilometres. Another hour, the music continued, Springsteen, the lady liked good music.

Gabi turned the music off, "You remember everything about last night?"

"Yes of course I do."

"What we were talking about, the introduction."

"Yes, I remember that as well." He smiled, she smiled in the mirror.

"We are going to meet in twenty minutes, you are okay, happy?"

"I'm still alive, so I suppose I should be happy."

"I am serious, this has to go right, I'm your friend, you want more cocaine."

"Yes, yes. I have done it before; I know what I'm doing."

They were silent as the vehicle was driven off the motorway a few kilometres North from Pontevedra, it was driven into an industrial estate. Gabi parked outside a large factory unit, Leon waited in the car and watched as she entered by the office door.

After a short wait the door opened, Gabi waved to Leon to enter the building. They went into the small office together, Leon quickly looked around the inside of the building, what he could see was empty space, a few pallets with large boxes stacked, not many. Leon was aware that this was the building where the slaughter had taken place on Monday, the drugs had been removed from the container and divided into the quantities wanted by each of the customers. They had made a good cleaning job of the unit after the slaughter.

Gabi made the introduction, "Leon this is Lucas, Lucas, Leon." the two men shook hands. Lucas was a typical businessman, dark suit, white shirt and a patterned tie, Leon thought he would be in his early fifties, fit, dark hair going grey, short and well styled, about 1.8 metres tall.

Lucas started, "Your friend Gabi tells me you need to step up your quantities."

Leon nodded, "I have had some delivery problems from Andalucía."

"I hope you did not lose too much Leon, sometimes it can be painful."

"I lost money, lots of money, but I still have my freedom. I can get my money back soon, with your help hopefully."

"Well maybe we can both help, Gabi and I."

Leon looked at Gabi, then looked back at Lucas, "The plan was, Gabi and I would go into a partnership and build up what I had lost."

"Leon that's an excellent plan, but you have no money, well not enough to get what you would want. Unless you have a plan to get some more money, rob a bank maybe."

Leon looked at Gabi, "You told me you would help, you would get me some money."

Gabi shook her head, "I told you, I would help to get you money, that's what I'm doing."

"No, no you're not helping me. Give me what I want and I'll pay off the debt straight away."

Lucas interrupted, "Just wait Leon, there has been a misunderstanding, Gabi can help, I can help you get the money for your requirement."

"What do you mean by help?"

"We need someone to do something for us, who would get paid very well, well enough to get what your requirement is."

"What do I have to do?"

Lucas, "Gabi has told me, you have worked on ships, yachts, you can read charts. You could go somewhere and bring back a cruise boat, there would be a small crew. Just one trip. Then you start again."

"I've done the hard shit man, start again." Leon was thinking, shaking his head.

Lucas continued, "You can get smaller amounts and build up, might take a year, two years, the others are taking your connections, it would be more difficult. The seas are good this time of year, think of it as a two-week holiday"

"When?"

"Soon."

"Where?"

"You will be told when you leave."

"Do I come back here, Europe, anyway?"

"You will be told when they give you the chart."

"Do the crew know what they're doing, I mean boat handling?"

"Boat handling, yes, they don't need to know about the cargo?"

"Do they speak English?"

"Yes, a bit."

Leon looked at Gabi, "Why didn't you tell me this before you brought me here, I could have said no?"

Gabi, "Because, I knew you would not say no when you met Lucas."

It looked as if Leon was in deep thought, they waited for his answer. "Lucas, I like you, you don't ask too many questions and you give no answers. I need to know this, if I do it, will I get my requirement without any payment, no cash, I'm not doing it and being done over?"

Lucas, "You can trust me, others do. What is the British saying, loose lips sink ships? There will be no loose lips, it has been done several times."

"One answer please, do I have time to go back to England?"

"You can go anywhere, as long as you will be in Madrid in 24 hours."

"That is a sort of answer." Leon was smiling.

The two men shook hands, Gabi was kissed on both cheeks by Lucas, Leon turned his back on Gabi and walked towards the door.

Gabi was smiling, "He's okay, he needs me, he needs a lift, he does not know where he is."

They both laughed.

They sat in the car, as they were driving away Leon said quietly, "That went well then. How long to get back to Madrid?"

"We're not going to Madrid, you will stop with me tonight at my villa, I trust you, and it would look better."

Leon looked at the car clock 15:39, it was too early to call Steve.

It took just over an hour to get to the Villa perched on the hillside overlooking the Atlantic, the automatic gates opened as the car approached and closed behind them as they entered. It was a modern box style white walled and glass villa, there was a pool at the front of the house, the patio furniture positioned with a view of the Galician Atlantic Islands towards the horizon. The sun had eventually broken through the clouds and the temperature was rising to a pleasant 24 degrees. Gabi opened the villa and entered the hall; Leon took the chance to contact Steve, he sat on a patio chair.

"Hi Leon, can you be quick?" Steve had heard the mobile and walked away from Sarah who was lying on a lounger listening to music through her pods.

"I'll try, but there's a change in plan."

"Explain?"

"I met Gabi, she trusts me, she came up with a plan to meet the guy who runs the importing and introduce me to him to get things started."

Steve was confused, "That was the plan we had, what's the change?"

"I didn't go back to Madrid after the meeting."

Steve interrupted, "Please tell me you didn't?"

Leon interrupted the speech, "We just stayed together, that's all, and talked about the plan."

Steve was angry, Leon could hear it in his voice, "She is not to be trusted like that, you know what she has done, Leon you have to be careful, what you are doing is wrong."

"Whoa, wait, that's enough. What I have done is wrong? What the fuck did you do then when setting this meeting up, taking her into your apartment? This is a way to keep you out of it. She trusts me and I trust her."

"Sorry Leon, you're right, but for fuck's sake be careful man, I've seen what she can do, what's the plan now then?"

"I've met this woman by chance, we became friends, we liked each other, she told me about drug dealing in Galicia, she knew some peripheral members of the organisation, she introduces me to one and I get asked to do a job for them, so get inside the OCG."

"It sounds believable I suppose, so when does this start? Who are you going to pass the info on to, your boss or Bert?"

Leon held his breath for a second or two, "It's started, I've had the introduction."

Steve was walking along the beach, well away from the sun worshippers lying on the sunbeds. It was idyllic, the high sun shining down on the mountain greenery, the golden sands, the gentle sound of the waves rolling onto the shore. Steve could feel an earthquake happening inside his body, "Have you been thinking with your brain or your dick, I told you what she is like, she's fucking clever, very clever, she uses her assets, as she told me, to get what she wants, she fucking told me she uses her assets. You have fallen for it; you have fallen for her."

Leon denied the truth, he lied, "I have not fallen for her or her assets as you say, we talked it through together, thoroughly. She respects you and is aware of the dangers that she put you in, this is possibly a way around it. You are out of it, totally, no need to involve Trigger and the lies about his incredible information. It's down to me."

Steve was shaking his head, listening, thinking, "Who's going to control it, us or the Spanish, they would recognise her at some stage if there's photographs flashed around the departments."

Leon continued, "We've thought about that, she is pulling out of the group and handing over to me, to run the business, she is history, no need to dig to find her."

"So, she is out of it totally now."

"Well, no, not exactly. Please listen before you blast off again. She will pass on the information to you, by phone, no meetings, like a liaison between me and you, then you do the action plan. Simples"

"Simples! I think you have got your head stuck in the ground, or somewhere else, fucking simples! It's serious this man," there was a silence for a few seconds, "so what happened at this introduction?"

"I got introduced to a guy called Lucas, I told him I wanted some supplies, as my other sources were taken out in Andalucía and I had lost a load of cash. He wouldn't accept laying on the drugs and offered me a way to pay for them."

Steve was anxious, "Come on, I can't wait to hear this bit?"

"I've just got to bring a small boat, yacht, from somewhere to somewhere else, obviously the boats going to be full of, probably 'charlie', then I take my consignment for the transport fee. Just like driving a wagon really."

"How big is the boat, you don't know the route?"

"No, I'll get told when I get to the boat and I don't know where the boat is. Just a cruise boat or yacht, he said there would be other crew but they wouldn't know there was cargo."

"So, you could be in the middle of an ocean, with no back up, no communication, do you think that's wise?"

"It is a risk, but I'm prepared to do it."

"When is this?"

"Could be tomorrow, I don't know, but soon."

There was silence again, Leon, "Hello."

Steve, "I'm here, thinking. You'll have to call your boss and explain the, the, circumstances of your meeting and how it's progressed. You'll have to get the go ahead to continue, which shouldn't be a problem as you have already had the introduction. Will they need to know the identity of the CHIS?" (Covert Human Intelligence Source.)

"They will, but not yet, they would only have her new identity, she's legal in Spain she told me."

"She might be legal but CITCO (Intelligence Centre against Terrorism and Organised Crime) might already have her recorded, the E.D.O.A. (Civil Guards Organised Crime Team) could be involved already."

"It's a big organisation she told me, so it is possible."

Steve thought for a few seconds then asked, "You say she trusts you; I need to know her new identity, d.o.b., her address if she will give it, did she tell you where she was living?"

"No mate, I didn't ask, just building up the trust." He lied again.

"Suggest me, as you're partner in Spain, we've worked together, know each other, I wouldn't come into contact with Gabi. She would have to keep clear and we could get the job done."

Leon continued, "Steve, what I'm doing is only one of the methods, a big one from what I have been told, possibly tons. There are ships coming regular to the Galicia region, you could possibly get involved with those, I could give you an introduction."

"You could, if I'm back before you leave for wherever?"

"I could at least get Lucas to accept you as my partner if I'm away."

"Give it a try, we've gone down the line now, I'll know nothing if Bert gets in touch with me, I'm sure he will agree. Leon, I must know if she's recorded in Spain before we do anything, get the details and call me back straight away, I can get it checked out."

Leon, "Okay will do. Where are you now?"

"You wouldn't believe it, but we've been dropped off at a remote beach on The Pearl Islands, looking out from the jungle behind, the beach down to the ocean to where Chapman was speared twice by the lovely Gabi and dispatched to the bottom of the Ocean." He momentarily could see the event happen in his mind. "Where are you?"

"I'm waiting for my train back to Madrid." He lied.

"Keep in touch, let me know what the score is."

"Will do, don't worry, enjoy your holiday."

Leon stood up and started walking around the pool, looking out to the Islands which could be seen clearly now, he made a call to England.

After the call was made, the introduction to Lucas was accepted, on the understanding that no further work was done with the OCG, until the full intelligence checks had been made with NCA and CITCO.

He walked into the modern villa, the hall had plain white walls where large bright alfresco paintings were on display. A large mirror was positioned opposite the staircase, the floor was highly polished white patterned floor tiles, a chandelier hung from the ceiling. The open staircase had wooden stairs leading to the upper floor, there were four doors on the ground floor. He walked towards the door that was open which led into the lounge, a large square room, the feature being the glassed security windows which were the width of the room affording the view over the Atlantic and the distant islands. The cream leather furniture was large with 2 chairs and a long sofa, they faced the wall where a huge television screen was hanging invisibly. The house was ultra-modern and expensive, Gabi was doing well.

Gabi was sat in one of the chairs. She had poured two glasses of cola, she added ice and a slice of lime. Leon sat on the other chair and took a sip of his cola.

She had been waiting, "That was two long phone calls, what do you have to tell me and ask me?"

Leon took another drink from the glass, "I spoke to Steve first, he is okay about what we did," again he was lying, "he wants to be involved in the operation, to protect my back I guess."

"Yes, that could be good, what did he ask you about me?"

Leon thought, "You, we, have to trust him, he wants to know your new identity and address."

"Did you tell him I live here?"

"No, of course not, I told him I was on the train to Madrid. He does need to know, to protect you and us, just in case the Spanish police know of your involvement already, that's all."

"Okay, did you tell him that you had stopped with me?"

"I told him we stayed in separate rooms in the hotel, he was okay with that."

Gabi was laughing, "He didn't believe you, did he?"

"No, you're right, he wasn't happy but told me just to be careful."

"Yes, in case I kill you." She was laughing again, Leon wasn't laughing.

"Please, tell me what he needs to know, it will be a big help, he is not trying to get you into jail, he's trying to keep us all out of jail."

Gabi stood and walked out of the room, she returned and handed Leon her Spanish identification card, a small writing book and a biro pen. He recorded the details from the DNI, Elena Gabriela Suárez, 14/6/89, the national identification number and her address. Calle del Seixo, Cangas, Vigo, Galicia. He sent a WhatsApp message to Steve.

CHAPTER 6

Friday 12th May

Gabi had dropped Leon at Vigo airport for the 09:35 flight back to Madrid. He was in the lounge with a coffee, in truth he didn't want to leave Gabi, but it was necessary to return to the capital and access the police computer. He had told Steve in a message that he would check out the details on Gabi, it would be authorised, as his meeting had already been disclosed to his department supervisor in the UK.

When he arrived at the Embassy, Leon spoke to Bert and was given access to the computer linked system with CITCO. The enquiry about Gabi was negative, she was not recorded on the system, he then checked the National Police intelligence, there was nothing known. Leon's shoulders relaxed, a slight sigh of relief, time to push on. Gabi had given three member names of the group, Lucas Alvarez, Miguel Torres, Javier Delgado. The three men were known, while there was little intelligence on Alvarez, Torres and Delgado were known drug dealers of large quantities, believed imported from South America. Time was of the essence to register Gabi as a CHIS, an informant, liaise with the Spanish Intelligence, CITCO, and commence the operation. Leon wasted no time, he spoke to Bert and told him the full story, minus the parts about the registered informant being a serial murderer, a prison escapee, his recent lover and was known to Steve. Bert decided to hold a meeting with the Spanish at the Embassy on Tuesday, this was to give Steve sometime to get to know the intelligence, he would have to use another intelligence officer as Sarah was not available. There was a plan.

It was 10:05 in the Gulf of Panama, Sarah and Steve were on board the quick boat to Panama City from San Miguel Island, the sun was already beating down, they sat beneath the canopy for some protection from the rays. They were having a great holiday, making fantastic memories, their tans had been worked on and Sarah looked like a local. They had rested on the beaches, had a visit into the jungle, Sarah loved the Islands and Panama City was so lively. They had done so much.

Sarah gave Steve a kiss on the cheek, "Thank you for bringing me here, I absolutely love the place."

Steve was happy, smiling, "I knew you would, we did." He stopped himself from saying more.

"I know, you both did, no need to hide or try and forget, it is how we ended up together."

Steve was apologetic, "I'm sorry, it hasn't entered my mind, well not much."

Sarah hugged him, "I think we need to maybe see some people you know and visit some places. We are here, we should do it."

Looking in her eyes, "Do you not mind, honestly?"

"I would love to meet some of both of your friends, I know Jessica was well liked here. I know you have a few numbers, give them a ring and meet up. I would honestly like that if they could."

Steve made a call to Jaime; Jaime was pleased to hear from Steve and was surprised that he did not call before. He arranged to meet up with some others he could contact at a bar in the city that afternoon. Sarah was excited at meeting up with Jaime and possibly Gloria and the others, but she was anxious for Steve. She had seen at times during the week that he looked troubled, deep in thought, it never crossed her mind that his thoughts were thousands of miles away in Spain. The less she knew the better.

They had time when they returned to the hotel to again top up their tan, relax on the beach, and swim in the ocean before heading towards the city. Steve was receiving calls on his mobile, he would walk along the beach when he was in conversation, Sarah could see him laughing on occasions, it made her happy.

Leon was one of the callers, "I'll keep it brief, the operation is on, Gabi is not recorded anywhere on Spanish police systems, all of them. Bert has liaised with the Spanish and is planning an ops meeting on Tuesday at the office so you can be back. The three men she told me about are known as big players but there's no one inside, until now, you and me mate. Here we go again."

"It sounds so easy, what could possibly go wrong?" Steve jested.

"If we play it right it should be spot on, and, you will not know anything about the informant. It's not Shakira by the way, the contact details have not been finalised, everything is going very quick."

"Do we still have control?"

"At the moment, the more we can put in, the more they will be reliant on our source and we retain control. They will be the arresting teams though, that could be soon."

"Where are you now?"

"I'm stopping in your place if that's okay? I need to be able to travel quick."

"Yes, no problem, please tell me she is not there."

For once Leon told the truth, "Honest mate, she's not here, I wouldn't do anything stupid like that."

Steve started to laugh, Sarah was watching and smiled, if only she knew.

Gabi was in the villa, she was sitting in the sun on the terrace warming her skin, the beautiful view towards the Islands in front of her. She had expertly made two large crystal glasses of Mojito, the way she did for her parents, brother and sister with fresh mint, cane sugar, fresh lime juice, Bacardi white rum, crushed ice and soda water. They were on the table next to her chair; she couldn't see the islands through her eyes, they were full of tears. All she could see was the farm building, Paco and Borja, what they did to her and Susanna, the slow-motion action of what she had done to her best friend, each time she pumped the sharp blade to cut through her skin, the throat, her chest, the tears were heavy, Susanna was lying on the floor looking into her face until death was in her eyes and could see no more. She was sobbing, her head was hanging down on her chest, she used her resolve to straighten her back and hold her head high, ignoring the tears, she lifted one glass of Mojito to the sky. "Susanna, my best friend, I love you still, I did it for you, please forgive me. I will get full revenge for you, for both of us. That I promise."

She took a large drink and sat back in the chair, her thoughts were clear, she was now watching the naked Borja die from his own poison, she was smiling and wiping the tears. She thought of Filipe and asked for his forgiveness, though she could never forgive herself, she drank more Mojito, the first glass was emptied. Her thoughts turned to the horror of the attack on the prison van, the explosion which disoriented her, filled her eyes with clouds of dust, the guard being riddled with bullets, his blood spraying through the metal fencing cell across her face, the attackers entering the van as she cowered in the corner of her small cell and hid her head, expecting the same as the guard. The gate being opened, dragged out roughly by the arm towards the clean air at the doorway. Jessica was running to save her, 'Pantera' was aiming and sending gunfire towards Jessica, she was pulling at his sleeve, it did no good as she watched Jessica hit with the gun fire then she fell behind the wall. Picking up the second glass, she raised it to the sky, "The future, revenge, Paco, 'Pantera', Manolo, fuck you all." She drank the full contents of the glass, then threw the crystal glass onto the terrace where it shattered into thousands of small pieces.

Jaime had sent a message to Steve to meet at the Blarney Stone pub in the city at six o'clock that evening, he was sending a police vehicle to collect them. He had given the driver specific instructions.

Sarah had dressed casually in navy blue shorts and a lime green top, she placed one locally bought coloured bead necklace around her neck, her long black wavy hair was shining and hanging loose over her shoulders. The bright colours highlighted her tan.

Steve was wearing cream shorts, a white and green leafed patterned collared polo shirt.

They had bought a bouquet of assorted flowers; sitting in the hotel foyer, they had a cold cola as they waited for their transport. The uniformed officer entered the hotel, Steve recognised him immediately as the officer who had collected him and Jessica from the hotel in Colon, he couldn't recall his name. They greeted each other and Steve introduced Sarah, the officer shook hands and looked at Sarah momentarily, then walked towards the waiting patrol car.

On the way to the city on the motorway, the officer activated the warning lights on the vehicle, moved to the inside lane and then the refuge lane then stopped. The officers alighted from the car and opened the rear passenger doors, ensuring it was safe, Sarah and Steve got out of the car and stepped through a small pedestrian gap in the safety wall. They immediately saw a number of small wooden crosses secured against the wall, there were flowers next to all of the crosses, messages had been written on the wall. They saw the cross with Jessica O'Brien carved into the wood, it was well cared for, varnished, and recently polished, some fresh local flowers were in a small bowl. Steve could read through his tear-filled eyes the names of Gloria, Jaime, Arturo, Stefanie, Paco, many more, all of the team had written messages. Sarah stepped back as Steve laid the bouquet next to her cross, he was crying, as to be expected. He touched the cross of every person that had died that day. They returned to the police vehicle and continued towards the city. Sarah was quietly pleased she had not put any makeup on her eyes and cheeks, they hugged each other in the back of the car.

It only took another ten minutes for the car to stop outside the Blarney Stone pub in the city, the officers opened the rear doors for Sarah and Steve to get out of the vehicle. Steve thanked the officers for their courtesy and transport and shook hands with them both, Sarah smiled and gave each officer kisses on both cheeks then they turned and walked up the steps into the welcoming airconditioned interior of the pub.

The first friendly face to be seen was Paco, he had placed himself near to the door to watch for them both arriving.

He had a large smile on his face when he saw Steve and walked forward to greet him, he opened his arms wide and they hugged then shook hands vigorously. Paco's mouth opened in surprise when he looked at Sarah, Steve made the introduction, Paco, "Sarah you are a beautiful lady, I am really pleased to meet you." They both kissed each other in the usual welcome.

Sarah, "I am pleased about that Paco, at first I thought you had seen a ghost."

Paco was apologetic and thought quickly, "Sarah, I was stunned by your beauty. I apologise."

Sarah smiled, "See Steve, that's what you should say to me, thank you very much Paco. You are a handsome man if I may say so."

They walked towards the group who had gathered at the far end of the bar, Sarah noticed that they were all looking at her as she got closer, she considered that this was just because she was not like Jessica. Jaime and Arturo arrived together and again the initial looks at Sarah were noticeable then the very warm greetings. Jaime was the first to broach the subject of Sarah's appearance.

"Steve, Sarah is a beautiful woman, I cannot believe how

much she looks like Maria, ehm Higuita."

Steve was thinking back to his recent meeting in his apartment, "I never really noticed, obviously the hair and face shape were similar, but since we have worked in Spain her tan has developed, she is similar."

"They could be sisters, twins, everyone is talking about the similarities in appearance, but Sarah is also a beautiful person, so much different to Maria. Does she not think so?"

"She has never mentioned it, obviously they have never met but she has seen photographs, Maria is younger in the photographs and Sarah is fuller bodied."

Jaime was smiling with a little laugh, "I would not describe Sarah as being fuller bodied, she is a woman."

Again, Steve was thinking to the recent encounter, "Maria's appearance that we knew would probably be different now anyway. She must have changed." He lied.

"Yes, that is very true," he started to laugh again, "however, if Sarah does not get stopped at the airport on the way out of the country, I will sack all of the officers on duty."

After a few seconds of laughter, Steve asked, "Do you have any idea where she may be?"

"No, none at all. Some think she is dead, killed by the Cartel, there have been no sightings, that is until she walked in with you." More laughs, then they joined the crowd.

Sarah was enjoying the company and the music, everyone was friendly, police everywhere she thought, work and party together.

Steve sought out Enrique who was the partner of Gloria, they shook hands firmly, Steve enquired, "Have you seen or heard much from Gloria, she's not here?"

"No, I have tried, I tried today, a call, no answer, I sent her a message, no answer. I thought it would be good for her to meet up with you, you know, she was very good friends with Jessica." He shrugged his shoulders. "She is not well, she never recovered from the incident, the injuries are bad but she blames herself for Jessica, you know."

"Do you never see her now?"

"No. I am sorry Steve, but she does not speak to anyone now, in fact she moved, I do not know where she lives. The mobile I have for her might not work. We are all worried about her," he thought for the words as he pointed his finger at his head, "brain health, if you know what I mean."

"Yes, I do Enrique, thank you for trying."

The party went on until the early hours, they slowly drifted away, there was only Paco, Barbra and Alejandro with Sarah and Steve. Paco was dancing a merengue with Sarah, the others were drinking shots at the bar, the last of the kitty, mostly paid for by Steve and Jaime.

Gloria entered the building and walked towards the bar unnoticed, she was casually dressed in a long sleeved dark blue shirt and denim jeans. It was Paco who noticed her first as he swung his body on the dancefloor, "I am sorry Sarah." He left Sarah still dancing and quickly walked to Gloria and as they embraced, he could feel something was different. They both kissed in greeting. He shouted above the music, "Steve, see who is here?"

He turned and saw her, she hadn't changed, the smile was great to see, immediately taking hold of her around her body, again for a big Geordie lad, rare tears were in his eyes. They held each other for ages, Sarah looked on, moved to tears again. Steve could feel the left arm of Gloria, it was solid, he recognised the feeling and started to cry. He hugged tighter, he whispered, "I am helping Gabi, we will get revenge."

She whispered in his ear, "Not for me, for Jessica, the guards, for Greg, Gabi and many others. Thank you." turning to the others, "It is good to see you, all of you. I could not cope with everyone, I need time, maybe soon," she smiled at Steve, "I can be happy again."

Sarah and Gloria embraced, "I am really pleased to meet you, this means a lot to me, Jessica really liked you and obviously Steve."

"I am pleased Steve has found happiness with you; you look

so much like Maria, Higuita."

"Do you know something Gloria? You are the first one who has had the balls to tell me, they've all looked and known and said nothing, of course, I can now see a resemblance, not back then. Watch." she winked at Gloria.

"Hey, you lot, Gloria thinks I look like Maria."

The four of them looked with open mouths, Steve was the first to speak, "Actually I was going to tell you," The others were nodding, "but I think you're bigger."

They all looked at Steve now with surprise he said what he had. He tried to claw back the words, "I didn't mean bigger, rounder, no, no, mature, I've had a few drinks." by now they were all laughing.

Sarah was smiling and jesting, "Go on son, keep digging?"

Steve, "I was just joking you know that?"

Sarah gave the twisted smile she did so well, "And?"

"More athletic, fitter, that's what I meant to say and taller, yes taller, and more beautiful as well, but similar sort off."

Sarah, "Steve, stop your slaver and get another round of drinks in."

Sarah and Gloria were quickly becoming friends, this could be awkward was in the mind of Steve, as he waved his finger around, the international sign for same again, at the barman for more drinks.

Sunday 14th May

The holiday was coming to a close, Saturday had been a day of recovery and some last-minute shopping in Panama City. Now there was still some time for relaxing on the beach and a swim in the ocean before the pick-up for the airport for the flight to Spain.

Gabi had been to the early morning mass; she took communion but no longer attended the confessional. She had driven the few miles to the Marina in Cangas, she had cleaned the external windows and decking of her motorboat. It was not as good as her fathers, the one that Martin Chapman had made use of, but it was big enough and easy for her to handle single crewed. A Princess 286 Riviera, a ten metre, diesel engine motorboat, it was second hand but had a reliable engine, good enough to get her around the Islands or further up the coast to A Coruña. She had spent some money replacing the old leather cushions, inside and out, and installed a new music system throughout. After starting the engine and idling for some time while the instruments were checked, she slipped the mooring and sailed out onto the Atlantic, at a steady rate she pushed along towards the Islands in clear blue skies on the very calm ocean. Having dropped the anchor near to the Isla Cíes, she rowed the dinghy to the beach then had lunch in the Restaurante Rodas. She would later return on the same route and after mooring up return to her villa.

Steve and Sarah had returned to Tocumen airport where Sarah was allowed through passport control with no problem. After depositing their suitcases, they had a couple of drinks in the bar before boarding their overnight flight to Madrid.

CHAPTER 7

Monday 15th May

They landed in Madrid at 6:30am, they had both slept some hours but not enough. Sarah had to be back at the airport at 11am for her flight to Newcastle upon Tyne.

They were in their apartments in an hour, Sarah wasting no time in emptying her flight bag and case then replacing it with the clothing she had prepared for the visit to her parents and the eight-week course. She set her alarm for 10am and lay on the top of her bed.

Leon had heard Steve enter the apartment and made a pot of coffee. They discussed the plans that had been made, there were so many, what ifs and buts, questions and possible answers, as he often said, no-one said it would be easy. The operation hadn't even started yet and their prospects were grim if the truth unravelled.

Leon showered and went to the Embassy; Steve would follow later.

Steve booked the taxi and together they travelled to the airport, he had a feeling of guilt about what he had not told Sarah but, it was for the best, the only way. He had an unusual feeling towards Sarah at the gate to departures, he suddenly realised he might never see her again, well possibly through iron bars if things went well. He held her in a passionate hold and kissed her for real, in public. Sarah was taken aback; it was good though. "I am coming back you know, nine weeks."

"I love you."

Again, Sarah was surprised and excited, "I love you too big lad, I have for a long time. It was a great holiday; we can do it again." She kissed him on the lips gently. "You will be good won't you, do not do owt daft, are you listening, promise?"

He lied, "I promise, enjoy the course if you can, I know you will be a success, watch, listen, learn and don't let your gob runaway, keep it shut, well, when you should anyway."

There was one more kiss, then Sarah walked into the departures lounge. Steve watched until she was out of sight, then leaving the terminal he took a taxi to the Embassy.

He walked through the door to see Leon sat at his desk, the pleasantries and greeting was said at once, "Nice to see you Leon, out of my chair and desk."

"Nice to see you as well Steve, I'm working on something."

Bert came out of his office, "You two, in here, now." He spoke in a stern voice.

They were apprehensive as they walked into the office, "That will have them thinking," he smiled, "good holiday Steve, did Sarah enjoy it?"

"Yes, thanks Bert, we did."

Bert interrupted, "Sorry Steve, tell me later, there's a new job in that I need you to get started on. Leon has done the donkey work."

Steve knew the kind of donkey work he had been doing.

"It's another UC job you will both be involved in, we currently have the lead, the informant into an OCG in Galicia importing, shit loads of gear apparently, is that the right expression Leon?"

"Yes boss."

"Call me Bert, everyone else does." Leon nodded as Bert continued, "I want to build on our success with Devil's Crossroads and our liaison with the Spanish, UDYCO and GRECO. It could happen very soon, any time in fact, is that correct Leon?"

"Yes b, Bert."

"Leon, the CHIS has been logged, so safe now, just make

sure you or the informant tell us everything, even if they are involved somehow, as long as it's minimal it will be okay. There're no skeletons I should know about are there?" Bert handed Leon the details required for the informant.

Leon lied again as Steve looked on, "Not that I know about, anyway once Steve and me."

Bert interrupted, "Steve and I." Leon looked puzzled. Bert continued, "not me, you say I."

"Oh yes b, Bert. Once Steve and I get working, the informant will not be of any use unless we tell the informant to contact the intelligence officer."

"Excellent." There was silence as Bert was flicking through his desk diary. "You have both been allocated this for three months, hopefully we can get a result before then, do not push it, let it take its course, and of course do not do anything that you should not do. Self-preservation is very important though; you both know the rules on that. Here in Spain, it is easier to justify actions than back in the UK. Can you both give me the answer, you have been told?"

Steve, "Yes Bert."

Leon, "Yes Bert."

"Well done Leon for remembering my name, God help us."

He was shaking his head and smiling with the lads. "Both of your cards have been loaded, as usual, do not go stupid, I don't expect receipts, just honesty, I have no doubts on that."

They both had a feeling of guilt but it didn't show, "Thanks Bert." Steve answered, Leon nodded.

"Now, I do not expect to see you in this office until the end of the operation. Keep in contact, careful with the phones, I don't have to tell you that, you know what you're doing. Keep away from the ladies, they can be very dangerous. Unless there's any questions, get out and get to work."

The three shook hands, Leon collected his jacket from the back of Steve's chair then they walked out without looking back. They collected their UC phones and credit cards from the secure storage in the Embassy, then returned to the apartment, both mobiles were put on charge, they were keeping a small amount of history from Devils Crossroads. Steve made a call on the UC mobile, the call was on speaker, "Hi Cass, it's Steve can you talk?" It was a stupid question when he thought about it.

"Steve, really, is that you, it's great to hear you mate. I thought you and Leon must have been arrested with everyone else when I hadn't heard from you, so I was fearing the worst. Is Sarah okay, and Leon, what's happening mate? It's all change here, but the business is up and running again. Michael's missus is now running it, well she owns it, I'm running it like before really, they've shut the other place where they did the repairs down, so it's just the car sales. I'm doing okay though, not so good for Michael, Mark and Jason, they're still inside. Mark and Michael are down Granada way, it's a pain in the arse for his missus travelling all the way down there and back to visit, he reckons he's fucked, those were his words, a long time in jail, she says she's lucky to have me."

Steve interrupted, "Cass, Cass, slow down mate."

"Yes, sorry Steve, I just got carried away a bit, not like me really, anyway, how's things with you and the others?"

Steve and Leon were smiling, "We are okay now, Michael set us up with the others, all because that driver was murdered in Newcastle. He needed a driver as a one-off, Leon said he would do it, looking at setting up our own transport company as you know. Michael had been locked up before we even got the wagon, we didn't know anything. I went along with Leon as I wanted to organise some pick-ups in the UK. Then we got lifted after we made the last drop off, near Newcastle."

"How did you get out?"

"We never went in prison. The cops locked us up when we parked the wagon to go to the hotel. They had been following the group for a while, the dead driver and the others. They didn't know us, eventually they believed us that it was our first trip and didn't know what the cargo was. It was corroborated by the old guys on the golf trip"

"You had a lucky break there, well not really if you weren't involved in all those drugs, loads of drugs, cocaine, heroin, cannabis, I never knew a thing. I thought Michael was legit mate, couldn't believe it when the Guardia came through the gate, fuck me Steve, I was shitting myself. They don't take any prisoners, well they do, but you know what I mean." Leon had to leave the room he was laughing that much. "Anyway, they didn't take me as a prisoner, they must have known I wouldn't do anything like that, I'm honest, you know that Steve, I told them everything I knew, which was about selling cars that's all I ever did, still do. Oh, fucking hell! Have you heard what happened to the Scouse bloke in jail yesterday?"

Kevin Wilson had returned from the shower block to his cell, the other occupant of the cell was still in the block, he had been prevented from leaving. Wilson was applying medication to his left shoulder scars and injury; he was grabbed from behind and a gag with a ball made from rolled up kitchen cloths was placed in his mouth and tied securely at the back of his head. He briefly could see the three attackers in the polished tin mirror on the wall, they were tall, muscular men, their skin was the colour of wet coal, black and shiny. The men forced him to bend over the end of the bed and pushed his shirt over his shoulders and head, he could feel his trousers and underwear being pulled down and falling around his ankles. Wilson was furiously shaking his head which was pushed into the thin mattress on top of the bed, whilst continually trying to resist, with only one arm it was futile. He could feel something wet around his anus, then he felt a penetration as his muscles contracted against the entry, it was pushed further and more powerful inside, it was pulled out and pushed further inside again and again, repeatedly, Wilson was sweating, he had stopped struggling. He could feel a coldness inside him then what he thought was a large erect black penis being removed from his rectum. Then the pain intensified, his attackers left the cell. He freed the gag with his right arm and screamed, alerting the prison guards. Wilson couldn't move, the pain was unrelenting but intensified again if there was any movement. The officers ran to the cell and saw Wilson, bent double over the end of the bed, the shirt still over his head and shoulders, the trousers lying around his ankles on the floor, "Fucking do something, help me, please." The officers then saw the barbed wire, 10 centimetres of which was extending from the anus, the points had been sharpened, the wire was old and rusted. There was a dark brown, black fluid, mixed with red blood coming from the anus and rolling down his legs. On the floor was a plastic tube which would be used for the plumbing repairs, about five centimetres in diameter, thirty five centimetres in length, it had been white but was covered in mixture of fluids, there was a discarded brown stained plastic bag next to the pipe. The guards sounded the alarm and stood back awaiting the arrival of the medical team, they could do nothing other than protect the crime scene.

Steve replied curiously, "No, how am I supposed to know? Tell me then."

"Apparently, he was beaten up in his cell, in a bad way apparently, something to do with the murder of the black girls they reckon, Michael's brief told his missus this morning."

Steve, "That's a shame then. Tough shit eh." He didn't know the reality of his remark. "Do you still have my car?"

Cass, "Well, the Guardia locked the gates of the compound and started searching."

"Cass, Cass, have you still got my car? If not, I want my cash back. That was the deal with Michael."

"Yes, but I've put it up for sale and someone wants it they're coming for a test drive and."

"Cass" Steve interrupted again. Leon was ill with laughter in the kitchen, "They're not getting it. It's my car, it might still be registered to the garage but I've paid, in cash, for that car. Sarah likes the car."

"Yes, of course Steve, when will you be collecting it? Are you in Spain now?"

"I am in Spain; I need my car."

"Steve, I like you, you have been mucked about a bit, not by me or this company, but by others. You know who did the stuff behind your back, the police, well, Mick as well. I'll deliver it personally to you, no hard feelings, mates, right."

"Are you sure about that Cass?"

"Yes definitely, I'll get my assistant to look after the plot tomorrow and I'll bring it to you. Are you in Benidorm again?"

"Madrid, I'm in Madrid."

There was an incredible brief silence from Cass, "Madrid, okay, it will be in the afternoon, where?"

"Make it outside the train station and I will pay for your ticket back to Alicante, no hard feelings. Shall we say 2pm? I will watch for you."

"Yes Steve, thanks, that's very good of you, see you tomorrow."

Leon brought two beers as they were laughing at the conversation and Cass.

Steve made a call to Bert and was told what had happened in the cell, the fluid was a mixture of sewerage and hot chilli powder. Needless to say, Wilson was still in hospital in severe pain, his wounds were infected. He didn't get any sympathy.

That evening, they went for an Indian curry, they were continually exploring the plan, what ifs, etcetera.

Leon had broken his poppadom and was liberally covering it with mango chutney, "I've just thought of this, another what if. What if, I stay here and then, I can keep in touch with Gabi, you would be nowhere near her, and you do the boat trip, you like boats, you always said you were better than I am with charts."

"No, you're just getting wet feet and you want to stay on dry land. What about, it was a risk I'm prepared to take, that's what you said."

"I've done the introduction, he couldn't give a fuck who

brings the boat back as long as they're reliable, two weeks holiday he said. You need a holiday." As he laughed and ate his poppadom.

Steve was spooning the spiced chopped onions onto his poppadom and filling his mouth, he started nodding, he finished his mouthful, "As much as I absolutely hate to say it, I think you're right. I'm starving. Keep the chat for later"

Leon quickly replied, "We haven't ordered chat, idiot." They started laughing and did a high five, food took the priority.

As Sarah would have said, "Boys will be boys, they never grow up."

Tuesday 16th May

After a light breakfast Steve made a call. "Good morning big lad, you haven't forgot me yet then, what's happening?"

"Hi Sarah, you alright? I've got some news."

"I hope it's good."

"Kevin Wilson has had a plastic pipe shoved up his arse a long way and then barbed wire pushed up the middle of the pipe," Sarah could feel her bum automatically squeeze tight in reaction, "The pipe was filled with nasty stuff, then pulled out leaving the barbed wire to cut into his insides and the nasty stuff to cause infection."

Sarah was screwing her face and clenching her bum cheeks together listening to Steve, "That's painful, I can't say I feel any sympathy, but I feel sick myself at the thought."

"Just to let you know, Leon and I are starting on the new job today, so might not be able to speak to you for a while."

"It was expected, do nowt daft, that's what you say."

"I'll not. You enjoy this week at your mams, it's going to be tough for eight weeks but I know you can do it. Enjoy the bits you can and learn all you can, it will be needed. You never know, next time we meet might be to go on holiday again."

"Bloody hell Steve, I hope it's not that long. I really enjoyed the holiday; I will miss you."

"I haven't seen you for a day and I miss you already."

"You're learning, who told you to say that?"

"Leon. Only joking, I mean it. See you when I see you."

"Love you big lad."

"Same here, okay."

The call was ended, Steve made another call to Trigger,

"Geordie boy, I've been waiting for your call."

"Sorry about that Trig, there's been a change in the plan and you will not be needed, well for the moment."

"No need to apologise mate, is everything sorted then?"

"It is for now; I can't go into detail but if I need you, I'll let you know."

"Anything I can do mate, I owe you, I will always remember what you've done for me and the family."

"You owe me nowt mate, well apart from the fish and chips I paid for."

Trigger was laughing, "Yeah mate, next time on me then. Get in touch if you need anything and I mean anything."

"Trig I certainly will, I promise. I'm going to be busy for a few weeks so I won't be able to call until the jobs done. You have some good times with Laura and the kids, I will catch up later."

"You look after yourself, see you when we can."

It was now Leon's turn to make a call, Gabi had just finished doing her work out in the small gym upstairs with the view over the Atlantic. "Buenos Dias Leon, it is a good time that you have called."

"Good morning, I need to meet up with you, soon."

"Yes, as I said it is a good time that you have called, can we meet today?"

"Yes, I was going to suggest that. Is something happening?"

"Yes, I can tell you when we meet. What did you want?"

"I will tell you when we meet but there is a change in the plan. Can I go out on your boat tomorrow?"

"Of course, if the weather is okay, I think so. Are you coming to my villa?"

"Yes, if I can remember the road."

"What time will you be here?"

"We are leaving Madrid at two, so however long it takes."

"Who is we?"

"Just a friend of ours, he will not be coming to the villa."

"I have no problem with him."

"Yes, I know and he knows, but you two cannot meet."

"I understand. It should take about six hours, maybe less if you share the driving and don't stop"

"Okay, I will be there about nine. Can you get us two phones, I will give you the cash?"

"I have them for you already, what kind of bad guy would you be without one. I hope you are stopping with me tonight, just to make it look good of course."

"I might just have to then. See you tonight."

The call was ended, "Something is happening soon by the sound of what she said, she will tell me tonight. She has two encro phones for us, we can use her boat tomorrow if the weather's okay."

"So far so good. Dump everything now, leave it in the safe, get our bags and wait for Cass." Leon Watkins and Steve Calvert left the apartment, each carrying their new identification cards, bank cards and one holdall of spare clothing. The operation had started, as they made their way to the Atocha railway station to meet Cass with the Range Rover Evoque. They both had a light lunch and purchased some soft drinks, water, sandwiches, crisps and sweets for their long journey. Steve had contacted Cass who was running on time and asked him to fill the car with fuel before he got to the meeting point.

Cass was early, they were waiting and saw him enter the car park. Steve ensured the conversation was brief, he gave Cass the train ticket to Alicante and €300 for the fuel and for looking after the car. They immediately set off to Vigo. Steve booked a room at the 'Hotel Inffinit' in the city centre, Leon would not be needing a hotel room.

It was after 8pm when Leon dropped Steve outside the hotel and continued his journey to the villa.

Gabi was drinking cold white wine and looking towards the ocean through the large windows which were closed, there was a cold wind coming up the hill from the west. She saw the Evoque stop at the vehicle gate and activated the remote opening of the gates. Placing her glass on the central table, she walked to the door and greeted Leon with a kiss on both cheeks. They walked through to the lounge, Gabi poured Leon a glass of white wine and placed the bottle back into the ice bucket. "It is good to see you." She smiled at him, Leon raised his glass, "It is very good to see you. Can we talk first?"

"Of course, what do you want to do second?" again she smiled.

She certainly did know how to use her assets, his smile widened. She was dressed in a loose-fitting yellow T shirt and grey leggings to just below her knees, "Well we could talk some more, who knows. But first what were you wanting to tell me"

"Okay, can we talk quick?" another smile. "Yes, there is another ship coming in, in the next days, maybe even tomorrow."

"When will you know?"

"Usually when Lucas tells me, he has not told me yet, so I think maybe the day after tomorrow, possibly Thursday."

"How much is on the ship, cocaine I take it?"

"Yes, coke, there will be a lot possibly, I don't know all the details."

"How much will you be collecting?"

"I don't collect anything."

"What do you mean, you don't collect anything, does someone collect it for you?"

"No, it is an arrangement, I never touch any drugs. I met Lucas when he was having funding problems. He was owed money, it never arrived, which is why he will not lay on the goods anymore. He liked me and thought that I was very rich, I didn't tell him otherwise. I gave him some money, invested in his business, he keeps my investment and I get regular payments, each delivery. So, I am not a drug dealer."

"You don't have to tell me, but how much did you invest?"

"Four hundred thousand Euros, it was what he needed to keep with the others, he soon made up his lost money like he said, without losing his contacts."

Leon gave a whistle in surprise, "So what?"

She interrupted the question, "Over two million so far, I don't count it, I don't need it."

"Why do you still do it? You know the dangers."

"It is setting the trap, not for Lucas or the others, they will get caught some time, they all do if they're not at the top."

"Who then?"

"El Pantera, the panther, he will come looking for me. He killed Jessica, he killed the policeman in the US, he has killed many, many. He kills who Manolo tells him to."

"He will kill you, you have said that, if he knows where you are, he will kill you."

"No, we will stop him first."

"How are you going to set the trap?"

"When you go to get the boat, it will be the big load. I know that Lucas sometimes tells me things he should not say, I think he believes I'm stupid. He is linked to the MMV Cartel, Manolo's, he gets his supply from Manolo. Not directly but Manolo's supplies."

"Wait just a second, there is a change in plan, Steve is going to get the boat, not me."

"That makes no difference, Steve, you, bring the boat back, it is coming here, or very close. One of you tells the police and they raid and take all the cocaine and the people. Manolo will be badly hurt, again, there will be a leak, possibly by me, that I was involved and he will send Pantera."

"Oh easy, when he comes to the door, we will arrest him. I don't think so."

"No, it will not be easy, but I will make it easy for him to find me. It is easy to find this villa, look, no other villas, no other people, he would come here to kill me. I will get revenge."

Leon was shaking his head, "We are supposed to let this happen, then kill him?"

"Hopefully, before he kills me. I am very tired of talking, come on, we can go to bed."

CHAPTER 8

Wednesday 17th May

Leon had collected Steve from the hotel and they were now in the car heading towards the Marina in Cangas. They both had their new encro phones, Leon told Steve of the imminent arrival of the next shipment. Gabi was arranging with Lucas to accept Steve as her presence at the next slaughter and had suggested that he do the transport in the boat that was being planned. She made it known that she and Leon would be spending some time together, Lucas had readily accepted what she had said, it would be natural, he would if he had been younger. She used her assets well again.

They boarded her boat and were impressed, it looked well maintained and well fitted out with the electric technology equipment that would be needed. They opened the cabin and started doing a refresher on chart navigation, they planned different routes, mostly from South or Central America to Northern Spain. They were checking the tides and drifts of the Atlantic where would they save fuel by getting pushed along rather than going against the drift. The basic route was head north to the Caribbean and Puerto Rico, turn right and travel due east passing the Cape Verdi Islands, towards the coast of Africa, Mauritania, head north passing between the Canary Islands and Morocco, then passing the coast of Southern Spain and Portugal. It was nearly 6000 nautical miles.

It was a bright, warm morning with a westerly wind flicking the top of the ocean. Steve started the engine, they manoeuvred slowly out of the Marina, they only did an hour away from the Marina then returned and made the boat mooring secure.

Leon received a message on his encro mobile, it was from Gabi. 'Ship arrives tomorrow, need to talk, get Steve with Lucas and come to villa.' He left Steve at a restaurant at the marina and drove direct to the villa.

She was sat on the patio next to the pool, Leon took a seat next to her. "Where is Steve?" she asked.

"I have left him in a restaurant in the marina, why?"

"Tell him, when he has finished his meal to get the ferry from near the marina back to Vigo, it is only twenty minutes, and you can meet him later. Message him on the new phone, he does have it. Yes?"

"Yes, he has it, he has his own mobile as well."

"Quick send him the message."

Leon typed the message out and sent it to Steve. "Okay, what are we doing now?"

"You come with me, we have some time to kill before you can meet up with Steve. There is news for him."

She stood and walked into the house; Leon followed as she climbed the stairs.

It was just after 4pm when Leon met with Steve in his room at the hotel. Steve was anxious to know what was happening, "What's kept you, it has to be good?"

"Yes, it was, is good." Leon replied.

"Tell me then?"

"Lucas has accepted you for the boat trip and you will be flying from Madrid on Friday, we haven't been told where to. The ship is coming in tomorrow, a cargo ship, so no container. It will be anchored out at sea, near the Islands until it can get into port on Friday morning. The packages won't be unloaded until all the cargo is taken off, so possibly Friday night or Saturday. You will not be here for that, so I will have to cover that one."

"It's go, go, go then. I suppose I had better head back to

Madrid. How will I get the tickets? Did she tell you the name of the ship?"

"No, but it has a cargo of iron ore, should find out from the port manifest. You will get your tickets at the airport they will message you, they have both our numbers, we're in mate."

"What are you doing, when the boat comes in?"

"I'm going with her for the first one, unless it's being covered by the surveillance, Guardia, Nacional."

"You are better off leaving her at her home, get her to tell you what you have to do, just in case. I'll get in touch with Bert, he can get the wheels in motion with the others concerned. You're going to have to be careful with Gabi, they might start following you, they don't know who you are."

"Yes, that's true."

They went for a walk and found an internet café in the central commercial centre. Leon stayed outside and ensured they were not being watched as Steve sent a detailed email to Bert. Leon was staying in the hotel tonight, they went for a few local beers, Estrella Galicia.

Bert had received the email and immediately started the research on the vessel and flight departures from Madrid on Friday. The ship was easily identified MV Colombus X, from Cartagena in Columbia with a cargo of iron ore, when loaded with the cargo she had a deep draft. Continuing the research on the ship, it was subject of a deep search just over a year ago by UDYCO (National Police drug and organised crime unit) when it arrived in Vigo. There was nothing found indicating any criminal activity, the ship was a regular visitor to the port.

Bert contacted his counterparts in the operation, which had now been given the name, Portcullis, (Rastrillo in Spanish) hoping that it would block one gateway into Spain and Europe.

The Guardia replied that they were prepared to do a search on the vessel when anchored at sea, in deeper waters than the harbour, if it would not interfere with the planned future development of the operation. It would need to be considered soon.

Thursday 18th May.

Leon drove Steve to Vigo airport in the morning for his flight back to Madrid. They both shook hands and gave each other a manly hug, Leon said to Steve, "Don't say it, I know, I won't. You have to promise me the same, I'm getting to like you, I wouldn't like, not to work with you again."

Steve nodded, they fist pumped and stepped back, Leon turned and walked back in the direction of the car park, Steve walked into the departure lounge.

Bert had held an online meeting to discuss the latest information on Operation Portcullis. It was decided to do a cursory search of the vessel, it had been done before and was usually expected by ships that sailed that route. While the crew were restricted in their activities, divers would enter the ocean and visually examine under the water line of the vessel unobserved by the crew. Covert surveillance would take place inside the port area.

In late afternoon, the MV Colombus X was seen to drop anchor in the estuary of the Rio Vigo, midway between Vigo City and San Martino Island. There was no facility to accept the ship into port at the time of arrival. It was a bright day with calm seas, perfect for what was required.

Guardia Civil had contacted the ship's Captain, they informed him that a deep rummage team would be visiting the ship for the purposes of a thorough search. It was requested that the crew be centrally located during the search, apart from members who would be needed to aid and facilitate the search. The patrol launch pulled alongside the larger vessel, the officers climbed the wooden ladder onto the main deck, the Senior officer spoke to the captain and the search was commenced, it would take some hours.

When the search was underway, two divers entered the

ocean between the two vessels unseen. They were being fed compressed air by line, this would enable the officers to stay underwater for a longer period should it be necessary, they also had a safety line attached.

The first diver approached the rudder which was held in position, as the vessel slowly moved on the surface tide and wind but was secured by the heavy anchor. In the ocean there was deeper, clearer water, it made it easier for the divers to conduct the search. In port there would be very limited space until the load of iron ore was offloaded. He entered the rudder trunk, an air-filled space above the water level where the rudder entered the sealed vessel, he raised his camera and videoed inside the void which was approximately 2.5 x 2.5 metres. Fastened with strapping to the sides of the void were several large packages wrapped in blue plastic. The diver informed the dive supervisor by radio.

The second diver was following the hull at a depth of nine meters, he stayed on the port side of the ship and found the sea chest, all ships draw water through the sea chest on the hull to cool the engines. Again, it's a big void with a metal grill covering, the grill can be removed or loosened so it swings open, another ideal place to hide packages. He could see similar packaging inside the void and took more video recording. The diver could feel the suction pressure from the chest pulling him towards the grill, the safety line was used to keep him at a safe distance. The Dive Supervisor recalled both divers, it would be too dangerous and unnecessary for the divers to continue to search the starboard sea chest.

The rummage team continued for another two hours and found nothing on board the vessel. The Senior officer thanked the captain and the crew for their assistance in the search then left on the launch.

On return to the port, the intelligence officer completed an entry on Operation Rastrillo and attached the video recordings. It was the first sighting of evidence, Bert was rubbing his hands together, Ken was the nominated intelligence officer in the Embassy office. Bert convened a group meeting at the Embassy on Friday morning.

The captain of the vessel sent a message, 'Yearly search found nothing unloading dock 5 tomorrow sailing Sunday be ready.'

He received the reply, 'Ready and waiting.'

Steve, after landing in Madrid had booked a room in the Air Rooms Hotel near to the airport, he was waiting again.

Leon drove to the villa and met with Gabi.

It was waiting time, again.

CHAPTER 9

Friday 19th May

It was 08:30 when the meeting started in the Embassy, it was to decide the best way to advance the operation. Bert was in the chair, Ken Nolan was the dedicated operation intelligence officer, Sub Inspector Josan Alvares represented the Policia Nacional Drug and Crime Unit, and Sergento Manuel Vidal represented the Guardia Civil Organised Crime Team.

They first discussed what had been found when viewing the recordings made by the divers. It was now estimated at approximately 400 kilos, almost half a ton of drugs were concealed in the hidden storage areas of the vessel. If the packaging contained cocaine, it would be worth €16,000,000 or €32,000,000 street value. This was too big a delivery to be allowed to slip through to the Organised Crime Groups.

Sub Inspector Alvares had organised the surveillance at the port of Vigo for any vessels approaching the MV Colombos X whilst in port. Sergento Vidal had prepared for a strike on the known warehouse, where it was anticipated the drugs would be taken to before the distribution. It was planned that when the three main subjects of the operation, Miguel Torres, Javier Delgado and Lucas Alvarez were in the same building as the cocaine, they would raid the premises, arrest those present and seize the cocaine. It all sounded so easy, a success in the first few days of the operation commencing. The CHIS would be receiving a substantial payment.

Steve was at the airport; he had received a message to go to the Mahoudrid bar in Terminal 1. Enroute to the bar whilst walking through the terminal he checked the departure screens; he noticed some interesting locations. He took a seat in the bar and ordered a black coffee and tostada. There were a few in the bar, he took particular attention to two other males sat on their own, both with one flight bag.

A man entered the area of the bar and took a seat next to Steve, then waved to the other two men to join them. This man was not much older than Steve, possibly fourty, Spanish, wearing a dark suit and a white open-collar shirt, he had a smile which could be described as, threatening. He made the introductions, "This is Steve, he is the captain of your vessel, he will chart the course and give instructions and make decisions." The two men looked at Steve but did not speak. He then indicated a man who was in his early thirties, he looked fit for a fight with a rugged face, "This is Juan, the engineer, technician, if there are any mechanical, radar problems, he will fix it." Nothing was said, they waited, "This is Pepe, he will do as he is told, he knows how to handle boats." Pepe was in his early twenties and looked confident, in reality, he was scared. Again, there was brief silence. "You have all been selected to do this job, you will be paid very well on your return." He handed Steve a large manilla envelope. He continued, "Your captain has your tickets for your flights, some instructions and importantly, some money to spend when you get to your first destination." He smiled at the three individually, "You will need to go now to check in for your flight. Do not fuck this up."

Steve opened the envelope, their names were on the tickets, he handed the other men their tickets and they followed Steve to the desk. The other male watched as they went through security and out of sight. Once inside the departure lounge Steve led the men to a bar and ordered three beers, he only spoke English, the younger man Pepe could speak English well, but there wasn't much call for translation, "Cerveza" and a wave of the finger.

Steve had been recorded by the airport CCTV system from the moment he had entered the airport, the meeting with the three men in the bar and entering the departure area.

It was a bright sunny morning in the Bay of Vigo, Leon could see the ship at anchor, it was being approached by a tug. There were several smaller ships, mainly fishing boats, either leaving or returning with their catches from the North Atlantic. Vigo has the biggest fishing fleet in Spain, the port is always busy. He had made use of the small gym upstairs and was finishing off his run on the treadmill, he looked at the wall clock 09:18, time for a shower and a breakfast.

The Policia Nacional had set up covert cameras on the area that the MV Colombos X would be docked. It was anticipated that the drugs would be removed during the hours of darkness, which would be after the cargo had been unloaded, to allow the divers to access the areas where the drugs were concealed.

The Guardia Civil had intended to conceal cameras inside the warehouse where the drugs would been distributed but they found that the empty building was now permanently occupied.

There was no planned surveillance on any of the individual subjects, just a strike and arrests when the consignment was delivered to the warehouse.

Steve was now sitting next to his new companions on a flight to Bogota.

In the villa, Gabi had suggested that she and Leon go on a four-day trip to Porto in Portugal using her boat, this would keep them away from the 'slaughter' of the drugs in the warehouse. Leon agreed that it would be sensible this early in the operation and would keep her identity unknown. Gabi used the encro phone and sent a message 'Going to Porto on boat, keep my interest until I return'

There was a short wait for the response from Lucas, 'Si'.

An hour later, just about the same time as the dockers were starting to unload the iron ore from Colombos X, Leon had slipped the mooring ropes in the marina and Gabi was slowly moving the boat into the Rio Vigo. It was a smooth day for the short cruise to Porto, sailing towards the Portuguese border, Leon used the boat's mobile to make a call to Bert's mobile.

Bert didn't recognise the number displayed on the small screen of his mobile, he pressed the accept green button, "Hola".

"Hi Bert, it's Leon."

"Hello Leon, I was wondering who it was, is everything all right?" he asked.

"Yes, just a bit info, we're not represented at the warehouse, today, I am going to Porto to build my story, I'm not rushing my introduction."

"Oh, that's good in a way, the Guardia are doing a strike there when the drugs arrive, so we should get a very quick ending to the operation and the CHIS will not be compromised."

"That's quick Bert, have I missed something?"

"We couldn't tell you or get in contact anyway. The Guardia did a search under the ship yesterday and there's loads of packages concealed in the sea chest and the rudder cavity."

"So, what do I do now if they're arrested," a thought came into his head, "what about Steve, did you cancel his job?"

"No, Steve was on the plane before the decision was made, we don't know what he is doing anyway, the boat would still need bringing back to Europe."

Leon was puzzled, "Why would a boat come to Europe if the persons buying the product are no longer there to pay for it? That's not right Bert, Steve is up shit creek without a paddle, when he gets to wherever he's going if that happens."

"It is out of our control, it was never in our control in a way, once Steve got on the flight, you both said you wanted to do it. Whoever is running the boat will still want to get the products here, hopefully in Spain, they have the crew now."

Leon was thinking, "Can I message Steve on the encro if he still has it, tell him what's happening."

"Leon, I don't think that would be wise, he shouldn't know what's happened before it happens. I can't see a problem sending him a message after, if it wouldn't compromise him, you would know that, that's if he still has the mobile, they might take it off him, it might not work wherever he is?"

Leon was angry but kept his temper, he asked, "How are we going to know where the boat is, if Steve does bring it back, if they have taken the phone off him?"

"That's a good question Leon, I've been thinking about that myself, I honestly don't know. Possibly the CHIS could find out, are you still in contact?"

Leon was shaking his head, "Not at the moment, there's a lot happening but possibly in a few days after the event is finished."

"I think you will have to make contact, not before the strike and arrests, well you will have to after, to organise the payment."

"Yes, I will do, it should be safe to. Bert, keep in touch I'll keep this phone I've called you on, let me know what happens."

"I will, as soon as anything happens, I'll be in touch with the good news hopefully."

The call was ended, Leon sat inside the cabin next to Gabi who was at the controls, they were heading south about four kilometres off the coast. She asked, "What have you found out?"

"The ship that is being unloaded. It has a big shipment of drugs in some hidden places. When they're taken off the ship to the warehouse, they're going to do the arrests."

"That's good," then looking at Leon's concerned face, "isn't it?"

"It is, it's what you were wanting but I'm concerned about Steve, he's on a flight to get a boat to bring back to people who will be in jail. What's going to happen now?"

"I will order it, I would be contacting them anyway somehow to give my location, so this is how I do it."

"You said they would kill you if they knew where you were."

"Exactly, so he will come when they know it is me."

Leon looked Gabi straight in the face, "Don't take this the wrong way, we know they want to kill you but what about Steve and the shipment?"

"They will not kill Steve, not before he has delivered the boat and the shipment. They are greedy, it's about money, lots and lots of money. I can use my assets in Panama to help get a message through. It is possible, maybe. We will wait in Porto and find out, for now open up some cava."

It was 13:45 when the Iberia flight touched down in Bogota, Colombia. Steve and his companions passed through passport, immigration and customs into the arrivals area of the airport. A man was waiting, watching for them coming through the doors. He identified Steve and told the group to follow him to the car park, he led them to a Mercedes van with the side doors open, they climbed inside and sat on the wooden benches along both sides of the van, then the doors were closed. They could not see anything as they were driven away from the airport.

The journey lasted 37 minutes, Steve made a mental note of the time. The doors opened, the sunshine was blinding, the air was clean and hot. They were in a courtyard of a large building, they followed the same man through a wooden door into a corridor and were shown into a room with three beds, a table and four chairs. There was a small window which allowed natural light in from a high elevation. There was no decoration on the plain walls, once painted many years ago. The man left the room, closing and locking the door behind him. There was a partition in one corner, Steve found it was the shower and toilet area, being the captain, he threw his bag on the bed of his choice, the one under the window where it was in the shade. In English he told the two others to take some rest but keep their shoes on, this was not going to be a two-week holiday.

A few hours later the door opened and a large pot of hot rice, vegetables, and a fiery sauce was placed onto the table with three plates and spoons and six cans of Aguila beer. They ate the meal which in fairness was plentiful and tasty, the beer cheered the spirits of the three men. Steve was trying to explain through Pepe, that this was a transit stop on the way to collect the boat, it would be better when they were on their own. Do not ask questions and don't annoy anyone. Pepe was still scared; it wasn't what he had been told or expected.

After the meal they played cards, Steve spoke, he asked Pepe to translate, "We have to stay together, they are testing us out, how we get on in tough situations."

They both acknowledged by nodding, "Si."

Steve continued, "I think we are in a transit house, they don't want us to know where it is, so we cannot tell anyone."

Pepe translated and they both nodded.

"If I am correct, this is good, it indicates, it looks like they don't want to kill us, they need us or want us to do a job."

Pepe was nodding, "Si, si, sí." Then translated for Juan who nodded.

"We should not cause trouble, do not ask questions from them, ask me first, I'm the captain, I will decide if the question is asked."

They both agreed.

"I am here because I've lost money and need to get some to get back into business. I don't want to be here; I have not done this before. What about you Pepe?"

Pepe explained, "This is my first time, I was not paid my money and I owe someone the money, this is my debt paid."

Pepe translated for Juan, "I was asked in a way I could not say no, I do it to protect my family."

Steve, "We all have a big reason to do this, together we can. Can you do what I have been told, fix engines, radio," he then looked at Pepe, "make coffee, cook beans, clean the windows?"

They all laughed for the first time.

Juan, "Yes, I am a good mechanic and worked on my father's boat fishing in the Atlantic in all weathers, I can do radios if there are parts."

They looked at Pepe, "I make good coffee and beans," again there was a laugh, "but I have been on boats for many journeys from Galicia to Azores, Cadiz, Canary Islands, I know how to handle controls a little mechanics and if there are computers, I can use a computer."

Steve continued, "We will try to keep our spirit high with each other, speak to me before you ask anything, we do not want to cause them problems, I think we all know the people they are."

They both nodded, Steve dealt the cards and they continued their game.

CHAPTER 10

Saturday 20th May

It was 01:47, the officers of the Policia Nacional were monitoring the cameras, they were covering the area of the port where the Colombos X was docked. The docks were quiet with no movement in the secured area, they saw a fishing vessel approaching the starboard side of the ship, it was in darkness, the tide was turning and running out to sea. The cameras were zoomed in on the deck of the vessel, the small crew had placed tyres along the port side of the ship to avoid making a noise, hitting against the bigger ship. One man who was dressed in a black wet suit with a mask and snorkel entered the water on the starboard side and swam towards the rudder. He disappeared under the surface; two other men were constantly looking in the area he was believed to be while a third man was in the cabin keeping the vessel close to the ship against the tide. After a few minutes, the man in the wet suit surfaced and signalled to the two men, they used a mechanical pulley to drag a length of rope through the water and over the edge of the small boat. After a few seconds, blue packaging could be seen being lifted from the water onto the deck and then dropped into the hold of the vessel, the diver was helped on to the boat. On the deck the two men were helping the diver to put a scuba tank on his back, he then sat on the edge of the fishing vessel and fell backwards into the water. Again, the two men were looking over the side into the dark water, it was now noticeable by the officers that the ship had dropped down in height from the side of the dock as the tide was running out.

The diver realising the tide was going out decided to swim under the ship and release the gate on the sea casket on the port side of the hull first. The visibility under the surface was not good, it was dark and the movement of the tide was disturbing the silt and spilled iron ore on the bottom of the river. He kicked hard to swim under the width of the hull and reached the sea casket where he could see the large packages inside. He started to remove the first fixing on the sea casket but the current was strong. Holding onto the gate with one hand, he released one fixing and he could feel the ship sinking lower with the tide ebbing, it was getting closer to the dock wall. He made the decision to return to the starboard side, swimming against the current he kicked hard to get through the rapidly narrowing escape route when a sudden movement by the ship pinned him to the riverbed. It was quick, he was crushed into the bed of the river by the full weight of the Colombos X and its remaining cargo. There was activity on the deck where the two men were pulling on a rope or cord, it was now twenty minutes since the diver had gone into the water but the rope was not moving, it was pulling against the side of the vessel. They released more rope and tried pulling again using the mechanical pulley but it could not be freed and pulled the vessel into the side of the ship. They released the rope, one of the men could be seen to cut through the rope, then the vessel was motored up the river away from the Colombos X. The officers never saw the diver return onto the fishing boat.

It was apparent that something had gone wrong from the observations, there was nowhere near the estimated quantity of packaging seen to be recovered from the ship. The fishing vessel was monitored by radar as it continued up the river and moored in an area used by the many fishing boats. The three men were seen to leave the vessel, the packaging recovered remained in the hold.

Gabi was awake, sitting watching the morning sun rise over Porto city, the smell of the fresh coffee coming from the galley. There was a message, 'No slaughter, delayed for month, diver dead, missing, $ safe'. Gabi took Leon a coffee and showed him the message, he had just showered. He fastened the towel around his waist and made a call on the ship mobile.

"Good morning, Leon, how is Porto?"

"Yeah, Porto is great, beautiful in fact," he smiled at Gabi, "I have some news which may impact your planned action."

"So do I, you tell me first."

"It doesn't look as though they got the stuff off the ship, the diver died if that makes sense and so it's delayed for a month."

"Yes, it does make sense, it was guessed something like that had happened. We were watching last night, well not me, and it looked as if something has gone wrong but it's good to get it from the horse's mouth. We were thinking of delaying the strike anyway."

Leon asked, "So does this mean we can wait for Steve to return with his shipment?"

"It certainly looks that way, he can enjoy his holiday now then. Keep in touch, occasionally." The call ended.

Leon turned to Gabi, "What do you know about the trip Steve is making?"

"Nothing, I can guess that it is coming from the MVB, it's who Lucas is in contact with, so it could be leaving from Colombia on the Atlantic side or any other country, Venezuela, Panama, the Islands. It is the first that I know of, it usually comes in on the ships."

"Why change what works?"

"They are always doing different methods, like the cruise liners, aircraft, sail ships, they will do everything."

"What more do you know about the cartels and their methods?"

"I know they are cruel, powerful and frightening. Not one person can fight against them and win but they can be hurt. I have hurt them, they will get revenge on me, I know it but not before I can hurt them some more."

"Are you not frightened?"

"Of course I'm frightened, very frightened, but I have to be ready and hurt them first. If they kill me quick, shoot me, poison me, good. If they take me alive, it will not be so good, I know that, I know what they can do to someone."

"What about the people here, Lucas, Miguel and Javier, what are they like?"

"You have only met Lucas, he is a nice man, a good businessman. When he takes his suit off, he would cut your throat and pull your tongue through the wound, he would kill your mother. If he really knew me, he would feed me to the pigs after doing so many horrible tortures. He hides behind the suit but he is not weak, do never think that, despite his manner he is not to be fucked with. He is a man of honour, he owes me, no he owed me, and he has more than paid his debt. He will continue out of honour until I walk away or I am buried. I will walk away soon."

"Honestly, why don't you do what your sister wanted and live on a paradise island for the rest of your days, find love and happiness. Leave the memories behind?"

Gabi looked at Leon, "Who says I haven't found love and happiness and I'm waiting to live on a paradise island, once I can kill the memories?"

Leon was smiling, he had found the same and could fancy living on a paradise island with that person, Lauren was a memory. "Maybe we can do that together, kill the memories."

Steve was awake, he had showered early and was sitting at the table playing solitaire. Pepe and Juan were still asleep on their beds, both wearing their training shoes, the sunlight was coming through the high window illuminating the ceiling of the room. It was 07:32, the door was unlocked, fresh smelling coffee, water, bread and fruit were brought in. Steve cleared the cards as they placed the breakfast onto the table, the others woke at the sound of the door opening. They were told they would be travelling in thirty minutes; they took turns using the bathroom and the shower, they poured coffee for each other, there were signs that they could help each other.

At 08:00 the door opened again and a simple wave of the arm signalled for them to leave the room pulling their flight bags. They all climbed through the open side door of the same van and took their seats on the benches.

It took 56 minutes to arrive at their destination. It was beautiful to look at, the river was 100 metres wide, blue and smooth running, surrounded by the rain forest with a small wooden slatted jetty protruding out into the river. They were transferred by a small rubber dingy to a waiting water plane which took off as soon as they had boarded. It was a one hour and twenty minute flight then they landed on a river surrounded by jungle. A long wooden boat with an outboard motor being piloted by a native Indian pulled alongside the aircraft landing floats. They disembarked from the plane into the boat which was then turned upstream and picked up speed, the aircraft took off as soon as the boat was a safe distance away. The native controlling the boat was dressed only in a loincloth, he knew the river well and negotiated the sweeping bends. It took another 24 minutes before they pulled alongside another jetty, deeper into the jungle. Steve could see the houses on stilts, was this the village that Gabi had described?

They took the one step from the boat onto the jetty and walked up the river bank towards the village, a group of five open wooden framed homes with thatched roofs. It looked as Gabi had described, there were no guards that could be seen, just the natives. The only access was the river which was now 60 metres wide. They climbed the steps into the shade of one of the houses, there were several hammocks tied between the wooden posts and some woven rugs on the wooden floor. The native pointed to an area in the trees for the toilet and towards some clay pots which contained cold water. The noise from the thousands of nearby birds and monkeys was never ending, after walking around the village watched by the natives, they returned to the shade of the house. There were women in this village so this was apparently not the same village as Gabi had been resident. They lay in their hammocks which were wide enough to rap fully over the body for protection from insect bites. Why were they here, miles from the sea?

Later in the afternoon, some native men returned from the jungle with their skinny dogs running ahead of them, the women were calling for the men and the dogs. They greeted the dogs; their bodies and tails were shaking in happiness at the gentle touch of the women. The men were carrying their bows with arrows in a quiver hanging over their shoulder. Tied over a long tree branch carried by two of the natives were several dead animals, a howler monkey, a sloth and a long anteater, tonight's meal. Steve looked for his encro phone in his bag but there was no power and there definitely would not be a signal but at least it was still intact. Juan, Pepe, and Steve watched as the women skinned then butchered the animals then dropped the meat into cauldron like pots on top of a flaming fire. The sun was dropping below the trees, the darkness was drawing in very quickly, a male walked from the river carrying a small net of mixed fish and some green plants, these were cleaned and dropped into other pots.

When the food was cooked the three were invited to sit at the fire and eat, Steve instructed them to eat what they could to stay strong and to not offend the natives. It was a tasty meal, some meat was tough but chewable, there was no meat on the animals wasted. Steve put his hands together in a prayer form and nodded at the women and men in thanks, Pepe and Juan followed his action. After the meal they returned to the house they had been allocated and wrapped themselves inside the hammock, the house was lit up by several burning torches, this would not only keep wild animals away but allow the natives to see their guests. The noise of the birds and wildlife could not stop them from falling asleep.

After a few hours, they were woken up by the natives entering the house, it was black darkness beyond the light of the torches. The native indicated to the three men to get their bag and follow him, again the wave of the arm, Steve was awake and alert as he followed the man towards the riverbank. He stopped at the top of the bank and looked down onto a blue semi-submersible boat, his first thought, 'Am I dreaming?' then 'Where the fuck has that come from?' Juan and Pepe were in shock, Pepe was saying, "No, no, no, no."

Steve took a hold of Pepe around the shoulder, speaking firmly he gave the instruction, "You understand me, you will get into that thing when they tell you or you will be killed, we might all be killed, just fucking do it."

Pepe nodded "Si, gracias, I'm sorry."

The vessel was 18 to 20 metres in length, a light blue fibre glass body and hull, near to the middle of the vessel was a small tower with four viewing ports and the access hatch, 3 metres in front of the tower was another access door. The vessel was floating high on the river. The hatch in the tower was opened, a man in a white t-shirt, not a native, climbed halfway out of the tower. He gave the wave for the three men to enter the vessel, Steve led the way, stepping onto the structure from the jetty then climbing down into the cramped space, the other two followed.

The cockpit with the controls was directly below the tower, a similar set up to most boats, a small wheel, levers for the speed control and gears, forward and reverse, the instruments for fuel, oil and water level. The only extra instrument and control was for the ballast tanks which would control the depth the vessel sailed at; it could not fully submerge. On the side panel was the long-range radio, GPS positioning screen, radar and sonar screens.

When they were all grouped in the tight space of the cockpit and cabin, the male spoke in Spanish. Steve could understand what he was saying but acted ignorant, Pepe took on the responsibility to translate for Steve, it helped Pepe feel useful. He explained how the ballast would work, the low profile would make the vessel invisible to radar from other ships.

Below the cockpit was the crew cabin with two bunks, one either side of the hull, there was a small two ring electric hob for cooking and there was storage space under the bunks for their bags, food, and water. A door separated the cabin from the diesel engine and diesel storage tanks towards the aft. At the front of the cabin, another door opened onto a large storage area which was filled from top to bottom with large sacks of what was believed to be cocaine. There was no head, toilet or washing facilities.

The male gave Steve an envelope with instructions then climbed out of the vessel, he was collected by a low-level boat which had a tow rope attached to the front of the semi-submersible. Pepe informed Steve that the boat would be towing the vessel through the night, to stay in the middle of the river follow directly behind the boat. Steve took control in the cockpit, he instructed the other two to search the vessel and find food, water and anything they were not sure about. Juan had to inspect the engine; Pepe was to find an electric source to charge mobile phones. They felt the first jolt as the tow rope tightened then the vessel was guided by Steve into the middle of the river and followed the boat by looking through the viewing port. Steve closed the hatch door to keep the river insects out of the very small, enclosed cabin, after thirty minutes he asked Juan to take the controls. Pepe took control after, they all knew the controls, they had to trust each other, this was a river, they still had to cross the Atlantic.

Steve took the opportunity to read the instructions, there was to be a refuel in the Atlantic on a date and time, he took out the charts and marked the position, approximately 40k from the coast of Porto Nova in the Cape Verde islands. He checked the satellite navigation screen; they were currently on the Rio Catatumbo heading towards Lake Maracaibo then entering the Gulf of Venezuela to access the Atlantic, by estimate travelling only at night, it would be another two days before they entered the gulf.

CHAPTER 11

Sunday 21st May

Steve looked at his watch; 05:13. It was still dark on the river but he could see the boat ahead. Pepe was asleep on one of the bunks, Juan was looking at the charts, the boat slowed as the vessel floated on the river. The boat turned left from the centre of the river, they could feel the vessel being moved left then the jolt as the rope tensed, they were heading for a small tributary to the river which wasn't named on the sat-nav system. They travelled a short distance up the river under the cover of the jungle, the boat had stopped, it turned in the river and gently pushed the vessel sideways towards the riverbank. Steve could see other men on the riverbank watching the securing of the vessel. Pepe was now awake, there was a banging on the hatch door, Steve moved from his seat and spun the securing lock to open the hatch. They climbed out onto a small jetty running down the side of the vessel, there were several men stood watching, they were all armed with automatic or semi-automatic weapons. They walked up the river bank in the direction of some low-level enclosed plywood huts, they were pointed in the direction of one of the huts, the door was open and they entered the hut. In the gloom they could see several metal beds and after they took turns to visit the toilet, they each lay on a bed, the door was closed and locked from outside. It certainly was not what was promised.

Sarah had packed her case for the next few weeks on the

course, it would be two weeks before she could return to her parents in Newcastle upon Tyne. She sent a message to Steve's mobile, 'I don't know where you are or what you're doing but enjoy the job, do nowt daft. I've done my prep for the course so ready to go, no-one said it would be easy, hey ho, missing you big lad, x reply when you can.'

She had eaten her mam's Sunday lunch and was feeling good and maybe a bit fat. After kissing and hugging her mam, she got in the car with her dad who was giving her a lift to the Central Station.

Leon and Gabi had finished their stay in Porto and were now sailing north on the return journey to Vigo. Gabi was on the leather seats at the rear of the boat soaking up the sun's rays and drinking cold white wine, the music was playing loud on the new sound system, Latino pop, Leon was dancing on the floor next to the controls, happy days.

The Colombos X left the port at Vigo having had the legal iron ore cargo removed, it was now returning to Cartagena with the cocaine packaging still intact in the sea chests.

In the wooden hut they were all awake, it was hot inside with no windows to open for ventilation, the door was still locked. Pepe was getting stressed, pacing the room like a caged wild animal.

Steve spoke to him, "Pepe, come and sit down, this will not do you or any of us any good, it will just be a few more hours until it's dark and then we will be on the move again away from this group."

Pepe was angry and irritated, "This is not what I was told, this is wrong, I should not be here, I want out."

Juan did not understand the English language but he knew that Pepe was causing a problem, "Pepe take it easy, it will be okay, they need us, I don't know what Steve has said but just a few hours, we will be on our way."

"They lied, they fucking lied to all of us, are you happy, both of you, no."

Juan stood up and punched Pepe in the stomach, he buckled, winded by the blow. Steve stepped in and pushed Juan back to his bed, he took hold of Pepe around the shoulders, he struggled but Steve held him tight. "The only way you will get out of here, is by working with Juan and me, one more day, once we're at sea it will be okay, I'll ask for some fishing line, we can get on the top, fresh air, a bit fishing, fresh fish every day, just the three of us, we will be okay and we'll get paid well."

Pepe "They fucking lied, didn't they?" he was still angry.

"Pepe, Pepe, if they told you the truth would you have come? Of course not, Juan and I wouldn't have come. We are here and want to get back, so calm it, don't annoy anyone and we will be on our way soon."

The door was unlocked and opened, the sunshine came through the doorway, fresh air, a guard was standing in the doorway with the automatic rifle in his hands, he indicated by swinging the weapon they were to leave the hut. Juan stood and walked towards the door, Steve released Pepe from his grasp, "Easy, take it easy."

Pepe walked fast, passing Juan he bumped into the guard, knocking him backwards onto the ground, realising what he had done he bent over the guard to help him up, "Lo siento." (I'm sorry) Another guard standing on the other side of the door saw Pepe reaching down and believing he was reaching for the weapon, he hit him on the back of the skull with the butt of his weapon knocking him unconscious.

Steve was shouting in Spanish, "Señor, señor, por favor, por favor." The guard pointed the weapon at Steve, he continued in English, "Accident, it was an accident."

The door was closed and locked, they could hear Pepe being dragged away.

Twenty minutes later the door opened again, the guard standing back from the door indicating for them to leave the hut. They walked out into the sunlight and the heat of the jungle; they were walked to the riverside where the vessel was tied to trees. They both saw Pepe at the same time, Juan turned his head from what he had briefly seen, he wanted to vomit, Steve looked at Pepe with pity. Pepe had been stripped and beaten, he had been slashed with sharp blades across his body and down his arms and legs, blood was running from his wounds down the length of his body and legs into the river, he was standing on a small post in the river, the water was red around his feet. He was tied to a longer post on the jetty, he could not move.

One of the men spoke in Spanish, "He should not have tried to take the weapon, if you do not want to go in the boat, we can get some other people who will."

Steve spoke in English, "It was an accident, he said he was sorry, can we take him down?"

One of the men translated the conversation, Steve listened and the translation was good.

"No, he is a dead man, tonight when the night animals come, tomorrow he will not be here."

Steve answered the translation, "It does not have to be like this." He was stopped by the man who was speaking raising his weapon at him.

"I am the boss; I decide how it is with him. I have a decision to make, you can help me. Can you two take this," pointing to the vessel, "to the destination or should I get another crew?"

Steve knew there was only one answer, he could do nothing for Pepe, "Yes we can."

"Okay, give them food and drink." He indicated to the guards.

They were taken to the central fire in the middle of the settlement of huts where the food was being cooked and sat on the ground. They were given flat bread, a bowl of some sort of meat stew with spice, and a cup of water. Juan could not eat, Steve insisted, "Juan, eat the food, we need strength, eat what you can." They could hear the sounds from Pepe as insects and birds were biting, the bigger animals would come in the darkness. After the meal they returned to the hut, they could still hear Pepe shouting in pain from inside the hut.

The camp was in darkness the next time the door was opened, a torch was shone into the hut, the signal was given to leave, Steve walked out first followed by Juan and they walked to the small jetty. Pepe was still alive and in agony, there were several bite marks on his face, torso and legs from the smaller animals, he was looking at both of them, Juan turned his head and climbed inside the semi-submersible. Steve could hear Pepe in a low voice, "Please, please. I'm sorry."

Steve looked at the man who said he was the boss, "Señor, por favor," he pointed to the knife on his belt, "por favor?"

The boss raised his weapon into the chest of Steve and stepped back, he removed the 15 centimetre bladed knife from its pouch and gave it to another guard to give to Steve. Steve walked to Pepe, "I am sorry to leave you here, I tried to stop it."

Pepe looked at the blade, "Por favor amigo." (Please my friend)

Steve punched the blade through the ribs into the heart of Pepe, he thrust it so powerfully his clenched hand around the handle was touching the bloodied chest, the knife had a pulse through the handle, then nothing. Pepe's head dropped immediately and the warm blood flowed freely through the wound down the arm of Steve, Pepe was dead or would be very quickly avoiding the long night of pain. He pulled the knife out slowly, Pepe didn't move or make a sound, Juan was watching through the viewing port, he was crying. Steve felt sick, he had never killed a man in close quarters, certainly not a man who was not trying to kill him, but it was what was needed to be done he justified to himself. He held the knife out to the guard handle first; the guard took the knife and wiped the blade clean of blood on Steve's shirt. He looked at the boss and nodded, Steve would remember his face then he climbed onto the vessel. He removed his shirt and threw it onto the jetty then entered the vessel. Juan had moved to give Steve space to climb down into the cockpit, he placed his hand on the shoulder of Steve, "Gracias amigo." The vessel was silent, thoughts running through his head. It took him back to a classroom when he had joined the police all those years ago, he could hear the trainer saying, 'Some people will never steal but in certain circumstances, everyone can kill.' The discussion he had with Sarah, 'How far do you go down the line, when do you stop, when do you know what's right and wrong, if you know it's wrong, do you carry on, who would know?' The Marines had taught him well, how to kill with a knife quickly.

Steve watched as the ropes holding Pepe were cut, his lifeless body flopped into the bloodied water. The vessel was pulled away from the jetty into the river, Steve concentrated on following the boat ahead, the journey continued.

CHAPTER 12

Monday 22nd May

Sarah was sitting in the bright modern styled classroom of the training college, there were 3 instructors and 6 students including Sarah. Prior to the start of the course, she was looking out of the rain marked window and wondering where and what Steve was doing. Who knows, in a few months she could join him in his adventures, she checked her mobile, no reply to her message, then switched the mobile off.

Bert and Ken were in the Embassy conducting an online meeting with their Spanish colleagues from the Nacional and Guardia, they were discussing Operation Portcullis. There was no evidence being gathered by the use of mobile phones, they knew they were using encrypted mobiles. The fishing vessel that collected the packages from the rudder void was still being monitored, the cargo was still in the fish hold, in the port of Vigo. The owner of the vessel had now been identified but it was not known who the crew were or the identity of the diver. No bodies had been found in the port; it was believed that the body would have been taken out to sea. There had been no activity at the known warehouse, the building would still be under surveillance. Further intelligence was awaited from the CHIS to proceed with the operation.

Gabi and Leon had finished their morning training session in the gym and were having their light breakfast at the table by the side of the pool. The sun was already warm, a few white clouds were floating by from the direction of the sea, Leon was looking west past the islands and was wondering where Steve was and if he had started his journey.

Steve looked at his watch 03:55, it was still pitch-black darkness on the river, he had to concentrate to see the towing boat, but occasionally some moonlight would brighten up the river then disappear as it turned one of the many bends. Juan had powered up the mobile phone, thanks to Pepe, who had inserted an additional USB port which was hidden in the engine room, there was no signal available inside the vessel but it would be checked again later. The radio had been switched on and worked, the electronic systems were working, the engine as yet had not been started, the sound would travel, even in the jungle.

Steve had been thinking of a work strategy for Juan and himself, they could both control the vessel, at the moment they were taking control for short periods of time, they were both finding anything to do that would take their thoughts from Pepe and the situation they were in.

The river valley started to brighten up giving them a bit more visibility, the towing boat had reached the next mooring point and turned into a tributary river, the vessel swung to the left as it was pulled into the river and immediately under the cover of the overhanging thick jungle. The next camp was only a short distance from the main river, 200 metres, it was positioned alongside a short jetty, a group of men were waiting to tie the vessel to the riverbank. The light was breaking through the canopy of the jungle as first Steve and then Juan climbed out of the vessel, Juan closing the hatch behind him. The men on the riverbank were not holding weapons, Steve and Juan climbed the steps that had been dug into the riverbank where they could see the familiar wooden huts. They were directed towards the fire in the centre of the camp where there was a long wooden table with benches on each long side, they both took a seat together with the crew from the towing boat. Coffee, taco's, cheese, and some fruits were placed on the table. After the meal they went into a hut which was allocated and eventually fell into a deep sleep, the door was not locked.

Juan was the first to stir, being quiet, he walked out of the hut and sat at the table, he was wearing a long sleeve shirt and trousers for protection against the insect bites. One of the men passing pointed to the fire, coffee, and metal pots, he helped himself to the coffee, using the nearby cloth to protect his hand from burning on the handle when he poured his coffee. He gazed around him, it was similar to the previous camp the night before, yet so different, the noise of the birds and animals, the colours of the trees. Picking up his coffee, he walked to the edge of the river, he could see large fish just a few feet from the riverbank, a caiman raised its head above the surface in the middle of the river, it was all new to him. Why was the previous camp so different, he looked over his shoulder back towards the camp, he was being watched by a man, maybe more. Why did they have to imprison them in the hut and kill Pepe? He looked again at the caiman, which was now looking back at him, tears filled his eyes, he tried to hide the images and his thoughts, he lay back in the grass and felt some sunshine on his face. There was a shadow on his face, he opened his eyes and saw a man looking down on him, he went to get up to his feet, "No, you lie there I will sit next to you."

The man, who he believed to be Colombian or Venezuelan had short cut black hair, he was slim in his early thirty's, he sat next to him. He was also wearing a long sleeve shirt and trousers with the hems tucked inside his black boots. "I have been told about last night at the other camp, it should not have happened."

Juan, "Why did he do it? I'm sorry, I've been told not to ask questions"

"Ah, your captain, he speaks the truth, do not ask questions, you do not get answers you do not want to know, I understand. It was wrong, your friend made an accident and their leader decided to back his man, it has caused problems. The hit on the head should have been enough, he wants to stay the boss, to show his power to his men. I'll tell you now, that man is boss of shit, he has six men, like me, sometimes more, he wants respect, he builds hate, the men don't like him, he does not pay them right, he keeps their money. It is a tough time in the jungle for many weeks, no girls, no drink, no mobile, you have to be good to the men. Look at me, same age as you, possibly, I have more money than I can spend, I am here in shit clothes, look at me, I have a beautiful girl, I cannot be with her. It is the business that needs to be done, soon I hope to do my business in the city, never to return here. He," indicating upstream with his thumb, "thinks it is the gringos, strangers, who will betray him, where his camp is, his men will kill him, soon, very soon. My boss, his boss, is angry with him, that means one thing, don't ask the question." He was shaking his head, moving his right arm, pointing at the river and the jungle, "Look here, look around you, where the fuck can you go? The caiman, anaconda will get you in the river, puma or snakes will get you in the jungle. I have only two more times in this place, he will not get out alive."

Juan looked at the boss, "I hope you get to the city, forgive me, but I hope he is food for the caiman."

"Thank you, they are both possible." He gave a smile towards Juan. "Your captain, is he a good friend, a good man?" he asked.

"He is a good captain, we are becoming good friends, I like him, we did not know each other until we came here."

"There is only two now, your work will be hard when you reach the ocean."

Juan asked, "Do you know when we can start the engines, they have not been tested?"

"You are asking questions, that is dangerous," he smiled again at Juan, "You will use the engines tomorrow when you enter the lake, the boat will guide you to the ocean. You should both eat and sleep until it is dark." He stood up and left Juan on the grass.

Juan looked across the river he could see the caiman slowly moving, he smiled, revenge is sweet.

Later that afternoon, a large meal was prepared over the open fire, a large bowl of rice with onions was placed on the table, a large piece of meat was roasting above the fire, some fish were on rocks around the fire cooking. They were all present, the boss, his men, the two men from the boat, Steve and Juan. The boss was the first to fill his plate, then Steve and Juan then the others, it was a good meal, too much to eat in one sitting.

As the sun was setting, dipping below the jungle canopy, they moved to the small jetty, the boat crew attached the tow rope to the vessel and manoeuvred into the middle of the river. Juan then Steve climbed into the vessel, one of the men passed the left-over food which was gratefully accepted by Steve and passed to Juan to store. The boss had one more instruction and gift, "You will have a difficult time at sea, just two of you. Keep clear of the islands, there are pirates that are looking for our boats, I have to give you these," he handed two Fara 83 rifles to Steve, "Do you know how to use these?"

"Yes, I've used them before or similar." They were very similar to Kalashnikov's; these were made in Argentina.

The boss smiled at Steve, "I thought so, that's why I kept the ammunition, they're not loaded." He handed Steve four clips of ammunition.

Steve smiled back at him, "That's a lot of ammunition."

"There are pirates, they will not be using swords." he laughed, "If they are seen, do not let them get close, shoot to kill." He waved to the boat which started to tow the vessel from the riverbank. Steve could recall his meetings with pirates off the East African coast during his rehabilitation period, it would need more than two Fara 83's to stop them attacking a small crewed vessel.

An hour later they entered Lake Maracaibo, the tow boat slowed and stopped towing, they released the tow rope. Juan went into the engine compartment and looked at the engine as Steve pressed the start button, it started immediately, the noise was deafening inside the compartment. Juan could not find any faults or oil spills, he left the compartment and closed the door, it was still noisy in the cabin and cockpit.

The boat continued to guide as Steve and then Juan maintained the distance behind the lead boat, eventually they were entering the gulf of Venezuela, the boat turned back towards the lake, they were on their own. While it was dark and having checked the radar screen, Steve used the ballast tanks to raise and lower the level of the vessel in the sea, when raised it would perform at 12 knots, when lowered the speed dropped to 10 knots. During darkness with nothing showing on radar where possible they would raise the level. They both got used to the controls at sea, obviously there was more movement than on the river. It was uncomfortable, there was no room to stand upright, the two bunks were the length of the cabin with just one metre between them. The toilet was a plastic 8 litre bucket, in the engine room.

Steve set a course on the sat-nav system, keeping to the South and East of the Caribbean Islands, Juan tried to get some sleep on the bunk. There was little to see out of the viewing ports, being so low in the water the range was limited. Steve switched on his encro phone, it showed full power but no signal, they were 30 kilometres from the nearest island, they had been at sea for no more than an hour and they were bored, which brought tiredness. The heat was growing in the cabin from the engine compartment, Steve opened the hatch, looking up on a clear Caribbean night he could see a small section of dark sky and stars, the cool air from the sea was welcome ventilation, Juan was snoring, sound asleep. He stood and looked out from the hatch, nothing but the ocean. He typed a message on his phone, 'Just left gulf of Venezuela, only 2 crew, heading towards Cape Verde islands then north to Spain. Very big cargo steady average 10 knots' he pressed send. No signal, it should be sent whenever a signal was available.

Friday 26th May

They were floating high in the middle of the Atlantic Ocean, the radar screen was empty, they had gone through two days of storms and choppy seas and rain. The sea was now calm, Steve had opened the hatch, the toilet had been emptied as the vessel drifted slowly. Juan was the first to climb out of the hatch onto the deck, he threw out the safety rope and jumped into the ocean, the first time in two days, the cool water against his skin was comforting. Taking hold of the rope with his left hand, he lay on his back and looked to the skies, the moon was crescent shaped and high, the stars were so bright, he closed his eyes and relaxed. After ten minutes, Steve called for Juan to return, he climbed on board using the rope, he stood next to the hatch drying himself off in the warm breeze. Steve dived into the refreshing sea, cooling down, he swam alongside the slow drifting vessel, then taking hold of the rope, he lay on his back and looked at the sky. His thoughts were miles away in England, he could see her face in the darkness, Sarah. He allowed himself the same time as Juan and climbed back onto the vessel, they both baited the four hooks with small pieces of left-over meat, fresh food was now gone, it was packets of dried food, rice, and beans. They threw the weighted lines into the ocean, then climbed back into the vessel, leaving the hatch open. At least another five days to go to meet up with the refuelling boat. Steve pushed the throttle forward, 12 knots, the fastest the vessel had achieved.

Juan pulled in the fishing lines, each one with a mackerel attached flashing through the surface, these were dispatched with a heavy knock against the hatch door and dropped behind Steve, the lines were set again, in all twelve fish were caught which would maintain their food levels for six days, when the rice and beans were added. So far, so good. They were making good progress with minimal problems other than a squally couple of days, Juan was learning the English language and Steve was doing surprisingly well at the Spanish improvised language class.

There had been no reported activity in Vigo, it appeared that they were all waiting for the next shipment after not receiving the load from the Colombos X. Leon had been in contact with Bert but there was little intelligence coming from any source into the Operation Portcullis system. There was nothing known about the whereabouts of Steve and the other two men. Leon was staying with Gabi at the villa, he did not disclose this information to Bert, he knew he should not be there. He had a room booked in a hotel in the city which he visited occasionally.

Tuesday 30th May

Juan was at the controls, he checked the screens, he saw nothing on radar, the ballast had been reduced to maintain 10 knots, checking his watch, it was 10:12, Steve was asleep on his bunk. He opened the engine room door and closed it behind him to reduce the engine noise, then started to use the toilet.

There was a sudden bump into the side of the vessel, not hard but enough to wake Steve, he couldn't see Juan at the controls and swung his feet off the bunk, another bump against the structure of the vessel. Juan emerged from the engine room, "There is nothing, I checked, nothing." They both looked at the radar, they could see nothing, Steve looked out of the viewing ports, all 360 degrees, nothing. Steve opened the hatch and climbed to look in the immediate area, he could see nothing, "It must have been ocean debris, check the compartments for any damage." Juan went back into the engine compartment, Steve climbed on to the surface of the vessel and grabbed hold of the safety rope, he shouted "Juan, Juan come here quick."

Juan quickly covered the few steps needed to climb to the top of the hatch, Steve, "Quick grab a rope, come out."

There was a very large Humpback whale swimming next to the vessel, just metres away, "No damage, I can see." said Juan. They then saw a calf swimming on the other side of the whale about half the size of the vessel. "They are curious animals it would not cause us danger unless we annoy the mother or the calf. I see them often when fishing in the Atlantic with my father." Juan went back into the cockpit, "We are ok still 10 knots, nothing close." He climbed out onto the surface of the vessel again.

Steve entered the cabin and collected his phone, he took several photographs of the whale and the calf, Juan smiling, which was a rarity, the vessel was not in the photographs. The visitors stayed by the side of the vessel for several minutes, the mother was so close Steve could see himself and the vessel in her eye. She turned her head and moved away from the vessel then began a dive into the depths. Steve took a close-up photograph of her tail in the air, folded with water cascading down from the full width of the tail onto the surface of the ocean. Then they were gone. The two men high fived, a moment of pure joy, a massive boost to each of them.

They were now good friends, Juan respected Steve, they got along with each other well, which was needed in the cramped space they had.

CHAPTER 13

Thursday 1st June

It was 01:24, an hour until they would arrive at the rendezvous location with the supply ship. Juan was at the controls, looking out of the viewing port, the ocean was calm and lit by the light of the half-moon through the clouds, nothing showing on the radar as yet, steady at 11 knots, high on the water level.

Steve was reading the instructions and radio codes for the meeting, he left the page open on his bunk, he retrieved the two Fara 83 rifles from the storage under the bed, he checked that both weapons were now fully loaded. "Juan, I hope we never have to use these," Juan was watching Steve with the weapons, "If we get into trouble, need to get into action, do everything I tell you to do, do not waste bullets, shoot in the chest, keep low." He indicated with his hands as he was talking.

A ship was indicated on the radar moving toward the meeting point, they were closing on each other, there would be no need to use the radio. The ship was holding its position, it was not showing any navigation lights, Steve saw another indication on the edge of the radar screen, which one was the supply vessel? He used the radio and used the password; the ship they were approaching returned their password. The supply ship was now visible, an ocean fishing boat. Steve moved the vessel to the port side of the boat, the hull was wooden with the bulwarks protected by steel plates against the damage that could be caused by the fishing equipment, the deck was only two metres above the level of the vessel, two crew were waiting. Steve opened the hatch and climbed onto the surface of the vessel; he passed two ropes to secure the vessel front and back to the boat. One of the crew passed a fuel pipe which Steve passed down to Juan, within seconds the diesel was being pumped into the tanks. Containers of fresh water were passed into the storage areas, as Juan was moving the water, he looked at the radar screen and saw the other vessel closing quickly. "Steve, there is another ship coming quick."

At the same time the skipper came to the side of the boat, he spoke to Steve, "You will have to go, pirates are coming, they must have followed us."

Steve was thinking quick, he knew the vessel could not outrun the pirate ship, "How many crew do you have?" he asked.

"Just three of us, we have some weapons."

"They will kill you and us if we split up, show me your weapons." He climbed on board; the skipper took him to the raised bow where he removed a tarpaulin from a .5 calibre Browning machine gun which could be mounted on a metal frame "That should give us a chance, do you have another one?"

"No, but I have a grenade launcher?"

"No fucking way, can your crew use them?"

"We have never had to; how hard can it be?"

Juan shouted, "It's 2 K, closing fast."

They completed refuelling the vessel, the water and food rations had been replenished, Juan handed out both Fara 83s and ammunition to Steve then closed the hatch and climbed on board. Steve took control, the skipper was responsible for keeping the starboard side towards the approaching boat to protect the vessel, his crew were positioned near the stern on the starboard side facing the oncoming boat, they had small calibre rapid fire weapons. Juan was positioned in the middle of the boat with both Fara 83 rifles, Steve was standing behind the Browning which had been mounted by one of the crew, the grenade launcher and a box of grenades was on the deck at his feet. He was afforded some protection by the heightened bow of the boat which was steel plated.

They could see the boat approaching, it was also in darkness, no lights visible. Steve was waiting, aiming down the sighting of the Browning into the small bridge of a smaller sized boat. The dark, quiet night exploded into deafening sounds of the rapid fire and was lit by the flames coming from the Browning, at the same time they were hitting the target, flashes of light and fire could be seen as the bullets hit the intended target, still out of small arms range, the attacking boat turned to port opening the starboard side of the target. At once Steve sent large calibre ammunition down the length of the boat causing small explosions. They were returning fire but their shots were falling short of the target and fizzing into the ocean, they were closing in about 400 metres, Steve looked down onto the deck which was covered in shell casings, he picked up the grenade launcher, his first shot was short and exploded in the sea creating a large spray, he added more elevation and sent another grenade towards the boat, two seconds, three seconds, a large explosion on the stern of the attacking ship. Steve then aimed the Browning again at the bridge, the attackers were attempting to get around the stern and attack from the back of the boat, the skipper was keeping low in the bridge as he maintained the starboard side towards the attackers. There was still returning fire but it continually fell short into the ocean, Steve fired another grenade which went over the attackers, the boat had again turned and was heading directly towards the starboard side at full speed, Steve opened fire with the Browning, he shouted at Juan to take over. The attackers' bullets were now hitting the ship, the bullets could be heard hitting the steel plating along the bulwark, the bridge and the gun emplacement were receiving most of the gun fire. The windows in the bridge were all hit with glass fragments exploding into the bridge and onto the deck. The two crew were hiding below the level of the bulwark, Juan maintained fire on the bridge of the ship which was deviating from the straight line, the crew at the stern started to fire towards the attackers. Steve took aim and fired a grenade, they were closer now, no elevation required, a direct hit in front of the small bridge, a big explosion. The boat maintained its line, more gun fire towards the attackers from all quarters, gun fire was being returned, bullets were hitting the steel plating or going overhead, some of which were hitting the fishing rigging, it was having little effect. Juan continued his relentless fire into the bridge which exploded in a ball of fire, it was now only 200 metres away and still closing fast. The sound of gun fire was deafening, it would have been heard halfway across the ocean. Steve suddenly realised that the boat was going to hit their boat in midships unless they moved quickly, he ran, ducking down to the bridge and shouted, "Full ahead now." He turned and faced the rapidly closing boat which was on fire, there were no weapons being fired from the boat, he doubted anyone was alive, could be alive. The skipper had the boat moving, the attacking boat was not moving offline heading for the starboard midships, Steve shouted and waved his arm to Juan who was still firing into the blazing ship and couldn't hear him. He ran to the bow deck of the small boat and grabbed hold of Juan, they both ran back towards the bridge, the two crew ran and hid behind the bridge. In seconds the flaming boat crashed into the stern of the supply boat, the boat rocked on the spot, the noise of the breaking wooden boards and decking as the two boats collided was immense, flames immediately engulfed the rear of the boat which was rapidly taking in water and starting to sink.

Steve shouted at the skipper, "Abandon ship, everyone into the vessel, now!"

They all quickly moved to the port side, Juan picked up one of the Fara 83s that he saw on the deck, he went first and opened the hatch. As he stood on the surface of the vessel, Steve climbed down and stood near to the control panel, the rear rope was released first, the crew member climbed into the vessel, the second crew member released the front rope and climbed into the vessel. They were sat on the bunks, the skipper climbed inside followed by Juan who closed the hatch. Steve pushed the throttle and moved away from the two burning, sinking ships, a minute later Juan and the skipper watched through the viewing port as both boats sank into the ocean, Steve didn't look back.

They didn't stop to look for survivors, it was highly unlikely there would be any. Juan took over the controls, the vessel was lowered into the ocean by taking on more ballast, to make a smaller profile should any shipping hearing the noise and decide to investigate the area. Steve and the skipper looked at the charts which were spread on one of the bunks, a decision had to be made where the skipper and the crew could be landed safely. The vessel could go into shallow water as it had done in the river. The nearest island was Santo Antâo, Juan headed south towards the island which would be two hours at full speed to reach in the darkness. The cabin was claustrophobic so the two crew were moved to the engine room, it wasn't ideal but Steve did not want the crew to see the size of the cargo.

Santo Antâo soon came into view, a large rocky mass growing out of the ocean. Juan was constantly looking at the radar screen as they closed in on the island. The skipper had indicated a bay that he knew, which had no population and a small beach near to the small village of Cruzinha. Steve was looking at the mountainous cliffs as they approached the beach, fortunately it was a calm ocean. The vessel was cruising at two knots when Steve opened the hatch, they were two hundred yards from the shore, the charts were showing a rocky, uneven ocean floor. The skipper and the crew shook hands with Steve and Juan before jumping from the vessel into the ocean and began swimming to the shore. Juan and Steve took the opportunity to empty the onboard toilet and freshen themselves in the ocean, each in turn. They waited until they saw the three men on the shore before climbing back into the vessel. Steve inspected his phone and saw he had a signal, he typed another message, 'leaving Santo Antao now direction Spain', they continued their journey.

Leon had completed his morning session in the gym then as an afterthought, he looked at both of his mobiles, nothing from Bert, checking the encro phone two messages.

'Just left gulf of Venezuela, only 2 crew, heading towards Cape Verde islands then north to Spain. Very big cargo steady average 10 knots'

'Leaving Santo Antao now direction Spain'

They were both timed at 04:22 earlier in the morning.

He opened his tablet and looked for the Gulf of Venezuela and then searched for Santo Antao, he did some calculations and worked out it would be another seven or eight days before the vessel would get to Vigo, if that was the destination. He made a call.

Bert answered, "Hello Leon, I was wondering when you would get in touch, I suppose you have been busy."

"Good morning Bert, keeping a low profile you know. I've received a message from Steve on the encro phone, two actually, but they both came through at the same time."

"Go on Leon I've got my pen ready."

"First one. Just left Gulf of Venezuela, only two crew, heading towards Cape Verde islands then north to Spain. Very big cargo, steady average ten knots."

Bert, "Only two crew, what's happened there then?"

"Second one. Leaving Santo Antao now direction Spain. They were both timed at 04:22 this morning"

"They sound very interesting, why only two crew and why go to an island, I'm sure we will find out. Sounds like a boring holiday, nothing but sea, or ocean should I say?"

Leon continued, "I've worked out it will be roughly seven or eight days before he gets to northern Spain. I'm sure we will get more messages when he gets mobile signal."

"Thanks for that Leon. I'll get the marine boys to check your calculations based on their knowledge and ten knots. Anything else happening up north I need to know about?"

"I'm keeping in touch with the informant regularly, it looks like they are all waiting for the delivery from Steve." It wasn't a lie.

"That's good news as well, I'll update the intelligence data, keep up the good work, occasional phone calls, okay."

"Yes, I will, I'll let you know as soon as I know."

CHAPTER 14

Sunday 4th June

They were sailing on calm seas, with clear blue skies above, to the west of the island of Santa Cruz de la Palma in the Canary Islands. It was just after 8am, there was some shipping showing on the radar but none near enough to cause concern. It was daylight and flights were passing overhead at cruising altitude. They were low in the water moving at ten knots. Steve took the opportunity to use his encro phone, it had a signal, 'passing Las Palmas Island Canaries good progress, Vigo Wed night early Thursday hours' The message was sent.

Gabi was making the breakfast when Leon's encro phone activated she called, "You have a message." as she whisked the eggs for the tortilla. Leon read the message, "I'll call Bert tomorrow, maybe we should call Lucas, Steve should be here on Wednesday night, Thursday morning."

Sarah was awake early in Newcastle upon Tyne. She had undergone a tough week on the training course and was looking forward to a day trip along the Northumberland coast, Seahouses and Bamburgh with her parents. She sent a message to Steve, 'Morning big lad, me, dad and mam off to Seahouses for a boat trip to see some seals, I'll probably get sick, again, then fish n chips and crab sandwiches, winkles and beer. Course is tough but doing well, I think. Travelling back down tonight. Hope you're ok, miss you. X'

Later that afternoon, Sarah was indeed sick on the boat trip around the Farne Islands. When standing on the platform for the train back to the course, she had enough dressed crab for everyone in a cool box.

Monday 5th June

Leon made a call to Bert, "Good morning Bert, I've had another message from Steve."

Bert was sat at his desk in his office, "Go ahead Leon, I'm prepared."

"Passing Las Palmas Island, Canaries, good progress, Vigo Wednesday night or early Thursday hours."

"That's excellent. That ties in with what the marine boys figured as well. Anything else?"

"I'm going to message Lucas for a meet and tell him the info as well, hoping I get some info in return."

"Good idea, keep it safe though. You know what you're doing."

"Yes, will do Bert, have they a plan as yet?"

"They have a few variations on the plan depending on where and how it gets unloaded. The boat will be monitored by the Guardia once it enters the Spanish local waters."

"I'll not tell Lucas that bit then. Hopefully I should know by Tuesday night."

Gabi made a call to Lucas and they arranged to meet in a bar in Moaña, not far from Vigo.

Gabi parked the Audi in the car park in Moaña marina and they walked the short distance to the bar, it was a glorious summer day. They both got attention from the people in the streets, Gabi in her short red dress and Leon in his white t-shirt and light blue shorts.

They entered the bar and took seats at a table in the garden, they both ordered sparkling water. Lucas arrived as the drinks arrived and ordered a small beer.

After the greetings, Gabi started the conversation, "We

received a message from Steve yesterday, he was passing Las Palmas Island, he should be here Wednesday night or Thursday morning."

"That confirms what I know," he directed his speech towards Leon, "you and your friend Steve might be getting a bonus."

Leon was puzzled, "That sounds good, is it a record time?"

"No, it's just good that he is here, well not him, the cargo?"

Leon was struggling to understand, "You have me confused, is there a problem?"

"I have been in contact with the suppliers. The skipper of the boat that was supplying the extra fuel for the journey, they were attacked by pirates and together they killed all the pirates but the supply boat sunk." Leon just looked at Lucas, he continued, "It was a miracle, all of the cargo is okay and the crew."

"How the fuck did the pirates know about the boat with the cargo?"

"They knew about the supply boat, one of the crew who didn't go with the boat told them, to pay off a debt. He will not tell anyone, anything, anymore." he took a drink of his cold beer, "The skipper made sure of that, before he called me."

Leon, "Is the skipper and the crew on the boat with Steve?"

"Steve isn't on a boat, he's in a submarine."

"You are taking the piss, a submarine?"

"Sort of, but only room for three people, Steve dropped them off near to an island."

"So, Steve and the other two are driving a submarine?"

"You mean Steve and one crew. Steve killed one of them, the young one, stabbed him in the heart."

Leon was shocked, "What?" he said with incredulity, "Why would Steve do that, I don't believe it?"

Gabi was silent and listening to every word.

Lucas leant forward over the table, "I have been told, the young one, had upset the leader of one of the groups and they tortured him, hung him out alive, to be eaten by the animals.

Steve killed him. The leader was killed by one of his men a few days later, they have a new boss. Steve killed most of the pirates as well, an ice cold killing machine."

Leon was calm, "We only do what needs to be done, we do not kill for fun."

Lucas smiled at Leon, "You do not need to work anymore, well not doing supply journeys, there could be other targeted work, if you were both interested?"

"We could be, but I will need to speak to Steve first, as you can imagine I don't like to upset him." They smiled at each other.

Gabi, "Okay, we have a hero, whoop, whoop. What about the slaughter of the cargo?"

Lucas turned to Gabi, "My apologies, it is in hand, it will be collected together with the two crew when it gets to the, location. You will get your large renumeration in five days, it is longer because it is bigger, will that be a problem?" They smiled at each other.

"Of course not Lucas, not now that you know my friends." She flashed a smile to Lucas, who nodded and smiled.

They finished their drinks and walked back to the marina in silence, it was also a silent journey back to the villa. Leon took a seat at the side of the pool looking out to the islands, Gabi brought him a glass of fresh orange juice and took a seat next to him. "What are you going to tell your boss?"

"I'll tell him about the submarine and nothing else."

"Nothing about Steve?"

"No, I cannot say anything until I've spoken to Steve. It's his decision if he says anything."

Gabi, "I can help a little bit; I have seen a submarine before. It does not go under water, under the ocean, the top of the boat is only maybe one metre above the ocean or less, it does not get shown on radar. It is like a long canoe; I saw one in the Pacific. I was watching the radar for anything; nothing was showing and it was at the side of the boat I was in."

Leon was shaking his head, "I was supposed to go and I

suggested that Steve do it, some two-week holiday."

"I listened to what Lucas was saying about the young crew man being killed, I know the submarines are built in the jungle, on a river, that's where they must have been. Steve was giving mercy to the man when he killed him," she thought of Susanna, "I can understand that as well, I know how easy it is to kill a someone with a knife." Leon was looking in her face, "A quick thrust of the blade in the heart, they die but it lives with you for ever. Mercy, necessity or want, may be the reasons to kill but it will last for ever."

Leon was nodding, "We have both killed before, in a war zone and probably some pirates off east Africa, we were not police officers then. He has some thinking to do, so do I when this is finished."

Gabi was curious, "What will you be thinking about?"

There was a short silence, "If we finish this when the guy comes to kill you, one way or another, it may not be possible to continue doing what we are doing now. We will have crossed the line, certainly if we stay in a relationship together."

"I would like that; we could go to the paradise island together."

"That's a great thought for later, I have to call Bert now."

Leon made the call to Bert and passed the information, Bert was aware of the semi-submersibles, the intelligence was logged on Operation Portcullis and disseminated to the Nacional and Guardia Police.

The vessel was heading north passing the straights of Gibraltar, there was more shipping in the area, Juan was constantly looking at the radar screen and making slight alterations to avoid any possible sighting.

Steve was lying on his bunk, a constant stream of thoughts were going through his mind: Sarah, how much he missed her, what would happen to their relationship when she knew what had happened, how could she possibly do her new role if she knew what he had done. The sights of young Pepe, the pulse feeling through his hand when holding the knife in his heart. What will the outcome be, if or when, they find out the real identity of Gabi? What is going to happen to Juan when the arrests are made, they had done so much together, trusted each other, were now more than friends. He recalled the early quote in his police career, 'no-one said it would be easy', this was fucking impossible was his opinion. The constant thought was to resign, he couldn't continue.

The Guardia had positioned covert cameras on the outside of the warehouse and had undertaken a surveillance on Miguel Torres. The Nacional were monitoring the fishing boat still moored in the port of Vigo, they had undertaken a surveillance on Vincente Escribe, the boats skipper.

During the course of the surveillance, Torres and Escribe had met in a small bar near to the port in Vigo, they were in conversation for a few minutes, Torres was seen to pass a folded piece of white paper to Escribe.

Lucas Alvarez was seen to visit the warehouse that afternoon, both Torres and Delgado were recorded as they visited the warehouse. The three were together in the warehouse for twenty minutes, they left the warehouse together and went their separate ways.

At 17:17, a Guardia civil CN 235-300 fixed-wing aircraft was conducting aerial surveillance over the north Atlantic. The semi-submersible was spotted fourty kilometres west of Cape Saint Vincent on the southwest coast of Portugal, heading north. From their calculations the vessel would be in northern Spain Vigo area in the early hours of Thursday.

Tuesday 6th June

The vessel had stopped, it was just after three in the morning. Nothing was showing on the radar, it was warm on the deck as Juan threw out the safety line, he had emptied the waste into the ocean then jumped into the clean water. He was hoping this would be the last occasion, he cleansed himself in the ocean and had a swim, after ten minutes he climbed back onto the surface of the vessel to dry off. Steve took his turn and jumped into the ocean, it felt good to have unrestricted movement, then he joined Juan on the surface of the vessel sitting against the small hatch. Juan brought two metal mugs of black coffee; they enjoyed the small amount of freedom outside of the vessel.

Steve spoke first, "This time in two days, we should be on solid ground."

Juan, "I am looking forward to seeing my mother and my girlfriend Verónica, who is waiting for you?"

"I have a girlfriend but she doesn't know I'm here, I would like to see her and a good friend is waiting. What will you do after this?"

"I hope to have enough to get my father's boat back and go fishing again, you can be one of my crew."

"Nice offer, but no thank you," they both smiled, "I have had enough of the ocean for a while. How did you get involved, you said you couldn't refuse their offer?"

"My father died, he, Torres, was at the funeral, he knows the family, we are not friends. He told my mother he was taking the boat, my father owed him money, it was bullshit, my father never owed anyone money. It was our living, our life, fishing, how we made the family safe, comfortable, not rich. I could get it back if I did this. Why are you here?"

"My friend and I had some bad luck, we made a bad investment in Andalucía and lost a lot of our money, it was a way of getting our money back."

Juan drank some coffee, "We could still be friends, I would like it if you come to my house to meet my mother and Verónica, would you do that?"

"Yes, if I can." Steve was feeling guilty thinking ahead to the arrests, "Come on, we better make progress or we'll not get there on time."

They both climbed into the vessel, Steve checked his phone, no signal.

The surveillance aircraft was regularly flying over the route and position of the vessel and sending reports back to the intelligence hub.

The surveillances were continuing on Escribe and Torres, there was little significant movement from either.

Alvarez was seen to enter the warehouse with two other men, a short time after their arrival, a wagon with a large metal container reversed into the warehouse. The container was removed from the wagon which was driven away.

At 15:28 Escribe left his home and drove to the port of Vigo, he walked to the mooring where the fishing boat was moored and climbed on board. The Nacional officers were watching on the monitors, when two other men were seen walking towards the boat and climbed on board. Images were forwarded to the intelligence hub; they were identified as the two men that had been seen at the warehouse. The three men went below deck, the engine was started.

At 16:04 the three left the boat and walked to the restaurant Pizzaria. They sat and ate together under the observation of changing surveillance officers.

Later that evening the fishing boat with Escribe and the two known men left the port and headed into the Atlantic, heading northwest, the boat was being tracked at a distance by another Guardia patrol boat.

CHAPTER 15

Wednesday 7th June

The surveillance teams were active during the day following Alvarez and Torres, there was no physical contact between the two men witnessed. The fishing boat had been busy fishing in the Atlantic, the Guardia surveillance aircraft had flown overhead on occasions and made recordings of the activity.

The vessel was still heading north and was now to the west of Porto, sailing low in the water with very little profile above surface level. Steve was at the controls, Juan was cooking, he was using the remaining beans, rice, spice sauce and what was left of the previously cooked mackerel, this would be their last meal together on the vessel. Steve checked the time, 19:38, another five, possibly six hours to go, he was thinking about Juan, how could they both get away from the arrest teams.

Gabi and Leon were sat at the table on the terrace, Gabi had made the meal, mixed salad, monkfish with prawns and mussels in tomato sauce, rice with mixed peppers and warm fresh bread. Leon had poured the chilled white wine into the crystal glasses, they toasted each other, then Steve as they looked out to the ocean. Leon, "I hope everything goes okay tonight."

Gabi nodded, "I certainly hope so, I haven't heard anything from Lucas, I'm assuming there is no problems."

"I know we're not going to the slaughter but is there any

way we can collect Steve when he lands, or are there plans for him and the other crew member?"

"I don't know, I usually don't ask questions but it might be expected to ask about Steve, now that we know he's had a rough time. I will message him after the meal, just ask if we can pick him up."

Leon made a suggestion, "Leave it until I have made a call to Bert."

They finished the meal, Leon looked at the screen of the mobile, it was 20:39, he made a call to Bert.

"Good evening Leon, is everything going well?"

"I certainly hope so Bert, is everything sorted for the operation tonight?"

"Yes, I've travelled up today so maybe we can meet up tomorrow, when everything is completed?"

Leon was taken by surprise, "Yes, would be a good idea to catch up, the three of us, but Steve might need some chill out time first, get pissed, good food, remember he's been on that shitty boat for a long time."

"Oh yes, of course, he needs time, psychologically and physically, it would be good to see you, then you two can chill."

"Do you have plans for Steve when the strike goes down?"

"The Spanish will be in control of that, certain people know about Steve, those on the strike will not know, he will initially be arrested with everyone else if he is in the warehouse, or wherever they decide to do the strike, we're hoping the warehouse."

"How long are you staying in the area?"

"Just a couple of days, we do not have any British involvement in the operation, apart from you two."

"Once it is safe, I will meet you somewhere."

"Fingers crossed; it will be a big result if everything goes according to plan. I will be in touch Leon"

"See you soon then Bert, good luck for tonight."

Leon turned to Gabi who heard one half of the conversation, "If Steve goes with the load to the warehouse he will get locked up, arrested with everyone, probably a few days in the cells, who knows what might happen when the Guardia raid the place?"

"I can message Lucas, no big questions."

"It's worth a try."

Gabi typed her message, 'all ok when will we see Steve?'

They sat at the table and drank more chilled wine and waited. After a few minutes the reply arrived, "yes when he is on land."

Gabi, "We can pick him up when he lands, wherever that may be, he hasn't said."

Leon was shaking his head, "No, we can't pick him up, you cannot be seen anywhere remember, you cannot be identified it's too risky, Steve would understand that."

Gabi was walking around the table, "You can send him a message and hope he gets it, he will when he gets close to shore. Tell him to go to the hotel room you have."

"Good idea. I was thinking that."

Leon sent the message.

Thursday 8th June

It was just after midnight; the fishing boat had started to return in the direction of Vigo from the fishing grounds. The vessel was now two hours south from Vigo.

Juan and Steve both had some sleep during the previous hours and were now fully awake, Juan was at the controls, Steve was reading the instructions for the delivery, again. He entered the cargo section and inspected the strapping, he turned the locking mechanism on the cargo hatch, which moved with ease. The rendezvous point was two kilometres west of Islas Cíes, the location was put into the satnav system, 1 hour 25 minutes travelling time. Steve took over the controls, he opened the hatch above him, they both welcomed the fresh cooling air as it entered the small cabin space, he looked directly above him to the dark star lit sky, there was a slight southern breeze which was pushing them on the final leg of their torturous journey. He stood with his head outside the hatch, he could see distant lighting from the horizon towards the mainland of Spain and Portugal. He tested his phone, it was on full power, after illuminating the small screen it took one minute for a single bar to show on signal strength, a few seconds later a message appeared: 'when you get to shore go straight to hotel Inffinit I have a room.'

Steve replied, 'ok me and Juan getting pissed'

A few seconds passed, he got the reply, 'and me'

It was an instant relief for Steve, for the first time in a long time he was feeling good, a possible escape route for Juan, certainly from the initial arrests, then mitigation could be put in for him at a later date if he was arrested. He looked ahead and could see the outline of an island in the distance, they pushed on.

The Guardia could now see that the fishing boat and the vessel were heading towards each other, the overhead surveillance aircraft was circling out of sight. The fishing boat stopped and was holding on a location in deep water two kilometres northwest of the channel that runs between Islas Cíes and San Martiño island. It was sheltered by the highest point on the island.

The vessel was approaching the meeting point, a distance of one kilometre to go. Steve looked at Juan, they both shook hands and hugged. Steve, "We are nearly done, when we go ashore, you are coming with me for beer, lots of beer, then we will visit your family, when we are sober." They both smiled and hugged again.

Juan used the radio to make contact with the fishing boat, they each passed their respective codewords, Steve positioned the vessel on the starboard side of the fishing boat, hidden from anyone watching from the island. The boat and the vessel were secured together with ropes to the front and rear by Juan and one of the boat crew, the vessel was raised in height above the ocean, it was now just one metre below the deck of the boat. After returning into the vessel, Juan secured the hatch and went to join Steve in the cargo section. Steve opened the larger cargo hatch, the ropes were dropped from the hoist on the boat through the opening, they both secured the ropes on the first batch of cargo. The move was easy as it was lifted and guided through the opening then placed the cargo into the hold of the boat, within seconds it was being repeated. When there were two more batches to be unloaded, Juan returned to the cabin and picked up the two bags of personal items that Steve and he had prepared, he opened the hatch and climbed onboard the boat.

The last batch was lifted, on the wooden floor of the vessel below where the cargo had been placed was the water valve, Steve opened the valve and the ocean began to flood the empty cargo section rapidly, he returned to the cabin, the ocean following him.

On board the fishing boat both ropes had been released, the vessel was drifting away from the side of the boat, Juan was looking at the hatch, Steve was climbing out of the hatch, which was now five metres from the boat. The two crew men were standing in front of him at the side of the boat, looking towards the vessel drifting away, they were laughing at Steve, Juan saw that one of them had a handgun and he was aiming the revolver at Steve, he had to do something to safe Steve, the sound of gunfire again hurt Juan's ears. He then looked towards Steve who was jumping into the ocean, he threw him a rope, looking down at the two bloodied bodies of the bullet ridden crew. He ran to the bridge carrying the Fara 83, opening the door he saw Escribe standing in front of him. He had stopped the engines and had his hands above his head, looking into the face of Juan. He went to speak, Juan then shot him several times in the chest and he collapsed in a bloody mess onto the wooden floor of the bridge. Juan ran to the side of the boat and assisted Steve to climb on board, they looked down on the crew, several wounds in the chest and back of both men, one was still alive, moving, moaning with the pain, struggling to breathe, he wouldn't live much longer. They both walked into the small bridge, Escribe was definitely dead, they pulled his body out of the bridge and lay him next to the other two then returned to the bridge.

Juan, "What have I done, I did this to protect my family, what have I done."

Steve, "You have saved my life my friend, mi amigo. We have to think." They shook hands and hugged, "Mucho gracias mi amigo, mucho, mucho, gracias. How did you have the Fara?"

"I was going to keep it in case I needed it in the future, if Torres came calling again, I think I might need it now."

Steve got his phone out of the bag he had a signal, he sent a message, 'BIG problem on board, collection boat tried to kill us after they got cargo, they are all dead, we have cargo, boat and bodies, wtf.'

Leon heard the mobile activate, he read the message, Gabi was awake, she asked "What's happening?"

"Shit, loads of fucking shit, I need to think, fuck me."

"I can help, what has happened?"

Leon read the message, Gabi replied, "That's shit, big shit, what are you going to do, what is Steve going to do?"

"Gabi, I want answers not fucking questions."

"Okay, message him and ask what his idea is."

"That's what I was going to do," Gabi was shaking her head in amazement, he sent the message, 'What do you suggest, can you still deliver the cargo'

Steve couldn't believe what he was reading, 'R u serious, they tried to kill us once wat d u think will hapn if we roll up with 3 dead. F'ing mad. wtf. think again.'

Leon, "He didn't like that idea. I think I should contact Bert"

Gabi, "That is the first thing you should have suggested,

give him the problem. Me, I think they should disappear with the boat and the cargo and negotiate with Lucas, they can possibly trust Lucas. He knows what Steve is capable of, you, and now the other man, I could do the negotiation."

Leon sent a message, 'I can tell Bert, u could disappear with the cargo and negotiate with Lucas.'

Steve read the message and discussed it with Juan, neither wanted anything to do with the cargo, he couldn't talk about Bert or Gabi. Something would have to be said to Bert, they were expecting the boat and the cargo to carry out a strike later in the day. He typed the message, 'have to tell Bert, skipper and 2 crew shot dead, they were sinking us with the vessel, self-defence, my crew mate saved my life, need urgent advice atm sailing away from area, possible negotiate with OCG's but believe that would end badly for my crewmate'

Leon made a call to Bert, "Hello Leon, you're up early expecting something to happen," he gave a little false laugh.

"Bert, something has happened, I need to tell you."

"This sounds ominous Leon; I've got my pen ready so go ahead."

"Okay, where do I start, fuck it. Steve and his crew member have shot and killed the three crew on the fishing boat in self-defence, they were going to sink them with the submarine, they don't know what to do." There was a pause, "Hello, Bert, Bert."

Bert had been thinking, in shock, "In Sarah's words, Holy Moly, are they both okay, uninjured?"

"As far as I'm aware they are."

"Well then, this is what I suggest, leave it with me and I will liaise with my Spanish colleagues, it has certainly put a spanner in the works, did Steve suggest anything?"

"He told me to contact you but he mentioned going somewhere with the boat and cargo then contacting the OCG's to negotiate getting the cargo."

Bert was thinking, Leon let him think without disturbing his thoughts, "That is a possibility but we will have to do a risk assessment on how it goes before we make a decision."

Leon answered immediately, "Bert with respect, how the fuck could you risk assess what he has already done and what he is about to do if you agree to that idea?"

"Leon, that's a good point, well-made I must say, eloquently put. Tell Steve to stay safe, I will get back to you as soon as possible if not before. I take it the crew member is on his side?"

"Yes, he saved Steve's life, sounds like best mates Bert, they've been through a lot together by all accounts." Leon knew Bert did not know half of what had happened.

"Yes, I'll get in touch."

Leon sent the message to Steve, 'Stay at sea, Bert will get in touch with me, making enqs now.'

They were both in the bridge, Juan had thrown a bucket of the ocean over the floor to clear away the blood that was sinking through the wooden flooring. A mobile activated on the workspace near to the wheel, a message had been received, it was in Spanish, 'Have you got the cargo'

They had a quick discussion, they decided on the answer, 'soon'

Another message was received, 'just cargo, no dead weight, clean up here after.'

Juan replied, 'Okay.'

Steve was again thinking, "Juan, I think Torres is going to kill the gangs when they get the load."

Juan, "He could do that, he is a bastard, I wish he had been onboard."

Steve sent a message to Leon, 'possible Torres is going to kill others and take all load from message sent to skipper of this boat.'

Leon replied, 'F'ing hell, I'll tell my mate, could be a blood bath'. He told Gabi the content of the message.

She agreed with the implied meaning, "I should contact Lucas and ask what's happening."

Leon, "I'm going to contact Bert first, give me a second." He made the call which was answered immediately, "Hello Leon,

I'm with the other agencies now discussing the update, its worrying."

"Listen, listen, listen Bert, it is probably worse than you think?"

"How can it get any worse Leon?"

"How about a Valentine's Day massacre type of worse."

"I don't usually do this, excuse me, what the fuck are you going on about now, Valentine's Day massacre, speak in plain English."

"The bloke Torres who is boss of one OCG has just sent a message to the skipper of the boat, I'll read it, just cargo, no dead weight, clean up here after. To me that means bring back no dead bodies and we will clear the rest of them when you get back."

"Yes, I can see where you're coming from now, why didn't you just say that in the first place?"

"Okay Bert, now, what the fuck does Steve have to do, because, if he turns up with the fishing boat there's going to be a fucking war on the quayside, then, if the cargo is landed there's going to be a bloodbath in the warehouse."

Bert replied calmly, "Again, eloquently explained Leon, tell Steve to stay at sea until he hears otherwise from me."

Gabi had been listening, "I should tell Lucas, he knows that you and Steve are in contact with the encro phones"

Leon, "What are you going to tell him?"

"I'll tell him what we know, he might tell us some more, he must be awake."

She messaged Lucas, 'Skipper and crew tried to kill Steve and crew man, they're all dead. Steve has read message on skipper's phone telling him to kill them and saying he's going to clean up when he gets the load.'

Lucas was having a coffee in his kitchen when he read the message, he replied, 'Do not deliver, I'll deliver this end. Thanks.'

Lucas Alvarez at this point did not know if Javier Delgado was involved in the conspiracy against him, he would take no chances. Delgado was not involved in the unloading and should not be at the warehouse until later that morning.

At 02:58 the Guardia officers conducting the surveillance on Lucas Alvarez saw him leave his home and travel to the warehouse, he was met there by six men who had arrived in a Seat van, the van was parked a distance from the warehouse, one of the men was carrying a black holdall, they all entered the warehouse together.

Juan was holding a position to the west of the island; another message was received on the phone. 'Have you got the load any problems?'

After a short discussion with Steve, Juan replied, 'yes no passengers, heading in.'

Steve passed the message to Leon who made a call to Bert.

Torres made a call to Lucas Alvarez and asked him to be at the warehouse for a meet in 20 minutes with his team, the delivery would be soon.

Alvarez positioned his men in protected positions in the warehouse with good vision of the floor area and waited. They were all armed with an Uzi automatic sub machine gun.

The Nacional Police picked up movement in the dock area at the same time, a refrigerated wagon entered the docks and moved to the area where the fishing boat would be docking.

Torres was seen travelling in convoy with two other cars in the direction of the warehouse, the two police agencies started to tighten the circle around both locations.

Torres arrived outside of the warehouse with his team of eight members all carrying handguns concealed in holsters under their outer clothing. Torres, thinking that Alvarez was the only person in the warehouse, as there were no other vehicles present told his men to enter the warehouse. He led the way through the small door into the brightly lit interior of the warehouse, the large container was in the middle of the floor with the doors open to receive its cargo. Alvarez came out of his office, "Good morning, you are early, my men are not here yet."

Torres was smiling, "This is good, men." He gestured for them to take out their weapons.

Alvarez, looked Torres in the eyes, "No, it is bad." He jumped behind the open steel door of the container. The gun fire was intense and deadly as his men started firing on the unprotected men of Torres. He was the first to be hit by several rounds, in the chest neck and head, it was over in seconds. They had no chance, standing in an unprotected empty space. The gunfire was heard by the nearby surveillance observers. The floor was covered in bright red flowing and pooling blood, the job was not finished yet, they were not all dead. The men gathered around Alvarez, looking down on their work, "Well done, thank you my friends, there is no need to use more ammunition, Sergio, your knife please." He held out his hand, Sergio placed the handle into his hand, he leant over the dead body of Torres, he was lying on his side, "Unfortunately, you are dead you traitor." He spat into the face of Torres then stabbed him in the back. The next man was alive, blood coming from wounds in his upper and lower body, he was conscious, Alvarez leant over his face, "You picked the wrong team, the wrong captain, can you see me?"

The man nodded, "Yes."

"Look into my face."

He raised his eyes and looked into the face of Alvarez, "Please, mercy, please."

Alvarez pushed the blade through his open eye, deep through the socket into his brain, "No, no mercy."

Two more were lying in their blood and the blood of the others trying to move, urinating through fear. He moved towards the next injured victim who was holding his hand up.

An extremely loud explosion rocked everyone inside the warehouse, the door was gone, the electricity had gone, there was no lighting inside the building, then a strong beam of white light penetrated the darkness through the enlarged doorway. The loudspeaker announcement, "Guardia Civil, put down your weapons, the building is surrounded. You have to drop your weapons and lie on the floor near to the door. We will use force." The blue and red lights on the vehicles outside were flashing in sequences around the upper windows of the warehouse, nothing could be seen from inside the warehouse other than the blinding white light. One by one, the men dropped their weapons and lay on the ground, Alvarez dropped his knife but remained standing, he didn't see anyone, he felt the blow to the back of his left knee and a push in the middle of his back, he was face down on the floor. His arms were pulled behind his back and was handcuffed, then after a quick body search, he was dragged by his arms out of the warehouse.

Bert made a call to Leon, "Yes Bert, what's happening?"

"You were right, it was another massacre in the warehouse, Torres is dead, Alvarez and his team are arrested. The Nacional are striking in the docks now so tell Steve keep away, now."

"Okay Bert."

Leon sent the message, 'STAY AT SEA DO NOT ENTER THE DOCKS'

The Policia Nacional secured the area around the fishing dock, then arrested the driver of the refrigerated wagon and three other men who they had been observing.

The operation was a success, one of the Organised Crime Groups had been killed and another OCG were under arrest for their killing. They just needed the fishing boat to be docked with the cargo to complete the excellent result.

Bert was in a briefing room at Vigo Guardia Headquarters with officers from the Guardia and Nacional. The initial discussion centred on the crew member of the semi-submersible, he had been identified from the recordings taken in Madrid airport as Xoán Uxio Mariño, Steve knew him as Juan. There was no criminal history recorded against him, he would have to be arrested and interviewed, it was known that he had saved Steve's life but the deaths of the three men on the boat would have to be investigated, as well as the transportation of the cargo. The conversation then centred on Steve. Bert wanted the true identity of Steve to remain unknown, to ensure that he would be able to continue in his undercover work. The Spanish agencies wanted to debrief Steve; he would also have to be interviewed about the deaths on the fishing boat. They came to a compromise agreement, the two men could come ashore together, they would initially be arrested and then interviewed separately, they could be bailed to attend another interview at a later date if it was required. Bert made a call to Leon.

"Hello Bert, what's the score?"

"I have spoken together with the Guardia and Nacional senior officers, it has been difficult, due to the circumstances of this morning's events."

Leon was impatient, "Yes Bert I can understand that, what the fuck is happening to my mate and the lad on the boat?"

"I'm aware that you are concerned."

Leon interrupted, "Concerned, me, fucking concerned, them two have had loads of shit, of course I'm concerned, you should be concerned, they don't need or want any more shit after what they've just gone through."

Bert being assertive, "Leon, if I may continue without interruption, please. We have made the decision, when the two men Steve and Xoán, come to the dock in the boat, escorted by a Guardia craft, it would look better, they will be arrested."

"Bert, but..."

"Leon, I have asked you once, remember I am not just a friend, I am your boss, so be quiet until I finish."

"Sorry, Bert."

"As I was saying, they will be arrested and interviewed then bailed, with assurances on Xoán's behalf to return at the time and date to wherever headquarters they recommend. This will give them a little time to refresh themselves after their arduous journey and frightful experience on the fishing boat. It will give Steve time to move away from Xoán and retain his undercover role which will not be mentioned. There should not be any problems once the facts have been verified by Steve. Could you please message Steve and ask him to come in with the boat and the cargo?"

"Can I speak now?"

"Yes, of course."

"Right Bert, how is Steve going to explain getting a message from the police telling him it's going to be okay? He has three bodies on the boat."

"Just send the message that the Guardia patrol boat is moving towards them now, we don't want any shenanigans with the Guardia, we know how that will end."

"Okay, okay, I'll think of something."

The call was ended, Leon started a message to Steve, 'Come in now, Guardia boat will escort, both arrested then bailed, go to hotel room, I'll book another one for your mate. Both will be interviewed separately. I will be at hotel let you know what happening.'

Steve read the message and was thinking when he saw the Guardia boat coming at speed to their position. They were both in the bridge he looked at Juan, "You are going to have to trust me again?"

"Yes, no problem, always."

"We have to go into port, we cannot do anything else, I'm sure we will be arrested but we have reasons why we are here, you and I have both been intimidated by the others or our family would suffer. We are taking the cargo to the police not hiding it. The three men were killed because they were trying to kill us, you saved my life, and the skipper attacked you, you defended yourself. Do not mention me killing Pepe, he was killed by the bandits, they don't know what happened and do not mention the pirates. If they are rough, do not resist, it should be okay."

Juan shrugged, "We are alive, that is a surprise, okay amigo, Capitan."

They sailed towards the port, followed by the Guardia patrol boat.

The armed Guardia officers were standing on the dock waiting the fishing boat arrival, Juan was in the bridge slowly manoeuvring the boat into position, Steve threw the ropes to the officers and the boat was secured alongside the dock. Juan stopped the engine then the two men climbed from the boat onto the dock, Steve first, he was handcuffed behind his back, followed by Juan who was also handcuffed. They were placed into separate vehicles and driven away from the area to the Vigo Guardia Headquarters. The Guardia forensic team boarded the boat and commenced their work, taking video recordings and photographs of what they found. The three men on the deck were dead, all killed by bullet wounds to the chest and back area, the handgun and the Fara 83 were recovered.

Upon entering the hold area, there was a decent catch of mackerel and tuna in iced boxes ready for the market. In the centre of the hold was the big catch, an estimated 4 tons of cocaine stacked on pallets and 400 kilos of drugs wrapped in blue packaging, quite a good haul. A street value in Spain of over €3 billion and the loss to the cartel of over $1 billion.

CHAPTER 16

Thursday 8th June

It was 08:26, Steve was in a cell, he had been stripped of all of his clothing and was wearing a white jumpsuit, he was lying on the wooden bench. He heard the sound of approaching footsteps and a key being inserted into the lock, he stood up as the door opened. The Guardia officer beckoned Steve to leave the cell and pointed him in the direction of the interview rooms. Steve walked in the direction indicated followed by the officer, he entered the room and saw Bert who was standing behind the table, the officer closed the door behind him.

Bert looked at Steve from head to toe, "I'm really pleased to see you, have they treated you well?"

"As well as could be expected Bert, it's good to see you, do you know what's happening?" they shook hands.

"That is why it has taken so long to see you; I have been in deep discussion with our partner agencies. First, they are all highly delighted at the result, magnificent work Steve and you will get the plaudits you deserve, two OCG's dismantled, three billion dollars of cocaine recovered, exceptional work by you on that small semi-submersible."

"Very good Bert, it was my job, what about Juan, what's happening with him? That's my concern, not plaudits."

"They are considering going very light on him in the circumstances, there is some explaining for him to do?"

"I can give you the explanations, the reason he was on the

so-called trip, how he saved my life, he doesn't deserve any time, Bert."

"Unfortunately, that is out of my hands, it's down to the Spanish partners, Guardia or Nacional to make that decision."

"It is not out of my hands, I want to tell them what he did, I'm as guilty as he is of doing anything, more so, I volunteered to do it, he had no choice. Without going too deep Bert, you and the Spanish lot haven't got a scoobydoo what the fuck we have gone through. We have just about survived to get here, by working with each other and protecting each other, that man, Juan, did what I told him," Steve was thinking of the shots into the chest of the three on the boat, "and because of that, we are still alive."

"Steve, I can understand that you have formed a kind of friendship with, Juan, you have been stuck together for a long time. You know when you take on the job, any formed friendships will cause problems at the end of the day, when everything is disclosed, including your identity."

"Bert, you don't have to tell me that, I've done enough. This is different, he was pressed into doing this to save his family, he is not in the OCG."

"I'm sorry Steve, it is out of my hands."

"Okay, so what is happening to me, when do I get out of here?"

"You just need to be debriefed by myself and a member from the agencies and that's it, you can have an earned rest."

"I suppose after that I could disclose my identity, be a witness for Juan or possibly even be his legal representative, that would be interesting."

"Steve, come, come. That would not be a good idea, disclose tactics, disclose your identity."

"Come, come, is that it! You have got two OCG's taken out, four and a bit ton of cocaine recovered, severe loss to a cartel, one young man is dead, which we have never talked about, because he was not in agreement with the cartel and you have a witch hunt against Juan. I've told you; he did nothing other than protect me and himself. You don't know half of it and you never will. The cartel will probably be looking for him and me now, they will blame someone."

Bert stepped back and raised his open hands, "Calm down Steve, you are going to have to be debriefed and then we can possibly talk some more about Juan, I can see that it is important to you."

Steve took a deep breath and slowly exhaled, "Bring in the Guardia or whoever let's get this debrief done." He sat in silence and waited as Bert left the room, then returned a few minutes later with an officer from the Guardia, Sergento, Manuel Chavez Vidal from the Organised Crime Team.

The interview was not recorded but both Bert and Manuel would make notes. Steve knew Manuel, they shook hands before taking their seats at the table.

Steve spoke first, "I think it might be easier if I start and go through what has happened, just ask if you want anything clarified?" both officers nodded in agreement.

"I was working with Leon who had managed to get an introduction to Lucas Alvarez. As part of the story line, Alvarez asked for one of us to do a boat delivery from somewhere, we both guessed it would be from across the Atlantic somewhere. It was decided I would do it, I had to go to Madrid airport, you have the dates and I would imagine CCTV recordings," Manuel nodded, "when I met a man, he didn't introduce himself and two other men, Juan and Pepe, Pepe was called Alejandro, I don't know last names, you don't ask. He gave us tickets; told us some lies and we got on a flight to Bogota. We were met at the airport and climbed into the back of a black Mercedes van, we were sat on benches, the journey was 37 minutes when we got out in the grounds of a large house, we stayed overnight. The next day we got in the same van for about an hour, then we got out at a wide river about 100 metres wide with a wooden jetty. We got into a plane on the river and flew south for an hour and twenty minutes then landed on another river, I believe it was called Catatumbo river, a native took us in a long boat, upstream for 25 minutes to the village where we stopped the night."

Manuel and Bert were scribbling down their notes and nodding, Steve waited for them to stop writing, then continued. "I got to know the two men and asked some questions they could answer, Juan, his family had their fishing boat taken off them by Torres over an alleged debt which Juan says does not exist. It was their means of living, he was doing the trip to get the boat back, nothing to do with drug money. Pepe owed drug money; he was working the debt off. There were only natives in the village, they were good people. We were woken up in the darkness and walked to the river, that's when we saw the submarine thing, Pepe was not going to get in, it wasn't what any of us was expecting, we were told a boat. Anyway, we had no option but to get in, it had a small control area where the hatch was with viewing portals, the cabin was under that, it had two bunks the length of the cabin a small gap between them. The separate section in the front had the cargo, the engine was in a section behind the cabin, really cramped. We were towed down the river overnight then pulled into a tributary just before the light came," he looked at Manuel, "I don't know the name."

Steve sat back in his chair, he was looking at the ceiling, Bert "Do you want to have a break?"

"No, can you get some water please?"

Manuel opened the door and spoke to an officer then returned to the table. They waited until the water was delivered.

Steve continued, "There was a group of armed men, there were a few groups every so far down the river, it's obviously a well-worn route for these vessels. You would stop during the day under cover of the jungle, then move at night. These were a bunch of idiots, kept us locked up in a wooden hut in the heat of the jungle, their leader was an arsehole, a right twat. Pepe was getting himself worked up, he was just a young lad, probably claustrophobic, didn't like small places being locked in. He was getting angry, I was trying to calm him down and Juan was doing his best, talking to him, then the door opened and he stormed off, as he walked through the door, he bumped into one of the guards and knocked him onto the ground, he was saying I'm sorry, I'm sorry, then bent over to pick him up, the other guard hit him over the back of his head and knocked him unconscious. We were saying it was an accident, they were saying Pepe was trying to take the gun, no way, they locked us in the room and dragged him away."

Steve waited for them to finish their notes and continued, "We were eventually let out of the room and walked to the river bank. Pepe was tied to a post standing on a wooden stump in the river, he was bleeding from cuts all over his body, arms, legs, his face was a mess, they really went to town on him the bastards. We watched, as they killed him and his body was thrown into the river." Steve closed his eyes and was silent for a few seconds, "The leader of the gang asked could two of us do the journey or should he order another crew. I knew what he meant, so I said we could do the journey."

Steve was tormented, he stood up from the table and took a plastic cup of water, he walked around the table and took his seat again. Neither Bert or Manuel said anything, they both had their heads down not wanting to look at Steve.

"We moved on again during the night and stopped at another camp, this one was okay, fed, watered, it was the last one, we were shown how to raise and lower the level of the vessel in the ocean, we were towed across Lake Maracaibo then we were on our own through the gulf of Venezuela and the Atlantic."

Manuel, "That sounds really bad Steve, we did not know."

"Yes Manuel, Juan and I survived the river and now had to cross the ocean, just the two of us, it was work and sleep, boredom, tiredness, a couple of storms, it was not easy."

Manuel asked, "What happened when you met the fishing boat?"

Steve had conveniently missed the part with the pirate

attack, "I had some co-ordinates to meet with the fishing boat, we saw the boat as planned and Juan pulled alongside, we got tied to the boat, we already had planned not to trust anyone, so when Juan had climbed back inside the vessel after tying it up, he closed the hatch so they couldn't throw anything inside the vessel. We both went into the forward section, I opened the cargo hatch and they began to lift the cargo out, it was quick using the heavy lifting gear on the boat." Steve was thinking about the explanation, "I told Juan to collect our bags and go on the deck of the boat, I had to open the flood valve after the load had gone. I opened the valve the water was coming in very quick, I walked to the hatch and I could see through the portal that the vessel was drifting away from the boat, they had released the securing ropes. I climbed through the hatch and saw the two crew with a gun pointed at me and laughing, one of them fired a shot which missed and I dropped back down into the control area, I thought I was going to die, drowned or shot, both, then I heard some rapid fire and looking through the portal I saw the two-gun men fall. Juan appeared and threw a rope over towards me, I jumped into the sea and swam to get the rope, I heard some more shots, then the boat engine stopped and Juan helped me climb onto the boat, he saved my life."

Manuel asked, "Where did Juan get the Fara 83 from?"

Steve was shaking his head, "It must have been on the fishing boat, we didn't have any weapons, they wouldn't trust us would they."

Manuel asked, "Why did they not use that weapon instead of a revolver,"

"I don't know, ask them, probably more fun for them, one at a time, I think they wanted me to drown inside the vessel, they didn't expect Juan to react like he did."

"Why did Juan shoot the skipper?"

"When Juan ran to the bridge to get him to stop the engine, he shot at Juan. Juan fired back in self-defence."

"When we have searched the boat there was only one

handgun, a revolver in the bridge, where is the other handgun?"

"The gunman on the deck who fired at me dropped it overboard when Juan shot him. Juan had shouted at them to stop them shooting at me, they took no notice, the gunman turned to face Juan, then Juan fired the gun, he has never fired a gun before in his life, he hit them both, he fell backwards and the gun went into the sea."

Steve was thinking back to the shooting on the deck. After he had been pulled on board by Juan, he had instructed Juan to place the dead men's hands on the Fara 83 to leave fingerprint marks, before Juan cleaned the floor of the bridge, he placed the revolver in the right hand of the skipper and fired a shot into the sea, leaving his fingerprints on the revolver and two bullets recently fired. The forensic evidence from the gunshot would be on the skippers clothing around his sleeve. Sometime it pays to plan ahead.

Bert asked Manuel, "Do you need to keep Steve in the cells much longer, any other questions can be sorted out later I'm sure, in a much more comfortable room."

Steve interrupted, "I would like to stay in as long as Juan is in. If he is released, even possibly on bail, I could be released in the same circumstances, if that would be acceptable Manuel, it would help with my story as well, my credibility for the future."

Manuel agreed but could not put a time limit on the length of stay, it would be dependent on what Juan had to say. Steve knew exactly what Juan would say, they had rehearsed it on the journey in the boat from the Islands to the docks.

Later that morning Juan was interviewed by Manuel and another Guardia officer, the interview was recorded. Juan stuck to the script that had been made together with Steve, it was the truth, with a few believable and hopefully undisputable lies.

It was just after 14:30 when Steve walked free from the custody area of the headquarters, he was still dressed in his white jump suit. Leon was waiting with a change of clothes, Steve changed in a small side room as he waited for Juan to emerge from the custody suite.

It was a short wait for the door to open and Juan to walk into the reception area, the two men immediately embraced each other. Steve introduced Leon, who passed a bag of clothing to Juan who stripped off on the spot and replaced the jump suit with new clothes. They walked out together and headed for the hotel.

The three men headed for the bar of the hotel which was quiet at this time of day, the sun was high and bright, a warm temperature with room to move, soft background music instead of the constant noisy rumbling of the engine, cold fresh beer. Leon handed Steve his work mobile and after one drink left the two to enjoy the freedom, friendship, beer and to discuss the memories of their recent history together. It was what was needed.

Friday 9th June.

It had been a long night, followed by a long deep sleep. Steve had woken up just before the alarm at 07:45. He was lying on the bed, reaching for his mobile, he sent a message to Sarah, 'Job done, great result, I'm ok. Hope you're enjoying the course and doing well. X'

Within seconds a reply was received, 'Fantastic hope you enjoyed it, never stopped thinking about you, sent messages on other fone. Loving it, doing canny. X'

He made a call, Leon answered, "Hi mate, have you got a bad head?"

"Just a bit, not as bad as expected, Juan can drink, had a good night, it was needed. I like the lad a lot. What's planned today?"

"Bert wants to meet up with us both, discuss the job and the informant."

"How are you two getting on, are you seeing much of each other?"

"I'll not lie mate, I'm living with her, I have serious decisions to make."

Steve was thinking exactly the same, "I have big decisions to make, I don't know if I can carry on doing this. I'm not going to get on your case, you know the dangers, you have to do what you want to do, I take it Lauren is history?"

"Shit mate, I feel shit but I can't explain my feelings, I guess it's what they call love, I think I've found it."

Steve was smiling, "I just wish it could be easy for you, I know one thing, you cannot stay in this work, not even the job."

"Steve, I know, it has done my head in. Gabi and I, I'm learning off Bert," he laughed, "we have talked about it and once the next bit is sorted, we are out of here, together, some paradise island or somewhere no-one would ever look for us, Skegness." They both laughed.

"Is she still under the radar here?"

"As far as I know, I check now and again but not enough to draw attention."

Steve took a deep breath, "That is for the future, what about today, now, when does Bert want to meet up and where?"

"He's heading back to Madrid this afternoon; he's suggesting about eleven in his hotel."

"That's okay with me, I've been invited to Juan's home this afternoon, if it's okay with you, just me."

"Fine mate, I can come to your hotel at ten, we can have our pre-Bert briefing then head on together."

"Great see you then."

Steve met up with Juan in the breakfast room, they were both subdued after the excesses of the night before, it did not stop Juan from eating as much as he could, fresh fruit, warm bread, local ham, cheese, it was never ending. Steve promised to meet up with Juan at four that afternoon outside the hotel.

Leon met Steve in the hotel lobby, they walked in the morning sunshine to the Evoque which was parked nearby. After getting in the car Leon drove to a car park overlooking the bay, Leon could see the villa on the hill on the opposite side of the bay.

Steve started the conversation, "How much does Bert know, what have you told him?"

"I've kept it the way I would want it, I've told him nothing other than locations and the shooting on the fishing boat."

"Has there been any circulations about the supply ship and the pirates."

"Not that I'm aware of, I know about it because Lucas told us, I believe he was told by the suppliers. He also told us that you stabbed the young lad in the heart and killed him. Ice cold killing machine was how he described you."

Steve closed his eyes and dropped his head, "We couldn't do anything, I was disgusted with myself, I couldn't help the lad. Pepe, he was a canny kid, he tried to brave it out but he was shit scared, he didn't like being locked in small spaces." He raised his voice and hit the dashboard with his clenched fist three occasions, "It was a fucking accident, the kid just wanted to be out of the hut. They were fucking animals, worse than anything in the jungle, they tortured him for fun, he was an absolute mess. Leon, I was sick when I saw him, he was stood on a post his feet were in the river, he was tied to a tall mooring post, he couldn't move, they had butchered him mate, slashed him all over, his blood dripping, running down his body, legs, feet into the shitty river. There's caiman, alligator things, piranha, snakes, the birds had already been pecking at his face and body, fucking disgusting. He looked at me and actually said sorry, what the fuck was I supposed to do, I know what I wanted to do." Leon had his head down, imagining the scene, he said nothing. "I wanted to kill every fucking one of them," Steve angrily thumped the dashboard again, "I would have put the fucking leader in the same position as Pepe and left him there to be chewed on by the jungle. He was fucking smiling, proud of what they had done to Pepe, then he asked me if the two of us could crew the fucking thing or he would get another crew. I told him we could, I asked him for his knife from his belt and looked at Pepe, he knew what I wanted to do, he fucking wanted me to do it, he gave me the knife, at gun point, I went to Pepe, he was looking at me, pleading me, please amigo, please amigo. He wanted it ending." Steve paused, he looked at Leon in the face, "I pushed the knife so hard through his chest into his heart, I could feel his heart beating through the knife, shaking the knife strong. Then nothing, his head dropped and the body sagged against the ropes. I pulled the blade out and handed it back to the twat. I looked into his face; I will remember him for a long time. We climbed into the, thing, and got towed away, we saw Pepe cut free from the post and crumple into the river." There was silence.

Leon spoke quietly, "That's tough mate, you did your best, the right thing, he wanted you to do it, you could not have done more." A brief silence, "The leader is dead, he was killed by the gang shortly after you left."

Steve was chewing on his thumb nail, "I'll never forget what I have done, how can I carry on, I did the best thing for him, I've crossed the line."

"You did what you had to do; I would have done the same. No-one needs to know, they will never find out, who will tell them?"

"I know Leon, I fucking know what I did to young Pepe, that is what matters. Who will tell his parents what happened to their son?"

Leon asked, "What about Juan, will he say anything?"

"No, I don't believe so, he wants to forget it, I might find out more when I meet up with him and his family, he might have had time to think, like I have, we've both bottled it up and just got on with what we had to do to survive. He was fucking brilliant when we got attacked by the pirates, did what I told him, then saved my life on the fishing boat. I owe him a lot, my life."

"Steve, you got him out of the jungle and back here, he owes you as well mate. Lucas told us that one of the supply boat crew had told the pirates about your cargo, that's how they followed the supply boat."

"That was a battle, just have to hope that doesn't get talked about."

Leon asked, "What should we say to Bert then, how are we going to go to the second part, they're all locked up, or dead?"

"Leon to be honest, I haven't even thought about the second part yet, I'm still thinking about what's happened over the last few weeks."

"Okay, we'll keep quiet about it for now. Gabi doesn't want any payment for the job, that will keep Bert happy, I don't think she will be happy if we don't push on with the next bit."

"Leon, why don't the pair of you just disappear like you said, leave everything behind, get a new life?"

"Sounds good to me but she is determined, she wants revenge, she's damaged the cartel again, no-one would know she had anything to do with it, but she wants this Pantera guy and others if she can."

Steve was in a thoughtful mood, "Okay, I know and understand where she is coming from. Can we leave it for a few days, maybe a week, then we can think again? I have a lot on my mind, decisions to make, without adding more problems at the moment."

They met up with Bert in the hotel, they made use of a small meeting room. Bert greeted Steve, "It's good to see you Steve, I gather it wasn't a holiday then."

Steve was calm and relaxed after having vented his anger earlier, "Well it certainly wasn't what was advertised but we have the desired result."

They each took a seat at the table. Bert continued, "I don't intend to do a full debrief now, sometime in the next week if you are up to it?"

Steve, "I appreciate that Bert, Wednesday, Thursday should

be okay, I just want a short break, recharge and then move on."

Bert, "I will start then, if I go on too much, please let me know." Steve nodded. "Are there any problems you want to discuss with me or one of our medical team?"

"I'm fine. I'm tired and annoyed about the possible prosecution of Juan for something he was forced to do, the man saved my life."

Bert reassured Steve, "I have spoken with the other agencies, in light of Juan, as you know him, he gave the same version of events that you did. Exactly the same, as if it had been rehearsed," Bert looked at Steve over his glasses, "there is nothing at this moment in time that can be challenged. I believe you are both singing off the same song sheet."

Steve looked at Bert, "You are not suggesting we made up the fact, that they were trying to kill me and he saved my life, are you, seriously?"

Bert, "No, no, no. Not at all, if something major, such as that incident happens in an otherwise boring crossing of the Atlantic, you would remember it clearly. That is what I am saying."

Steve, "I'll not deny we spoke about it after it happened, he was in shock, acted on impulse, if the weapon hadn't been there, we would no doubt be the ones that were dead. Which would you prefer?"

"Steve, please, I totally agree with what you are saying, it has to be investigated, I'm sure it will have a good ending. That is all I can say."

Steve persisted, "Is that a guarantee, he's done nothing, it's not a kind of Stockholm syndrome, I'm wise to that, he's a good man who just wants to earn a living fishing."

Bert, "All I am saying is, he will be fine, that's all, it is the Guardia who will make the decision in due course. Moving on, the Guardia have suggested that the vessel must have been refuelled during the course of the crossing, it is too far to travel without refuelling."

Steve, had to think quickly, "Yes, of course, we took on board more diesel."

Bert continued, "It is just that neither of you mentioned it when you were interviewed in the headquarters, is there a reason?"

Steve had now expected this question, "I don't know about Juan, I don't know what he was asked. For me, it wasn't mentioned by you or Manuel, it was not an important part of the story as it unfolded, I would have discussed it at my debrief with you. We met a ship, it didn't have any identifying marks or name, 100 k north of the Cape Verde Islands, the meeting point was on the notes I was given. We filled with fuel and fresh water, food and moved on."

"Excellent Steve that fills that gap in, anything else happen we should know about?"

"Yes, there is, we were nudged by a large whale and its calf, it swam next to us for a few minutes. I enjoyed seeing some sort of life in the middle of nowhere. That was the highlight of the otherwise shitty, uncomfortable, crossing."

"I appreciate it was hard, very hard. Is there anything you would advise if the job came in again or similar?"

Steve thought for a while, "Yes, do not ask me."

"Quite, I will remember that." Bert looked at Leon, "Leon have you been in touch with the CHIS?"

"I have Bert, the informant is very happy with the result and is not wanting any financial award for the information?"

Bert was surprised, "Really, it would be a substantial payment, it's the informant's decision."

Leon, "I spoke briefly with the CHIS and they are moving on, possibly away from the area."

"Well, that will keep the accountants happy, please pass on our thanks."

"I will do Bert. Then I doubt if I will be in contact with the CHIS again."

"Will you be coming back to Madrid or heading back to the UK?"

"I intend to have a day or two with my mate and then fly

back to the UK."

Bert, "I would like to thank you for your work in Spain and hopefully we may meet up again, I will certainly bare you in mind if there is good work to be done."

Leon was smiling, "Thank you Bert, anytime, I like it over here and this lad."

Bert closed the meeting and left for his flight to Madrid.

Leon and Steve took their seats again, Steve, "When are you planning on going back to the UK?"

Leon sat back in his chair, "I'm not, I'm not going back."

Steve, "Does Gabi have a future plan, for both of you together?"

"Yes, we've talked and talked but it's the revenge, she wants revenge."

Steve, "At the moment she can live the rest of her life here, she is legal. That would not be a problem, if she brings the cartel or this Pantera guy here, it will be trouble for her, both of you. Especially at the villa with both of your DNA all over the place."

Leon, "I agree, she has picked the villa because of its location, it's isolated with good views, that is her choice. I have suggested that it probably would not be a good place to take him on, because of the same reasons, a decent sniper could take her out on the pool terrace."

Steve made a suggestion, "It should be safe for the three of us to meet up now, somewhere out of the way, preferably. I'll keep the Evoque and you two travel together, we can meet and discuss some options, obviously not today, tomorrow or Sunday?"

Leon, "Can we make it tomorrow, then, if need be, we can continue on Sunday."

Steve "That's a plan. Do you want a lift or can you get the ferry?"

Leon decided to walk to the ferry, while Steve prepared for his meeting with Juan and his family.

That afternoon Juan met Steve outside the hotel and drove

to his family home in Mogar, near to Pontevedra. He met his mother and girlfriend Verónica - he looked like his mother, fortunately Verónica did not - in their detached, modest home with a view over the Ria de Pontevedra. It was great to see Juan being relaxed and happy, they were smiling as they met Steve, more hugs and kisses. They had prepared so much food for just the four of them, it was spread out over the table in the garden under the sun shade. Juan took Steve inside the home and showed him some photographs that were hung on the hallway wall, photographs of him and his father, at work fishing in the Atlantic, the fishing boat owned by the family and now back in their possession. Steve had the comfort feeling of being in a family, he had missed that, he had missed Sarah. They had some private talk when the ladies were clearing the second course in preparation for the dessert. Steve explained what he had told Bert about the refuelling ship, it had no identification marks and the distance from the islands. They discussed Pepe and when his family would be informed of what had happened by the Guardia. Juan eventually broke his external hardened shell, which gave way to raw emotion, he was crying uncontrollably. They were sat on the chairs at the front of the garden, farthest away from the house, Steve placed his right arm around his shoulder and pulled him closer, nothing was said. He took the bottle of beer from Juan and placed it on the lush green lawn next to his, they both stood and held each other so close. Verónica came from the kitchen with a large cake, she saw them both and walked back into the house. They were not disturbed.

Juan was wiping his tears with a handkerchief, "Gracias, gracias, mucho gracias Steve. You have brought me back to my family alive, I will never forget you and what you have done for me, my family and Pepe." He was still sobbing, taking in deep breaths trying to control himself and then letting go again.

Steve kept hold of him close, "Juan, I have to thank you, for me being here, you saved my life. We, we will never forget the time together, we have survived, the past is gone, a memory, a memory to forget, the future, you have the fishing boat and many things to look forward to. Now, is the present and we have the present of being here together with your mother and Verónica. What better present could you have?"

"Si, si, si, si, the best present. Forgive me, I do not cry, apart from when my father died" Juan gently broke free from the grip of Steve, he picked up the bottles of beer, "To you my friend".

Steve replied, "To you, my friend." They both hit the bottles and drank the contents.

It was after eleven that night that Steve got into a taxi and headed back to the hotel. A friendship had been forged forever.

CHAPTER 17

Saturday 10th June

The meeting had been arranged for 2pm at Barra Beach, at the headland of the north side of the Ria de Vigo. It was a typical very warm sunny day; Leon had suggested that they should all pack their swim wear.

Gabi and Leon were the first to arrive as they only had a few kilometres to travel. The beach was long, with white soft sand and was not crowded, they picked their spot and placed the sun beds and towels on the beach. Leon placed the sun shade behind the beds and placed the cool box in the shade. They were both in beach attire, Gabi was wearing a dark blue and white patterned swim suit, Leon was wearing yellow patterned beach shorts.

Steve arrived twenty minutes later wearing his beach shorts. After the usual greetings of kisses and hugs which he accepted from Gabi, the fist pump with Leon, they sat on the sunbeds facing each other.

Gabi had a big smile on her face, "I am really pleased to see you Steve, I was very worried about you, now you are here safe, that's great."

Steve, "It is good to be here, I want to forget about it really but I know you might have something to say, so just say it and then we can continue."

Gabi took the smile from her face, "I can understand how you feel, honestly," she raised her hand to stop Steve from speaking, "We have both killed in similar circumstances, I want to forget, I try but you never forget. I know it is difficult. That is all I want to say."

Steve, "Gabi, I am not a murderer but I feel like one, it is difficult. I don't agree with what you say about similar circumstances, unless there is something I don't know about, you are correct in saying it is difficult to forget."

Leon made his attempt to change the conversation, "Who fancies a swim, come on." He got off the sunbed and started walking towards the ocean.

Steve looked at Gabi, "Do not hurt him."

"I have no intention to hurt him, I love him, seriously. Come on, lets swim together."

They got off the beds and followed Leon, then they ran into the ocean together. It was great to lie in the ocean without holding a rope, so relaxing, no restrictions as he floated on his back, occasionally doing a swim parallel to the beach, then back to the group. They were stood together in the ocean, the water was up to the shoulders of Gabi, there was no one near them.

Steve started the conversation, "This is fantastic, a good way to live, no worries, no OCG's, no CHIS, no UC work, no need to look over your shoulder," then looked at Gabi, "to see who's following you from The Covent Garden pub."

They all laughed and started splashing water at each other for a short time. Steve continued, "You two could have a permanent life like this, like your sister Carmen suggested, just go and find the paradise island and live a happy life."

Gabi, "We will, it will not be long before we can go."

Steve, "No, you should go now. Do you honestly believe that if, and it's a big if, you manage to get this Pantera guy, that will be the end of it? They will send more."

Gabi, "I don't know them, I don't want revenge against them, just Pantera and Paco, they have fucked up our lives Steve. They are pieces of shit; they need cleaning away."

"I know where you are coming from, I'm sure Paco and Pantera will meet their maker someday soon, they all will but it will not bring Jessica back or heal Gloria's injury. They will both be replaced the same day they are killed, a never-ending conveyor belt of pieces of shit, as you say."

Gabi continued, "Manolo has killed my brother, which killed my mother, he sent my father to kill you, he was not a killer as you know and he failed and died, nothing against you, my sister is forced to be his prisoner lover. I have been raped by his lieutenants and forced to kill people, changed my life. Anyway, I belief Paco will be coming here."

Leon asked, "How do you know that?"

"Delgado told me."

Leon continued, "When did he tell you that?"

"Yesterday morning when you were meeting Bert, he called me and told me."

Steve interjected, "Gabi, this is serious, what was said?"

"He called about the killings and everything, mainly the loss of the cargo, that was his concern. The money has not been paid, not in full anyway and he had been called from Colombia."

Steve, "And?"

"Javier told me that a meeting would be held here to find out what has gone wrong, who is to blame. He is shitting himself; he is the only one who is not in jail or dead."

Leon, "I think I would be shitting myself in his shoes."

Gabi smiled, "I think Javier is going to point whoever comes in my direction."

Leon, "You had nothing to do with the deal, just some money, you knew nothing."

Gabi continued, "I had nothing to do with the deal that the Cartel knows about. Yes, just money, and a man on the submarine. I think the man could be Paco or maybe even Pantera to get the answers to the questions. They will not get the money back but they will get as much as they can and give out plenty of pain to get it."

Steve, "They cannot see you, you will be identified, then they will come for you. When is the investigator arriving in

Spain?"

"It will be this week, they do not wait, if the word gets out that they are not quick, other groups will do the same. They have to be quick and show force to keep the fear and control."

Steve, "Did he name Paco as the one that was coming?"

"No, but I know Lucas was talking to Paco, I heard him on one occasion."

Lucas in hope, "It could be another Paco, there has to be a lot of Paco's."

Steve, "We have to take this threat seriously, the first suggestion is, you two, just go, leave now, no-one will be any wiser. Hand your notice in Leon and fly somewhere nice."

Gabi, "Steve that is not happening, I can do this by myself if it is just Paco, you two can get on with your lives."

Leon, "That's not happening, I'm going nowhere without you. What is your second suggestion Steve?"

"Leon, we are supposed to prevent crime and protect people remember, I'm thinking about it." He lay on his back with his eyes closed, the sun was bright, the insides of his eyelids were red from the sun beating down on his face. The sound of the ocean was relaxing, his head was full of hatred, he had to think. He stood up and swam the short distance back to the loving couple.

"Gabi, can you use your assets in Panama or Colombia for a name and address for Pantera? Have you asked before? There could be a cash incentive."

"Yes, I can try, I've never asked before, it was dangerous to ask when in the jail, there is no escape."

"We have to start making preparations now, just in case."

Leon, "In case of what?"

"In case he is here now. Like Gabi says they will not hang about, they want answers and cash."

Steve started to walk out of the ocean. The others followed and packed away the beds, sunshade, cool box and dry clothing then walked to the cars. Steve went back to the hotel while Leon and Gabi went back to the villa. Gabi started to make phone calls.

Steve was in his room in silence, the window was open allowing the breeze to enter the room, he lay on his bed. Despite what he had been through and had done, he was not an ice-cold killer. He would like Pantera to be dead; he wanted revenge for Jessica and the others, including himself. Whichever way Gabi wanted it to go, it would not keep herself and Leon safe. It was unrealistic to think the cartel would not seek revenge against her again. Gabi would definitely be identified by the Spanish police if she was involved in any way which would mean a lifetime in prison and ultimately death. The only way would be a lawful way, keeping her and Leon out of it, well certainly Gabi. His first and second option became clear. He would inform Bert that the Colombian was being sent by the cartel to discuss the loss of the cargo with Delgado, set up surveillance and identify the man and his killing companion, then allow the Spanish police to conduct arrests before he reaches Gabi. He was writing his options down on the hotel provided stationery.

His mobile activated, it was Sarah, "Hi, are you not working on the course today?"

"I've just finished an exercise over the last three days, so got some time off until Monday, what are you doing?"

"I'm just chilling out for a couple of days, be heading back to Madrid on Monday, not doing much, sleeping, drinking. Where are you?"

"I'm just staying in the college, it's not worth going to my mams in the time I've got. Are you feeling better, now the jobs done?"

He lied, "Yes, taking life easier, you will find out what it's like soon enough no doubt, how's it going?"

"Like you said, it is tough, I'm developing my identity but it does take time, being a different person, and they test you every day, looking for mistakes, calling your real name and stuff as you know. I think I'm more the other person than me sometimes, it is scary, they give loads of advice, psychological profiling, testing. But hey, I'm still me, not long now and we can meet up. I'm looking forward to that."

"I am too, can't wait to see you, I have really missed you."

"I'm on a week test starting from Monday so I'll be out of contact, just to let you know, but I will be thinking of you, I do really miss you Steve."

"I'm sure you will do a good job, be natural, be your new person, listen, learn if you make mistakes, don't say too much, never give anything away. Don't ask too many questions, let them tell you, think about Cass."

They both laughed, Sarah said, "If only everything was that simple."

"I have to go, your mate candy features is picking me up downstairs about now for a day at the beach and beer."

"Okay give him my love, enjoy today you deserve it, don't get into trouble, love you."

"Love you as well, I said it."

"That's great big lad, divvent do nowt daft. See you soon."

The call ended, he lay back on the bed and drifted into sleep.

In the villa, Gabi had made some calls, she had spoken to Gloria and some of her acquaintances in Panama. The lure of American dollars was a big incentive but not immediately productive, there was hope of information being forthcoming but no certainty.

Steve had been asleep for nearly two hours when his mobile activated and woke him up. He didn't recognise the number displayed, he answered the call, "Hello."

A Spanish voice, believed a female asked, "Is that Mr Steve?"

He didn't recognise the voice, "Who is asking?"

"My name is Veronica."

"Yes, it is me Veronica, is there a problem?" Steve knew there must be a problem if she was calling, he had given his number to Juan's mother.

"Yes, yes Steve." she spoke slowly, he could hear a panic in her voice. "Some men have taken Juan from our house." She was crying.

"When was this Veronica?"

Steve immediately went to look out of his window onto the street below, he could see nothing that took his attention.

"Now, Steve, mama has given me the number to call you."

"Do you know who they were, did Juan say anything?"

"We do not know but we think it must be the gangsters, he gave us the signal of the phone, so I called you, he trusts you, we are very frightened for him."

"Did Juan say anything to them, or you and mama?"

"He was telling them they were wrong, not him, not Steve."

"Do not telephone the police, I will do what I can, if need be, I will call the police, I will do what I can, I promise, he is my friend."

"Yes, yes, he told me all the time you were his best friend, he owes you and trusts you."

"Yes, Veronica, please trust me. I will have to go and do things now, I will keep in touch with you, I will find Juan."

"Thank you, thank you."

Steve made a call, "Leon, you and Gabi have to leave the villa now, they have taken Juan from his house, just now they may be on the way to the villa.

"Fucking hell, are you coming?"

"Just get away from the villa, I'm leaving my room now, we will meet up later."

"Okay, we might go on her boat and get away somewhere."

"Just go now, get what you need and leave. This changes things, we might have to take action; I have to get to Juan, find out where he is."

Steve filled his bag, although there wasn't much to put in it, and left the apartment. He decided on taking the stairs instead of the lift. As he approached the second floor, he heard a door open further down, he stepped inside the second floor and quietly closed the door and listened. He listened at the door and heard the footsteps on the second-floor landing, he quickly pulled the door open and saw a tall male in a dark blue jacket and jeans with his back to him. The man turned to face Steve; Steve landed two heavy blows to the left side of the head of the male who was knocked unconscious. Steve leant over him, then hit him one more time to the head to ensure he was unable to take any further action. He took a pistol from the belt of his jeans and continued to the basement of the hotel and left by the pedestrian exit, leaving the Evoque in the garage.

He made a call to Leon as he was walking, Leon answered immediately, "They've been for me, I've took one out, just knocked him out, I've collected a pistol of some sort, get away from there now."

"We've left the villa and we're on our way to the boat. Gabi had a bag packed; I've just left my stuff. Keep in touch."

Gabi had a pre-packed bag for such eventualities which she had always expected and she had taken the encro mobile that was used by Delgado to contact her.

Steve walked to the train station in Vigo and took the train to Pontevedra which was only a thirty-minute journey. He was in a carriage with very few passengers, but he was sat away from the other travellers, he was certain he wasn't being followed. He made a further call to Leon. "Are you both away from the villa okay?"

"Yes, no problems so far, we haven't seen anyone, we're on the boat, Gabi is starting the engine so we should be on the move soon. Where are you?"

"I'm on the train heading towards Pontevedra, I'll hire a car, I'll use the company card. If you get somewhere with the boat, I'll pick you both up. It will be better if we get away from any known places or transport."

"Yes, that's what I was thinking. I'm sure we are not being followed; we are on the move."

"Is Gabi okay?"

"She is, she was expecting it sometime, not yet though."

"Let me know where you are heading as soon as you can. I

need to try and get something done with Juan; I need to find him."

Juan had been taken from his home by members of Delgado's OCG. This had been requested by the MMV cartel who were travelling to 'interview' anyone who had been involved. He was currently being held in a locked room inside an isolated finca, near to the hillside village of Balai a short distance from A Coruña. It reminded him of the room in Colombia with one metal framed bed without bedding, one metal chair and a small table. There was a small barred window, it had a view of the fields and hillside. He knew there were two men, armed with small automatic weapons similar to Uzi guns that he had seen in the films, inside the finca, there could be more.

Steve had hired a white Kia Sportage at the train station. They are very common on the roads and big enough for three or four people. He drove away from the station and stopped in a back road and examined the pistol, a Berreta 92, fully loaded with 15, 9 x 19 mm parabellum bullets. He placed the pistol in the glove compartment. He received a call from Leon saying they were heading to Bayona marina which was south from Vigo. He headed off in that direction.

It took 40 minutes for the journey from Pontevedra to Baiona where Steve picked them up from the Marina and headed back north, Gabi had told them that Delgado was based somewhere in A Coruña on the North Galician coast.

Gabi received a call from Delgado on the encrypted mobile, the call was in Spanish. "Hola Javier."

"Good evening Gabi, how are you?"

"I'm good, you haven't called to ask me how I am surely?"

"No, have you seen your man on the submarine?"

"No, I have been out all day, I still am, why, is it important?"

"He has attacked one of my men."

Gabi feigned surprise, "What, why would he do that?"

"My men went to collect him from his hotel, to answer some questions from the Colombians."

"He is not your man, you should have asked me, I would have brought him in, he has nothing to fear, he has done nothing."

"Well can you bring him in?"

"I could, are the Colombians here now?"

"They will be here soon; we need to be here."

"Who is we, Javier?"

"Well of course, I have to be here and you and the people concerned."

"I was not concerned Javier, I took no part in anything that was arranged, ask Lucas. The only persons who knew anything were Lucas, who is in prison, Torres, who is dead, that leaves you, Javier."

"You are involved, your man on the submarine was involved."

"My man on the submarine knew nothing, ask yourself. He did not know where he was going, he did not know it was a submarine, he was told it was a boat. He did not expect the jungle, he killed a man in the jungle, he fought against the pirates and saved the cargo. He killed Torres's men on the fishing boat. Yes, he was involved, he can prove what he did and the other man on the submarine. Can you?"

"Gabi, the Colombians are not taking this good; they are sending one of the top men, Paco Verdu, and his interrogator, he has a reputation of getting the truth."

Gabi's eyes widened at the sound of Paco, she knew who the interrogator would be, "I have nothing to fear Javier, where do you want me to travel to?"

"I will send the location, there will be a car to follow."

"What time? Tomorrow or Monday?"

"You must be here on Monday, better still tomorrow."

"I will travel if I can find my man as you call him."

The call was ended, "Juan must be somewhere near to A Coruña, that is where Delgado will have him, a good airport for the Colombians, near his home."

Steve, "We need a room to discuss this and get some work done, we need information."

They stopped at a small hotel in Santiago de Compostela. Steve booked a twin room for the night for Leon and himself, then they bought bottles of beer, pizza and fried chicken which they took to the room. Gabi entered the hotel later from the underground vehicle access and went to the room, she had her hair tied up and was wearing a wide brimmed sun hat to protect her from recognition and cctv coverage.

They sat around the room table and ate their meal while they discussed what they knew and what might be expected.

Gabi, "I am going to have to go to meet Paco and Pantera."

Steve, "You will be nowhere near hopefully, we can go as your representatives."

"Paco will not accept that, you know that."

Steve ignored what Gabi had said, "We could possibly still involve the Guardia, it is a kidnap, Juan has been taken against his consent. I dread to think what will happen to him if we do not act quickly." He looked at Gabi, "Who do you know, who would know where Delgado lives, where he could hold Juan?"

Gabi, "Do you not think I have been thinking that, I didn't ask questions, I know he lives in Coruña, it is a big place. I didn't tell him where I lived which is possibly why they did not come for us."

Steve, "We have tomorrow to get to Juan before they get here."

Gabi, "Lucas said he didn't trust Javier, that he could be working with Torres. Maybe he was right? He is the only free one now who can profit from what happened and continue the trade of all of them."

Leon, "Could we visit Lucas in prison, he might help us?"

Steve, "Gabi couldn't go, they take fingerprints and photographs of all visitors and it would take too long to get a friends visitor pass. Does he have any relatives who could visit him?"

Gabi replied, "He does have a sister, I have met her, she is a good woman, she knows what he was doing and didn't approve of it but still took his money and lives well."

Steve went to continue, "Do you?"

Gabi interrupted, "Yes, I know her, and, I have been to her home, I have her number, I'm sure." She retrieved her mobile from the bottom of the bag and started searching, "Yes, here it is, Jennifer, should I call her?"

Steve, "Wait, we need to know what to say."

Gabi, "I know Jenni, she is a lot younger than Lucas, she is not involved in his work, she is not naive but she does know what can happen and I'm sure she will be worried about her brother and maybe herself."

Steve, "Okay, but what we need to know is where Delgado lives and where he might be keeping Juan. We have to let her know, that Delgado is planning to tell Paco that it was Lucas who was responsible for the loss and they are taking revenge. They have already taken Juan and tried to take me."

Leon, "Will she be able to visit Lucas?"

"Yes, she can. Family visitors just have to turn up and wait if it's a glass visit, talking through a glass screen, less security needed. She could go tomorrow and just hope there is a slot available, the earlier she gets there the better."

Gabi, "Should I ring her now or would it be best to visit her?"

Steve, "Give her a ring, if she answers, suggest we could come to her home or meet somewhere, see how it goes."

Gabi pressed the numbers and waited, it was on speaker, it was eventually answered, the conversation was in Spanish "Hola is that Gabi?"

"Yes, it is Jenni, are you okay?"

"Hi Gabi, no, I'm not okay, I'm worried and scared, what is happening, I thought they were all friends?"

"In the business that Lucas was in, it is not easy to tell your friends from your enemies, it is greed."

"Why did they try to kill him?"

"They were wanting to cut him out of his very large share

of money that would have been made. He told me, that you would have been rich for ever after this deal, I know he looks after you well, he was not greedy."

"Lucas was very generous to me, I did not ask questions, I did not want to know."

"I was a good friend of Lucas and I still am a good friend of him and his family. Have you seen Lucas in prison?"

"No, I can't go in there, it is a horrible place."

"I was wondering if he had told you, that I told him Torres was going to kill him at the warehouse, that is why he is still alive today?"

"I have not seen Lucas since the day before, you know."

"Jenni, can I come and see you at your house or maybe meet somewhere? It is very important to me and could help Lucas and you."

"Am I in danger?"

"I am trying to stop any danger, really it would help a lot if we could meet."

"Yes, okay, can you come here?"

"Yes, I will come now, the sooner the better, we need to talk. Are you on your own, I'm not worried but it would have to be kept secret?"

"Yes, I know about secrecy, I was not involved with the business of Lucas, but I did keep secrets."

"That's good to hear Jenni, I will be there about eleven."

The call was ended, Gabi picked up the encro mobile and her own mobile. Leon and Steve left the hotel together through the front door, Gabi left by another exit then they met up at the car and headed for Pontevedra.

Steve parked the car a short distance from the villa, it was surrounded by a light pink painted two metre-high wall. Gabi pressed the bell and the pedestrian gate was opened. Gabi and Jenni hugged and kissed each other on meeting, she could see that Jennifer had been crying. She was in her mid-thirties, 1.62m tall with short dark brown hair. She was wearing a grey sweat shirt and bottoms. Gabi told Jennifer about Steve and

Leon in the car but she did not reveal their names. They were both invited into the house, Leon stopped in the car to keep observations on the villa, just in case. Steve entered the villa, they all sat in the comfortable large chairs in the living room, they declined drinks.

Gabi, "Jennifer, what we have to tell you, and ask you, is very important for us in this room, Lucas and some others."

"Yes, I do not know anything about his business though."

"Do you know Javier Delgado?"

"I know of him; Lucas spoke about him and that Miguel Torres."

"Did you ever go to his house or any of his properties?"

"No, I never met him or anyone, other than you, he told me you were a friend. He never, ever, involved me in his business, he kept me out of the way."

"My friend here," indicating Steve who was sat next to her, "He saw a message about the plan of Torres to kill Lucas, he had already tried to kill him and another man on a fishing boat. They won on the fishing boat, they told me and I warned Lucas that Torres was going to kill him in the warehouse."

"Thank you." Jennifer acknowledged Steve.

"Since these events, Delgado has kidnapped the other man who was on the fishing boat and tried to take him," indicating Steve, "they lost again. They want them, as the Colombians are coming here, to hold an inquest into what happened to the cargo and the money that has been lost. It is a lot of money, they want answers."

"I have heard bad things about them, Lucas would say you do not upset them. He did not do anything."

"You know that, I know that," again indicating Steve, "he knows that. The only person making anything out of this at the moment is Delgado. My friend and others, including me, want to get the other man out from where they are holding him, before they torture and probably kill him."

"That is terrible but I know nothing, how can I help?"

"We would like you to visit Lucas in prison tomorrow, as

early as they will allow it. He would be really pleased and surprised to see you; it would do him good."

"I do not like prisons, I have never been in one, they look so frightening."

"I agree Jenni, they are not pleasant places; some are worse than those in Spain." Gabi didn't elaborate on the prisons in Panama. "They are not meant to be nice. They are however really safe for visitors; you would be able to see Lucas but not touch him."

"I would not take anything in, I would be scared."

"Nothing like that, we want you to ask Lucas some questions and hope you remember the answers."

"I am good at listening. What do I have to do?"

"Do not be scared or upset when you get to the prison, the officers see visitors all of the time, a lot like you, are good people. The doors will be locked behind you, but the rooms are big and light. They will take your photograph and fingerprints and then, you just wait in a room until there is an empty glass booth you can use. It is really important; this man's life depends on it; we can't go to the police. I believe Lucas will know where the man will be held."

Jennifer was apprehensive but willing to give it a try and desperate to see her brother. "I will go. What do I have to say?"

"Tell Lucas what has happened to the man taken hostage by Delgado, ask if he knows where he would be held for the Colombians? I know he has a good memory but give him my mobile number."

"I don't think I would remember it, Lucas would, as you know."

"I can write my number on your arm, wear a long sleeve blouse, just roll your sleeve up."

"How will he call you; he does not have any mobile, the police took them all?"

"If he wants or needs to call, Lucas will get a mobile, believe me. It is very important, that you can remember the location of the place where the man might be held, we only have a short time."

"Will I be able to write it down"

"If you write anything down the guards might take it off you, or read it and take a copy. It is better if you can remember."

"Yes, I think I understand."

"It is possibly better if you ask the questions at the end of the visit, repeat in your mind. Will you do that Jenni please?"

"Yes, I will, what time should I go?"

"Get there for about nine, you will be one of the first visitors allowed in. We can take you there if you want?"

"Yes please."

Gabi stayed with Jennifer; Steve returned to the hotel with Leon.

CHAPTER 18

Sunday 11th June

Leon was parked outside the villa; he was waiting for the ladies and Steve to exit the gate. It was 08:17 on the dash clock and already 24 degrees with blue sky and no clouds, they emerged through the gate. Steve opened the rear door for Jennifer, Leon did the same for Gabi. They headed to the prison a twenty-minute drive, according to the satnav system.

At the car park, Gabi, Leon, and Steve stayed inside the car out of the view of the security cameras and watched as Jennifer entered through the first security gate. It was waiting time again.

It happened as had been explained, Jennifer had to show her Spanish identification and confirm that Lucas was her brother. She had to leave her mobile phone in a secure box, the contents of her small handbag were examined, she was then photographed and had her fingerprints taken. She sat in the waiting room and tried to do some quizzes in her small paperback book. After 40 minutes she was given access to the visitor room and directed to the glass booth. She sat and waited, the area was covered with cameras, two officers were also present, they were sat on chairs on a raised platform with a view of the monitors and the persons involved in the visit, on both sides of the glass partitions.

Lucas walked through the inside section of the visiting room, he immediately smiled when he saw Jennifer. She had dressed well for the meeting in long-sleeved white blouse and black trousers, she tried her best to smile and look happy when she saw Lucas. He was still wearing his own clothing which had been laundered, he was very smart, not at all what Jennifer had expected. Lucas took his seat and pulled up close to the window, "I did not expect to see you Jennifer, thank you for coming to visit me. You are beautiful as always."

"I had to come to see you, I've been worried about you and myself since that day."

"I am sure you have nothing to worry about, I'm sure."

"I have something to tell you from Gabi."

"Yes, go on tell me."

"She came to see me last night, she told me that she warned you about Torres going to kill you."

"Yes, she did, she saved my life."

"She told me that Delgado has sent men and they have taken one of the sailors from his home, they are keeping him in a house somewhere, for the Colombians who are coming to interview him."

"So, Delgado has shown his colours, I thought he was with Torres."

"She is asking if you know where he might be, Gabi and the big man and a black man, I don't know their names, I'm sorry, they want to go and get him before the Colombians get here?"

"Gabi and her two men, are they okay?"

"They tried to get the white one but he beat them."

Lucas smiled, "He is a tough one, he is good to be on your side."

"Gabi told me they were good men."

"I know of them, they are good men, it must be the other man from the boat, he is a tough man as well."

"Gabi has given me her mobile number," she leant forward and pushed her left sleeve up towards her elbow revealing the number. Lucas studied the number for a few seconds and then nodded, she pulled the sleeve down.

"Do you know where the man might have been taken?"

"I know exactly where he will be. Delgado has a large finca

at the end of a road. It is called Balai, Santa Maria, near to the village of Boedo. It is next to the woods, a long way from anyone. It is close to the airport. I have been there before, maybe four or five buildings, the big house and others, he will not be held in the house. Can you remember Balai, just south of the airport?"

"Yes, I can remember Balai."

"I have a present for you, if you go to our beach home, ask Gabi to take you today, go today," he emphasised "there is money for you and some things for Gabi and her friends. The money is all yours."

"Thank you Lucas, even in this place you are thinking of me and your friends."

"And my enemies Jennifer. Look in the kitchen in the big cupboard under the floorboards."

"I know the cupboard; it is a long time since I have been in there."

"I visit quite regularly, my safe haven. If there is enough for you, you can give some to the others but you take what you want first. It will have to go anyway, the Policia will find out and take everything."

"Do you need anything in here?"

"I would like you to visit regularly if you can, it would be great to see you, only when you can, you could possibly bring me fresh clothing, shirts, underwear. I will get a prison account soon and you could put maybe 500 euros in, it would keep me going. You cannot put more in. I don't want much."

"Of course, I will do that, anything for you."

"I would like to see Gabi, but I believe she might have to move if they don't kill her."

"I will ask her."

Lucas tested Jennifer, "What is the name of the finca?"

"Balai"

"The village?"

"Boedo."

Lucas recited the mobile number correctly. "I am going, you

give them what they need, give them my good luck and give Gabi my love. Thank the two men, give them what you can spare, I would have liked to do that in person, they saved my life. I hope they get there before the Colombians. Go, go, remember, I love you my sister, just us two now."

It took 25 minutes to get out of the prison and into the car, Jennifer immediately wrote down the name of the finca and the village in her note pad, then ripped out the page, without speaking. "Lucas is so happy to help, I have to take you somewhere," she handed the paper to Steve who searched on the satnav. "I have to take you somewhere before you take me home."

Leon started to drive away and followed Jennifer's instructions; it would be 40 minutes from the Centro Penitenciario Da Lama near Pontevedra to the beach house.

Leon was driving along a narrow road with large villas either side, he was approaching the end of the road. Jennifer told him to stop at the gates of the last villa on the ocean side. The villa was protected by three metre high white walls, there was an ornate stone sign on the wall. They got out of the car together, Jennifer pressed the code into the gate control, the highly varnished wooden vehicle gate began to slide open. Leon got into the car and followed as the three walked towards the main door of the villa.

The villa was extensive with large lawned gardens which were obviously regularly maintained. There were no trees near to the walls which would assist access over the walls, the flowers were colourful. The villa was in the old Spanish style, marble columns at the top of the steps leading to the main door, pristine white balustrades on the verandas of the upper floor rooms. The dark blue shining roof tiles a contrast to the white outer walls of the building.

Jennifer again entered the code for the security of the main door which opened slightly. They all entered into the expansive hallway; a large white tiled staircase curved to the first floor. They walked through the hallway to the back of the house and the kitchen. There were glass curtains halfway across the width of the kitchen, they could see the top of some sand dunes, the Atlantic was only 50 metres the other side of the protecting wall. It was a magnificent residence.

Steve got straight down to business, "Jennifer, which is the cupboard Lucas mentioned?"

Jennifer, "It is not in here," all three looked at Jennifer, "It is the outside kitchen, I had to deactivate the alarm for the property or the Policia would attend."

Leon, "That's a good idea Jennifer."

Steve was being impatient, "I'm not wanting to watch 'homes in the sun', can you take us there, now please?"

Jennifer, "Yes, I need a key first."

Steve was apologetic, "I am sorry Jennifer, we just need to move on a bit."

Jennifer collected the key from a drawer, she opened the glass curtains and walked onto the immaculate highly polished light grey patio and walked towards the outside kitchen. It was built with sturdy oak beams supporting a similar blue tiled roof, it was fully fitted with a large Belfast type sink, gas hob and oven, barbeque, pizza oven, large fridge, light grey marble work surface, and with storage space below for all equipment and utensils. There was a stand-alone solid oak preparation area in the centre of the kitchen and to the right of the preparation area was a solid stone cupboard with an oak door extending two metres from the wall. Jennifer opened the lock on the door, the light automatically lit up the inside of the cupboard. It was full of tinned food, fruit, dried goods, quality Ibérica hams hanging from the ceiling, spices and herbs. On the floor was an assortment of sandals, flip flops, seat cushions, neatly positioned.

Jennifer, "It is under the floor, I have never been in there since my mother died, only Lucas uses it now. You have to be inside and close the door, the light will go off, you switch the light on and it will release the lock on the floor."

They cleared the shoes and cushions from the floor. Steve

stepped inside then he closed the door and switched the light on. The floor raised slightly along one side of the cupboard floor, he pulled the floor up and saw the steps to the lower level, he opened the door for Leon to accompany him. They descended the wooden steps into a large void under the structure, there were several tall metal cabinets visible and a large safe, a long solid wooden table was in the middle of the floor. Leon opened the first cabinet and whistled.

"Have a look at this!"

Steve was now looking at a firearms cabinet, neatly stacked with Uzi sub machine guns, there were some empty slots, Glock pistols, 6 Remington 870 pump action shotguns. He opened the next cabinet; the ammunition was stored for each of the weapons on neat shelves. In the next cabinet that opened there were black jumpsuits hanging from a rail, black latex gloves and black head coverings on the shelves.

Steve, "Lucas was indeed looking after himself and preparing for anything that might come."

Leon, "He prepared for it definitely, it hasn't helped him much though."

Steve, "He is still alive, not like Torres. What would you prefer for your weapon?"

Leon after thinking, "Personally, I would take one of everything, it would be good if there were some silencers."

"I think you're right, good choice, we haven't finished looking yet, still two more cabinets and the safe."

One cabinet was full of possible torture or break in equipment, ropes, wire cutters, pliers, assorted cutting implements, jump leads and cleaning equipment for the weapons.

They found silencers for the Glock pistols and the larger Uzi silencers and cleaning materials in the last cabinet, they closed the cabinet doors and called for Jennifer.

Jennifer came down the steps followed by Gabi, "We have found what we were looking for, what Lucas had suggested would be useful, if you want to open the safe for what you want."

Jennifer dialled in the 8-digit combination and the 1-metre square safe opened, she pulled the door back. It was full of currency which had been vacuum packed. 100 Euro notes in bundles, US dollars of high value and sterling. Leon opened the cabinet where the clothing was stored, he took four black heavy-duty holdalls from a shelf, he started to pull the cash from the safe into the bags. They carried the bags up the steps and placed them on the outside kitchen floor, Jennifer and Gabi followed them up the steps.

Steve loaded two black holdalls with clothing that would fit, guns, silencers, ammunition of their choice and the cleaning sprays and cloths. Steve and Leon carried the bags upstairs and placed them on the top of the oak table. The floor was locked secure, the shoes, flip flops and cushions were put back in their previous position and the door was locked. Jennifer locked the house and set the alarm, they packed the bags into the boot of the vehicle and left the villa, the vehicle gate closing behind them as they left.

When they arrived at the home of Jennifer, they all went in with Leon and Steve carrying two bags of cash each.

Jennifer, "I do not need all of this money, Lucas told me to give some to you, for saving his life and hopefully the man you can rescue."

Steve was agitated and wanted to move on, "That's fantastic Jennifer, we really appreciate it. If you can hang on to it, we can meet up in a day or two. Keep it somewhere safe. We really do have to go."

"It will be okay here, no-one visits, I can wait for you all to return with the other man." They kissed and hugged in the formal Spanish manner.

They got into the car and headed back to the hotel room in Santiago de Compostela. They parked the car in the underground car park of the hotel and carried the black bags to their room.

Steve, "We need to clean down these weapons, bags,

anything we have touched." He unzipped one of the bags and took out a box of black latex surgical type gloves and an alcohol cleaning spray. "We never touch anything without these gloves on." He pulled the gloves tightly over his hands then unpacked the weapons and clothing from the bags.

Leon, "Have you got a plan yet, what are we going to do?"

Steve replied as he was lifting a shotgun out of one of the bags, "I want to do it properly, get the Guardia, Nacional in. The main priority is getting Juan out of that place fast, before any damage is done to him. We can do a reccy, if it looks do-able we can get him out, if not we will have to call the Guardia. I will not let them torture Juan."

They started cleaning down the guns and ammunition, removing any forensic markings or previous DNA trails which may have been left, then reloading the ammunition.

Gabi asked, "What about Paco and Pantera, when can we get to them?"

Steve, "One thing at a time, let's see what we can do with Juan first. One thing that's for sure, he cannot still be in that place when they arrive, that's not happening."

Leon, "They will probably have started putting pressure on him, he knows nothing, does he?"

"He knows fuck all, but if he, allegedly, says something, then dies, it would make it easier for Delgado to explain to this Paco guy, take the blame away from himself."

Leon, "Delgado could say that Juan set up Torres or was an undercover cop."

"Do you not think that's what I'm thinking? I know what happened to Filipe, he had done nowt, ask Gabi she will tell you what they are capable of."

Gabi had her head down looking at the Uzi gun she was cleaning, "She was nodding, I'm sorry Steve, they do horrible things Leon." She lifted her head and looked directly into the face of Steve, "Yes, we have to get him out, get him out quick."

Steve, "What we could do, let's talk about it. Gabi you could call Delgado and tell him we were ready to travel meet his car somewhere, well away from the finca."

Gabi, "I could do that, what time?"

"I will get a time later, Leon, you and me."

Leon interrupted, "It's you and I, remember what Bert said." He smiled at Steve.

Steve shook his head and sighed, "Yes of course, Leon, you and I. We need to get there and reccy the place, from the map on the mobile it can be approached through the woods to the rear of the finca. Hopefully we can get a decent view of the place, count numbers, identify the building Juan is in and do an effective extraction, quick, quiet and accurate."

Leon, "That takes me back a few years mate, sounds good. Are we talking killing force extraction?"

"Yes, look," Steve was shaking his head in disbelief at what they were planning, "we've crossed the line, we're goosed if we're captured. By them, we're dead, eventually. If by the police, we're going to jail for a long, long time. We are in a no-win situation unless we do it properly, leave no evidence, we have to be careful of DNA, CCTV, nothing left behind, no one that can talk or identify us, leave no trails."

Gabi, "What about me? What do I do, just sit here? That's not happening, I've got you all, including Juan, into this fucking mess as you would say Steve."

Steve, "No way Gabi, you are important to this, when we are in position, you make the call. You stop at the RV point, sorry, the drop off point, that is where you will pick us up from, unless there is a call to say otherwise."

Gabi, "Then what, just sit there?"

"Somewhere where you will not be seen or draw attention to the car or yourself. You might have to answer a call from Delgado asking where you are, tell him you're on your way, keep them away from the finca. It's important that you do that."

Leon, "So if it all goes to plan, we get Juan, he's okay, we leave the finca. What happens then?"

"There's two options, we wait until they return and take

them all out and leave quietly and get on with our lives."

Leon, "What's the second option?"

Steve thought for a few seconds, "I'm thinking, we might just have to find somewhere like that unknown paradise island and keep looking over our shoulders."

Gabi, "I am not going back to jail, not without getting Paco and Pantera."

Steve, "None of us want to go to jail, if I could get Juan out of there, making sure he would be safe I would call Guardia, that's not going to happen. If we are doing it, it has to be done properly, we've already marched over the fucking line, the Rubicon has been crossed, no turning back."

Leon, "What's the Rubicon?"

Steve, "It's a stream in Northern Italy."

Leon was puzzled, they continued cleaning the equipment.

Gabi left the room to purchase an ordnance survey map of the area, they continued cleaning everything down with alcohol wipes. On Gabi's return they studied the map, picking out a rendezvous point (RVP) and an approach route through the wooded area, skirting the hillside towards the rear of the buildings. They packed the bags into the boot of the Kia and left the hotel. They stopped at sports store and bought new shoes suitable for the terrain, then they headed towards the RVP.

It took an hour to reach the location, a long narrow country road just one kilometre from the buildings. Steve stopped the car in a small turning into the gateway of a field next to the wooded area. There was a small car park on the grassed area that hikers would use a further kilometre from the RVP, Gabi could park in the car park after the drop off. They waited for over five minutes, there was no traffic passed along the road.

Steve and Leon slipped on the black latex gloves. Steve took his shoes off inside the car, he stepped outside of the car and tested the ground. It was firm and covered in short, lush, dark green grass. Steve got the clothing bag out of the boot; they stood in the cover of the trees and bushes and placed the black overalls over their clothing and then put on the new shoes, they placed the head coverings in their pockets. Leon collected the weapons bag and they fitted the silencers onto the Uzi and Glock and checked they were fully loaded, they each carried spare ammunition for each weapon. The Uzi was on a shoulder strap, the pistol fit into the deep trouser pocket of the overalls, they picked up one shotgun each. They were almost ready to go.

Steve collected Leon's phone from Gabi, "We will ring you when we are in a position, then you call Delgado. You must stay nearby, be ready to pick us up, we might be in a hurry. Under no circumstances do you leave the car, keep your hat on at all times, do not get into conversations with anyone, if we do not come back, it will be better if you get out of here for good. I'm sure we will be back."

"I will be waiting, I promise. Please, both of you come back."

Leon was holding Gabi very close, "I'll be back, I promise, I love you. If by any chance something goes wrong, just do as Steve said."

Gabi, "I love you; you must come back."

Steve had the map in one hand as they moved away from the RVP, he was picking the hard grass covered ground, they were soon inside the cover of the wood and hidden from the view of Gabi. She drove the car to the car park and waited.

It only took ten minutes to walk the distance to the rear of the buildings, they sat behind a bush with thick green foliage. It was a sunny, bright day and now the temperature was hot for the north coast of Spain, they had an excellent view of the buildings. The large two story finca was on the left of the plot and stood alone, there were three single story stone buildings on the opposite side of a pebbled courtyard, these buildings were where they believed Juan was being held. They were solid stone buildings, all with orange roof tiles, each building had a door and windows facing onto the courtyard. There was no sign of any dogs which was a bonus, they slowly moved towards the rear of the three buildings keeping in the cover of the woods. They could see that each of the smaller buildings had a single window facing onto the wood. There were two large black Mercedes saloon cars and a black Mercedes van, similar to the one Steve had seen in Colombia, parked near to the finca on the pebbled courtyard. As yet, they had not seen any signs of anyone moving in the plot. There were no obvious signs of cameras visible on the outside of the buildings, they moved back behind the bush with a full view of the courtyard, Steve made a call to Gabi.

"Hello Steve, everything okay?"

"So far, you can make the call now, tell him we are all there, ready to travel but we're not trusting anyone unless he is there, we know what happened to Torres."

"Yes, I have been practicing the call."

"We have a view of the buildings. Once they leave, we will do what we have to do."

"I will call him now."

Gabi used the encro mobile to call Delgado, "Hello Javier, we are ready, Steve and Leon are with me, can you meet us somewhere near to Santiago de Compostela?"

"I will send my men to meet you somewhere near there."

"It's not that I don't trust your men, but I would prefer it if you came as well, it would feel safer after what happened to Miguel."

"Gabi, that was not me, that was the idiot Torres, he got what he deserved. You will be fine with my men, trust me."

"We will not come without you, or we will come tomorrow and talk independently to the Colombians, different stories, we have nothing to fear, as I told you, my man saved the cargo."

"Okay, okay, I will come, I was preparing a surprise for you all, a party, good food and wine. I will leave it to the housekeeper." He lied.

"That is good, how long will you be?"

"I will be maybe, 45 minutes? Be in the car park of the Biblioteca de Galicia near to the first roundabout."

"It will take us the same time to get there."

The call was ended, Gabi called Steve and told him she had made the call.

Within minutes there was movement at the finca. Four men came out of the main door, one of them walked over the courtyard to the nearest building to their position and entered, the door had not been locked. The others opened the doors of the saloon cars, they were all carrying a pistol in a holster over their shoulder, they removed jackets from the boot of the saloon and wore them over the holster to conceal the weapons. Two more men walked out of the finca. Steve immediately recognised one of the men, the male he had met at the airport who gave him the tickets who had the threatening smile, "Delgado, that bastard" he whispered. The rear door was held open as the man believed to be Delgado sat in the rear seat of the saloon, the door was closed. The two saloon cars were driven away together.

Steve, "That has got to be Delgado. I counted one walking into the building, there could be more inside but I bet that's where Juan is being held."

Leon, "We could possibly look through the rear window, see who's inside."

Just as they were about to move towards the building, the male with the gun pulled a chair outside of the door and sat in the sun.

Steve, "I'll line up the guy in the chair, you have a look through the window, see if you can see Juan or anyone else."

They moved slowly and silently towards their positions, they could see each other, they slipped the face coverings over their heads. Steve was in a kneeling position concealed by bush foliage, the male guard was targeted through the Glock sight, he signalled to Leon, thumb up. Leon crept low towards the window, keeping to the shade side of the window so as not to cast a shadow into the room. He was very close to the window but could hear nothing from inside the room, he leant back from the window to open his vision and slowly scanned inside the room, peering through the steel bars and dirty window.

He saw Juan. He was naked, suspended from a wooden roof beam with a rope around his wrists, his head was down on his chest, his toes were touching the tiled floor. He could see bruising to his body, head, and legs, with dried blood covered some wounds. "Bastards." Leon whispered to himself. He moved a few metres into view of Steve, he gave him the signals they prepared, thumb up, Juan was in the building, Steve acknowledged. Thumb and finger together, forming a zero, no men in the room, again he acknowledged. Finally, one man at the front, the point and trigger action, bending thumb. Steve acknowledged again, the point of no return, there was no further thought. It was what was planned, looking down the sight, no more than thirty metres, slowly breathing out, maintaining the target he pulled the trigger. Two quiet explosions as bullets sped the short distance into the left side of the head of the unsuspecting guard, the instant wide spray of blood from the exit wounds as he fell from his chair onto the courtyard, the chair resting backwards against the wall of the building. The Rubicon had definitely been crossed, he was now marching on Rome with no way back, they had to win.

Steve broke cover and started walking towards the door of the building, he was being covered by Leon. He looked briefly at the body, the male was dead, he had seen the man once before in a stairwell. The door was open, he entered a short corridor, there were no other guards. He turned into a large open room and saw Juan hanging from the roof beam, he looked unconscious, he moved quickly towards him, "Juan, Juan, it's Steve, you're leaving now." Leon stayed at the door of the building covering the escape route.

Juan was trying to help, "Gracias, gracias."

Steve asked Leon to come to the room, he made one more sweep of the courtyard then entered the room, taking a knife from the table then climbing onto a chair, he cut through the rope holding Juan who immediately slumped but was held up by Steve. Juan had no strength in his body or legs, Steve lifted his body over his shoulder in a fireman's lift. Leon picked up the rope and gathered together his clothing from the small bed. Leon led the way to the door, he signalled it was clear, Juan was carried away from the building into the woods. They took turns in carrying Juan towards the RVP, Leon called Gabi to meet them as they made their way through the woods, they never stopped until they reached the edge of the woods, they saw the car. They sat down in the woods on the comforting grass and gathered their breath, they looked at Juan. He had taken a beating: he was in a bad way but he would survive now. Gabi brought some bottled water which she slowly poured into Juan's mouth; he was slowly recovering. They pulled his denim jeans on and slipped his shirt over his body, putting his arms over their shoulders they carried him to the car and sat him in the back seat.

Juan, "He is trying to blame you and me, he is the bastard who gave us the tickets at the airport. He lied then. Thank you, I would be dead tonight, I can help when I'm okay."

Steve, "Yes, I saw him, Delgado, he's fucked everybody off. How many men have you seen?"

"Him, he is always with the same two other men, they have done this to me, that smile he has, I could clear it from his face. Three others, they take turns in guarding me, as if I needed guarding, hanging from the roof beam, not one would take me on, not on their own, cowards."

"Have they said anything about the Colombians?"

"They were going to kill us all, then put the blame on us to the Colombians, they are coming tomorrow morning."

"Did they tell you who they are?"

"No, I wasn't expected to meet them."

"How did they cause these injuries to you; did they use weapons?"

"They used a metal bar on my legs and used me as a punch bag with metal bands on their hands."

"We still have some work to do here, you will be okay to stay with Gabi?"

"I'm okay, I'm in pain but again my friend, I'm not dead, thank you."

Steve turned to Gabi, "I think you should call Delgado now, tell him I've changed my mind and we are not going until tomorrow."

Gabi made the call, "Javier, my men have changed their decision, they want to come tomorrow. We will not be meeting today."

"Why have you changed the decision? You know you can trust me."

"I can trust you, but these men have never met you and don't trust you. Steve was on the submarine, they tried to kill him when they got the cargo, what about the other man, where is he?"

"He is waiting to meet you all again, I told him you were coming; he will be upset if his friend does not come."

"They can see each other tomorrow; he will be pleased then. Same place tomorrow, just let me know the time. I will be there. I want this sorted out; it has nothing to do with me."

"Gabi, it makes sense to meet up before they come."

"I will see you tomorrow."

The call was ended, Delgado was an angry man, he was furious, he was being manipulated by a woman, "She is the whore of Alvarez, she should be dead now, fucking Torres could do nothing right. She will be dead tomorrow, all of them will be. Get me back to the finca, we can start by killing the fisherman." The two cars travelled in convoy at speed back towards the finca.

They jogged quickly back through the woods to the finca, sticking to the route they had made, Leon was carrying one of the empty black holdalls, they made a full 360-degree reconnaissance of the property from the road entrance to the rear fencing. It was completely private and not overlooked, other than the area to the rear where the woods were. They lifted the bloodied body of the guard from the front of the building to inside the hostage room where they dumped him on top of some blood stains which they presumed were from Juan. It should conceal his presence for a while. They collected the metal bar and knuckle duster from the tabletop and placed them inside the bag, Leon collected the remaining clothing and shoes of Juan and placed them in the bag, then left the building and closed the door. They could not hide the blood on the pebbled courtyard or sprayed on the wall, from 40 metres it would not be immediately noticed, that was the hope. They decided on the killing zone from where they had seen the vehicles parked earlier, Steve would move to the left of his previous position, 30 to 40 metres from where it was anticipated the first car would park. Leon was hidden in the undergrowth of the woods towards the road, about a similar distance to Steve from the second vehicle and would prevent any car from leaving the plot. The plan was to wait until they were out of the cars, then fire into the killing zone with their own responsibilities. Steve, the closest car to him, Leon the car nearest to him and the road access. They would fire on Steve's signal, the first shot. It was a beautiful summers day; the birds were singing it was so peaceful.

It took 20 minutes for the cars to turn off the road onto the private road towards the finca, Delgado was still furious about his wasted journey and being pissed off by a young whore. They didn't notice the blood on the walls or the ground as the cars slid to a halt on the pebbled courtyard outside of the finca. The driver and front seat passenger got out of both cars; Delgado waited for his door to be opened. Steve had targeted the first man, he fired his Uzi towards the front car passengers, a fraction of a second passed as Leon fired at his group. Delgado saw the blood on the walls at the precise moment the silent gunfire entered the zone, one by one they fell to the ground, blood, brains, pieces of bone bouncing against the car, the bullets shattering the windscreen and some of the passenger windows, Delgado pressed himself hard into the rear full-length seat. Not one of them fired a shot in return, they were all hit in the body and head, they had no chance. He lay there, he waited, it was silent, four seconds, that is all it took to kill four men. He didn't want to look above the seat, maybe they thought he was dead, he might be lucky.

He did not have long wait to find the answer to his thoughts, his hopes, there was a solid knocking noise on the rear passenger offside window. He didn't want to look but felt powerless to stop himself, he lifted his head slightly and saw the figure dressed in black, black face covering, black gloves and a black Uzi gun pointing at his head. The gun was being pulled, indicating for him to get out of the car. He reached forward and opened the internal lock on the door and the door opened, the seat was wet from him pissing himself, his threatening smile had disappeared. The man in black with the Uzi pointed at his chest, stepped back away from the door as it opened, another man in black was stood to his right side also aiming at his body, nowhere to run, the car door to his left, the car behind, two Uzi holding killers in front and to the right. He stood at the door, "It had nothing to do with me, it was the men on the submarine, they told the police. I have money, not all of it but you can have what I've got. Torres and Alvarez got the men not me. It is his whore who set it up. You must believe me. I have done nothing."

Steve and Leon said nothing, Leon was standing in front of him, he indicated for Delgado to get on his knees. He was momentarily brave, he didn't move, he showed resistance, but Leon stepped closer and pointed the Uzi at his forehead. Delgado moved slowly, leaning on the open door as he dropped down onto his knees, "I'm begging you please, it was the Englishman and Torres's man, with the whore of Torres, they must have been set up to do this. I have done nothing, I will kill them, I was going to kill them for you."

Leon indicated for Delgado to turn towards the other man, he shuffled on his knees to face the other man, "Please, please, it was the English man not me." He was looking towards the masked face of Steve.

Steve lifted his face protection, Delgado looked in shock at the face in front of him. Steve spoke slowly and quietly, "You said, do not fuck this up, remember?" He smiled at Delgado, then he fired a single bullet through the forehead of Delgado, the hair, skull, blood, and brains exploded with the bullet into the car window and beyond.

They examined the others, they were dead, retracing their steps, they could still hear the birds singing in the trees and on the roofs of the buildings, a silent, deadly, force. They returned to the RVP and waited for Gabi. They removed their black clothing and headwear as they waited, placing it back into the black holdall. Gabi parked the car in the gateway to the field, they took off the new shoes and placed them inside the bag, then they checked the area to ensure nothing had been dropped. They all kept their latex gloves on, they walked to the car, they placed the bag into the boot, then the weapons inside their holdall. They got into the car and Gabi drove steadily towards the motorway, the car was silent.

Leon was the first to speak, "I suppose that went as well as could be expected."

Steve answered, "It did, you do realise what we have just done?"

Leon, "Yes, yes I do. It is against the law, fuck knows it is, but nearly every copper, or polis as you say, would have fucking loved to have done it to some bunch of twats in their neck of the woods. Tell me if that's not true."

"There is a big difference about thinking and wanting to do it, to actually going out and doing it. About 40 years in a Spanish jail."

Leon replied, "Well then, we had better get rid of the evidence we have in the boot fairly quickly. There is no-one left alive to say anything."

Juan, "We should visit my boat now and have a little cruise, that might help, I want to help, you have done this for me."

Steve, "That sounds like a good plan if you are up to it?"

"I am, I want to, let's go." Juan gave directions to the location of his fishing boat; he then made a call to Veronica.

It took just less than an hour to arrive at the port in Marin, just south of Pontevedra, they had made a short stop at the home of Juan to collect the boat keys and some prepared food for the short cruise. Juan took the chance to change his clothing without Veronica or his mother seeing his injuries. Veronica stayed with his mother, she didn't ask any questions, she was just happy to see him.

Juan led the way climbing onto the boat, then helping Gabi on board before being handed the two black bags and the prepared food by Leon and Steve. Juan wasted no time in starting the boats engines and heading into the Ria de Pontevedra towards the deep Atlantic.

It was a well-cared for and maintained boat, recently painted, white hull and red bulwarks the same colours were used on the small bridge, 20 metres in length with all the requirements needed for a week's fishing in the Atlantic. A good size, fully equipped galley, room for four bunks if needed and a clean head, with shower facility. They were stood in the bridge; Gabi had been to the galley and brought the food up on plates to pick at in the bridge. Juan stayed at the controls in the bridge, the others went out onto the deck. Gabi took her hat off for the first time in the day.

Leon spoke, "What happens now?"

Steve had been thinking the same, he answered, "We get rid of our cargo in a short time, enjoy our day out together, it could be a part of our alibi should we need one. Then, I'll head back to Madrid and you do what your plan is and wait for the news."

Gabi, "I thought we were going to meet Paco and Pantera."

Steve, "Gabi, I know you have a need for revenge, I do, but this is not the right time, we are riding our luck as it is."

"But they are coming here, we do not have to look for them, it would be easy, like today."

Steve was angry, "It was not fucking easy today, not at all. They probably will not come now, who can they visit, who can they talk to? They have no contact, they're all dead or in jail."

Gabi, "They will want answers, they have lost a lot."

"I am aware of what they have lost, I've seen how much they have lost, but really, it is a drop in this ocean to their business and they have maintained their fear and power, as hopefully, everyone will believe it was the cartel that killed Delgado and his gang."

Leon, "Steve is right, listen to him, now is not the time. I can pack the job in and we can live together, we could stay here in Spain. They don't know who you are, you are legal, we can make a plan for our future, I would like that."

Steve softened his tone, "You have asked questions about this Pantera, you might get some answers, that would help in the future but we need to just keep a low profile now."

Gabi looking at Steve, "You want revenge, I know you do, we will get revenge."

"There is still a chance we can get revenge on Pantera, you, and us now, we have hurt them. We have taken billions of dollars from the cartel, their OCG partners have been eliminated, one way or another. We do not need to make mistakes by doing more. Think of the alternatives, life in jail if you are lucky, if we are lucky. No doubt about it, there will be a massive investigation into what we have just done, we have covered our tracks but there's always something, somewhere, we just have to hope they don't find it. That's why we have to be as normal as we can be."

Leon, "If I resign, would you move from here, we could go anywhere and be happy together."

Gabi, "I want to be happy with you, but I will never be happy until those two are dead."

Leon continued, "Think about what Steve has said. We could go to our paradise island and maybe, you get the call you want about Pantera, who he is, where he is and we could do something then. I am really fucked up at what Steve and I have done, we're coppers, we are supposed to be stopping it from happening. I did it, because they had Juan and would have killed him and I heard Delgado say to me and Steve that he was planning to kill all of us tonight."

Steve added, "Gabi, I've known you a lot longer than Leon. You have told me, Jessica, and Gloria, you are not a murderer, you killed because you had to, because of circumstances. I can understand that, I have done the same, like you said a few days ago. I am still a polis, despite what I have done today. I might suffer the consequences; it was worth it today to save Juan and protect us. I killed Pepe to stop his suffering, some might not see it like that. I killed the pirates in self-defence, they were going to kill Juan and me. We have done enough killing."

Leon, "Steve, its Juan and I, I've told you." He started to giggle, Gabi started to laugh, Steve started to laugh. Gabi went into the bridge to get some drinks.

Steve, "Seriously, what are you going to do, we can't go on doing the job, not after today?"

"I'm thinking about resigning, definitely, I want to spend my life with Gabi."

"What are you going to give as your reason?"

"I can't say I'm in love with an escaped murderer, they would accept that though." He smirked, "I'll tell the truth, it's been tough, I want to change my life and travel."

Steve, "The second one sounds reasonable, I know you would be good together but how long do you think it would last?"

"Forever mate, I wouldn't let her go back to jail, no matter what happened to me. We can keep our heads down, enjoy life while we are young enough, I'm hoping time will repair the revenge thoughts, I doubt it though. What about you?"

"I would like to say I'm disgusted at what I have done today but I'm not. It was a case of kill or be killed, we did what we had to do. Would I accept that as a polis? No, I don't think I would. I can't carry on getting into situations like we have been in the last couple of months, it's crazy. We volunteered for it but I have crossed the line big style, fucking huge leap, I can't carry on as a polis never mind the stuff we do."

"So, are you going to resign?"

"I'm seriously considering it, but not yet. I will wait and see what the outcome from the investigations are, see if anything turns up. I can possibly deal with it, give it a few weeks, have the debrief with Bert then decide."

"What would you do, what about Sarah?"

"I don't think I can stay with Sarah," Steve was thinking. "Those fucking bastards Leon."

Leon remained silent.

"I've never loved a woman until I met Jessica, I know she loved me, if she had never met me, she would still be alive. I'm not having a go at Gabi, but that cartel, fucking Pantera he killed her, an unarmed woman running to help her friend, Gloria. Now, the same bastards have ruined our lives again. Sarah, she is the best thing that has ever happened to me, I can't imagine life without her, I couldn't let her do the job she is training for, what can I say to her? Everything will be okay? When I've done what I've done?"

Leon, "Just quit the job, leave it behind and get on with Sarah."

"I would like to think it's that easy mate, it's in my head, even if things go our way after today, we will still be expecting a knock on the door. Sarah deserves better. I'll ride it out for a few weeks, there's the enquiry about the killings on the boat, Juan is on bail, if it is finalised with no charges against Juan which there shouldn't be, I'll make my decision then."

That ended that conversation. They went back to the bridge for more of the prepared food and listened to Juan's music playing.

After an hour, the contents of the weapons bag and the Berretta from the Kia glove box were emptied into the ocean as the boat sailed across the top of the calm water. The clothing was placed onto a small oil drum barbeque on the deck and burned, there was nothing left to chance. The remnants of the shoes and the ashes from the clothing were dumped overboard.

They all sat around the table in the galley and discussed the events since Juan had been taken from his home. Every part was broken down and discussed, who, if any, knew locations, timings, travel. The major part was the discussion about the killings at the Finca.

As far as anyone knew there were no witnesses to the shootings and no one alive to say anything. There was a possibility that there would be DNA found that would match up with Juan being in the building, the possible answers to any questions. The shell casings would be recovered, these were cleaned and would not give any identification, everything used in the incident had been destroyed and sunk to the bottom of the ocean.

CHAPTER 19

Monday 12th June

It was just after 07:00 when Juan pulled alongside the dock in Marin, the four left the boat and headed to the car. Juan was dropped off outside his home, Steve then headed towards Vigo and dropped Leon and Gabi near to the ferry terminal. They had all said their goodbyes on the boat, further hugs, kisses, and fist pumps before they went their separate ways. They had plans made but needed to get back to normality if possible.

Steve took the car to a nearby valet centre and had the car expertly cleaned throughout, he stayed and watched it being done. He topped up the petrol tank and took it back to the hire company without any problems. He took a taxi to the hotel in Vigo, paid the hotel bill, and met up with Leon. Steve drove Leon to the airport in the Evoque for his flight to Madrid and his connection to London. It was a strange day, waiting for a call while hoping they didn't get one, they had made their plans.

Steve had a coffee with Leon in the airport as Leon waited for his flight. There was a silent hug, then a fist pump as they said their possible last farewell, everything had been said and done. They turned their backs on each other, Steve walking towards the terminal exit, Leon towards the departure gate. Steve set off on the drive to Madrid.

It was 17:18 when Steve walked into his apartment, threw the bag on his bed, and sat on the sofa with his head in his hands. His mind was racing, going back over everything, the television was on the Spanish news channel but nothing was being reported. He remembered his personal mobile phone, the battery was flat, he put it on charge then took a diet cola out of his fridge, the mobile started activating. He lifted it up and looked at the screen, message after message from Sarah, it brought a smile to his face and a worry in his mind. 'Miss you', 'Going to Seahouses,' 'fish and chips, crab' sounded fantastic. 'Been in London', so many messages, he was missing Sarah. "What the fuck have I done?" He repeated, "What the fuck have I done?" He couldn't reply to the messages, not now. The images were still in his head, his eyes were closed. Pepe was standing on the post, asking him to kill him, the moment he forcibly pushed the knife through his heart, his right hand was automatic in shaking in memory of the feeling, "fuck, fuck," he said silently and threw his head back. He was watching Pepe falling into the dark river, he was shaking his head. The bright explosions on the deck of the pirate boat as it sped towards the refuelling ship, firing the Browning along the deck of the ship as it turned, the explosion as it rammed into the ship, jumping into the vessel with the crew to safety, shaking his head, "for fuck's sake". His mind sped through to the shooting on the fishing boat, "I was gone, fucked." Yesterday was still so clear in his memory, it would be forever, shooting the guard on the door, he was mirroring the action from Leon, bending the thumb, looking down on the guy he knocked out on the stairwell landing, a bloodied mess, but he felt nothing. Entering the room and seeing Juan, "Bastards." The sunny day when birds were singing, the black cars stopped and he fired into the killing zone watching his two targets drop without touching their weapons. The slow crunching walk over the courtyard to the Mercedes, Leon getting Delgado out of the car, the begging, the promises to kill them, him and Juan, the shocked look on his face when he recognised the man behind the mask. Steve smiled again and clicked his thumb. He dropped the mobile next to the charger and sat on the sofa with his head in his hands for a few minutes. He stood up, then left the apartment, walking to The Covent Garden.

Gabi was sitting in the lounge when her mobile activated. Looking at the screen, the number showed as unknown, the time showing was 21:27. She immediately looked outside through the large windows and could see nothing, she answered, "Hello, who is this?"

"Good evening. Did you find what you were looking for?"

"Ahh," Gabi recognised the voice of Lucas, "It is good to hear you, yes we did, thank you."

"I take it what you found came in useful?"

"I cannot say."

"Yes, of course. I have some information for you."

"I will get a pen."

"You do not need a pen, just listen and think."

"Yes, okay."

"I have heard that two men have gone back to their country for some reason and no one would answer their call last night."

"That is strange."

"I have heard that something happened and they have disappeared, everything cleaned."

Gabi asked, "Disappeared?"

"Yes, gone, they cannot be found."

Gabi had a realisation of what was being said, "Ahh okay. I know one man but I don't know the other man who has gone, do you know him?"

"Yes, I can tell you sometime."

"That would be good. Do you want anything?"

"Nothing, thank you, thank you very much."

Gabi, "No, thank you very much."

The call was ended.

Gabi was wondering how had Lucas arranged a clean-up operation from inside the prison, she didn't care, could it have been Jennifer? She couldn't have done it, she might know someone that can, Jennifer was worth a visit.

Gabi sent a message to Leon, 'Contact me.'

He was walking back to his apartment with a pizza in a box in his hand when he got the message, he went into the 24/7, he selected a six pack of lager and a pre-paid sim card, then he continued to his apartment. He put the lager into the empty fridge and placed the pizza in the oven to keep it warm. After changing the sim card, he made a call, "Hi, it's me, are you missing me already?"

Gabi ignored the question, "Is the mobile safe?"

Leon, "I've just put a new sim in, nobody knows your phone, do they?"

"No, it's okay then, Yes I'm missing you but that's not important now."

"Oh thanks, I guess you have got something to tell me then that is important."

"I've just been told by someone that everything has been cleared away, they've gone. The problem has been moved, taken away."

Leon was thinking momentarily, "How, if you're saying what I'm thinking?"

"I don't know but they can't be found, anywhere."

"How the fuck did..."

Gabi interrupted, "I told you, I don't know but he was grateful."

"That's possibly why it has not been on the news. I have seen before how clean he keeps his place. Have you called anyone else?"

"No, you can. Might see you soon."

"I hope so."

The call ended.

Leon made a call, Steve answered the unknown number in Spanish, "Buenas tardes."

"Steve it's me, new mobile, just in case."

"Okay, go on then, it must be important."

"My friend has just told me there has been a clean-up at a

location and nothing can be found, gone, for ever."

"What the fuck, how, who? Never mind, is your friend sure?"

"Yes, definitely."

Steve was amazed, "There's nothing on the news over here. I'm going into the office tomorrow, I'm sure to hear something then."

"Yes mate, I was just warning you about what I've been told. Say nothing."

"Leon, I would say nowt anyway, we know the script, stay behind and keep ahead. Good heads up though, this might change things. I've had a few beers tonight, thought about it but I think I'll still jack it in, I've had enough, I just wish I could take Sarah with me."

"You still have a few weeks before she's finished on the course, see how things work out with Juan, it might be okay."

"I'll still be here for a month possibly, unless something happens before I want things to happen. Have you decided what you're doing?"

"I am definitely packing in, just got to get things sorted and not draw attention to anything then slope off, be happy, get pissed, enjoy life."

"Sounds great mate, hope it happens. I'll keep in touch."

Steve set a message to Sarah, 'really missing you, just a few weeks.'

Tuesday 13th June

It had been a restless night for Steve, far too many thoughts in his head. He showered early and walked to the Embassy, he stopped off for a coffee and tortilla on his way.

Ken was the first to greet Steve as he entered the office, "Good morning Steve, have you got your land legs yet?"

"Still working on them Ken, I've just walked in, it's nice

out there and nothing is moving, that's a bonus." Ken gave a smile, Steve continued, "Anything happening today, or can I concentrate on doing my debrief report?"

"Nothing new that I'm aware off, the Guardia are considering trying to recover the vessel, they have had a look but it's quite deep. Other than that, nothing. Not on your job anyway, cracking result, you must be happy."

"It wasn't easy but it's almost done, just the paperwork."

Ken raised his eyes, "Bert told me it hadn't been easy but he didn't expand much on it, I didn't ask. You okay now?"

"Getting there Ken."

Steve took his seat at his desk. He took out the UC documents, passport, driving licence, credit card, and placed them into a large manilla envelope which he took out of the bottom drawer. He placed the mobile phone he had used on top of the envelope. He opened his work station and started to catch up on the intelligence that was coming into the system, there didn't appear to be anything that would cause a problem.

After twenty minutes or so Bert walked into the office carrying several folders, his face broke into a smile when he saw Steve, "Good to see you this morning, have you had enough R and R, (rest and recuperation) you are looking in a better condition than the last time I saw you."

Steve was relaxing, "Yes Bert, thanks, I have had some more sleep, a shave and long showers."

Bert, "Get two coffees, it will give me a chance to file these, come into the office, we will have a chat."

Steve walked in carrying the coffees, "Do you want the door closed?"

"No, no, not much business, just welfare and bits and bobs, unless you want it to be private?" The door was left open as Steve took his seat opposite Bert.

Bert started, after having a sip of his hot black coffee, "I know you are a tough lad, as you say. I know from what you have said, this latest operation has been both physically and mentally testing. I just want to ensure that you get all the help you need, to assist you to recover from the torrid experiences you have endured on that torturous, treacherous journey. The sights and the shocking near death experience."

"Thanks Bert, I really appreciate that. I volunteered for the job, I expected it to be difficult but not as bad as it turned out to be. Just goes to show you cannot trust OCG's."

"Quite. We do have a debrief to go through, none of our Spanish colleagues, just one to one with me. Obviously, they would like to know faces, places, anything that would help in any future operations."

"I was just about to start writing up my report when you came in, I can continue with that now and do the debrief this afternoon if that's okay."

"Yes, that would be excellent, if it can be done in time?"

"Bert, to be honest, there's not a lot I can tell you about faces, I could possibly identify a few places using google earth. I'll do what I can. Have the other agencies come up with anything that might be useful?"

Bert, "If they have, they have not shared it with me, yet. Have you been in touch with Sarah?"

"I've sent some messages but I believe she's on a task for a few days so she will not be getting any comms."

Bert was smiling again, "Just a few weeks until we see her face again, I wonder how long Sarah will stay with us?"

Steve shrugged his shoulders, "Who knows Bert, I'll crack on with my report then." He picked up his coffee and returned to his desk.

Gabi had made a call to Jennifer and then travelled to her villa. They were sat on high stools at the large square marble table in the centre of the kitchen, the windows were open allowing the warmth and a slight breeze into the room. Jennifer had made a large jug of fresh orange juice which was set on the table next to two matching stemmed glasses.

Jennifer poured the juice into the glasses, "I was hoping to see you again, did you find the man you were looking for in time?"

Gabi was smiling at Jennifer, "With your help and Lucas we did, he will be forever grateful, you both saved his life."

"That is excellent news." There was a slight smile on her face.

Gabi continued, "Yes really good news. I have received a call from Lucas so he remembered my number."

Jennifer, "Lucas has always been good with numbers, a very good memory."

"Lucas is a very good magician as well, he can make things disappear, even from inside prison." Gabi lifted her glass of orange juice, smiled at Jennifer and silently toasted her.

Jennifer had a slight smile on her face, "Lucas only does his magic for people he really likes." She returned the gesture.

Gabi again smiling, "Just one call."

Jennifer replied, "Just one call."

They both touched their glasses together and sipped their orange juice.

Gabi continued, "I take it you will be visiting Lucas again, now that you have been in once."

"Yes, of course. I would not be a good sister if I didn't visit my brother, there is just the two of us."

"Lucas told me that he would give me the name and possible location of one man. Could you ask him and remember the details for me during your visit?"

"I am sure I will remember one name and location. I told you I'm good at secrecy."

An hour later, Gabi loaded two black rucksacks into her car and headed back to her villa.

Steve had completed his report and printed off four copies, his copy, one for Bert, and one for each of the Spanish agencies. It was 16:16 when he walked into Bert's office and took his seat, Bert closed the door.

Bert, "Do you want me to read the report and ask questions

as I go through it, I think it's the best idea?"

Steve, "Yeah, whenever you're ready, I'll follow your pages."

Bert opened the report on his desk in front of him and started reading.

After the second page, "This operation involves Lucas Alvarez, Miguel Torres, and Javier Delgado. Which of these have you met?"

"None of them, I was supposed to meet Alvarez at a drug slaughter instead of Leon but the drugs didn't come ashore."

"Are you sure?"

"Yes, I'm sure. Why? I was on a flight to Colombia a couple of days after." He lied.

Bert, "You did not know it but you met Delgado at the airport, he was the man who gave you the tickets."

"Was that him? I didn't like him, arrogant man. Typical OCG boss with a threatening smile. So that's Delgado."

Bert, "He gave you three tickets with names on, can you recall the names?"

"No Bert, like it says in the report, the tickets were in white envelopes, mine had Steve, one with Juan, it may have been written Xuan I can't recall and Pepe which wasn't even his name. He was called Alejandro. No other names. We had a little meeting in the bar as it says, I instructed them to say nothing and ask nothing, that's the way it works, drip feed, it's not noticed."

Bert, "I'm just asking as I know I'll get asked but it is as explained."

Bert read on, "No further identification for the black Mercedes van I take it?"

"No, as it states we got into the vehicle through the side doors, possibly to stop us seeing any number plate. They parked side on to where we were heading when we got out, so no chance to see any i.d. marks."

"Again, no further way to identify the villa, house, you were at?"

"No, just 39 minutes of heavy city traffic, a bit quieter at the end of the journey possibly a suburb of the city, local cops will have an idea, I'm sure."

"You have identified the river from the onboard sat-nav system, you have given a possible area to look at, is that is as exact as you can go?"

"It's a huge river Bert. From what I saw it looked very similar, widened out in places."

Bert was silent as he read the next page, "That is very thorough and harrowing, we do not need any more detail on this. Are you okay?"

"To be honest Bert, no, I'm not. It is something I will always remember. I'll get on with the job, it helps, as they say." Steve had lied in the report that Pepe was killed by the leader of the group, Bert readily accepted the explanation. "Has Pepe been identified yet; his parents should know."

Bert, "I believe the Spanish colleagues are making the enquiries, they're not expecting any help from Torres or Delgado."

Further reading, "Two good locations for the possible camps you stopped at."

"They were on the sat-nav but as I have said, there will be more and will possibly move between them."

Steve sat and read through his report as Bert was turning pages. Bert, "Exact location for the supply vessel, and a decent description of a fishing boat in the dark and the skipper, that might help in the future."

"There's not a lot to write about is there Steve?"

"No Bert. Most days it was wake up have some turns in the cockpit, eat some mackerel, rice, and sleep. It was hard to stay awake."

Bert, "Okay, let's go through this together."

Steve, "Okay, it's written down as it happened."

Bert read on, "You've got the co-ordinates, you have seen the boat, then Juan takes over the controls, why?"

"He is a proper skipper; he could handle the boat better than me."

Bert nodded. “You open the cargo hatch as the vessel is tied up, Juan closes the cockpit hatch, you say to stop someone dropping something in, why do you say that.”

“I just think belt and braces, cover all eventualities. Anyone could drop a small incendiary or explosive after we had unloaded, I was protecting us, or so I thought at the time.”

Bert read on as did Steve. Bert, “You told Juan to get the bags and climb on board the fishing boat as you were unloading, explain.”

“There was just one load to go. I could manage it and I didn’t know how fast the vessel would fill with water so I told him to get on the boat, it would be a faster, unobstructed exit for me.”

“What about dropping something inside the vessel?”

“It was a possibility but the two crew and the skipper were busy with the lifting equipment.”

“As you were climbing out of the cockpit you noticed you were drifting away and sinking, then one man fired from a pistol at you from 5 metres and missed.”

“I saw him raise the pistol and point towards me and I dropped into the cockpit as the shot was fired, then I heard the gunfire.”

Bert asked, “You didn’t have any firearms on board the vessel?”

“No, what good would they be, the size of that thing? A bigger boat would just run over and sink it, it’s made of plastic like a canoe. I didn’t know what was happening on the deck, I was getting dragged by the boat, holding onto a rope Juan had thrown as it sailed away.”

Bert, “So, we have to take the word of Juan, there’s no-one to contest it.”

Steve, “That man saved my life, the three on board made a fatal error, on their behalf thankfully, of leaving a gun visible. Why? Who knows, who cares, it saved my life, Juan saved my life.”

Bert, “That’s a comprehensive report Steve. I am recommending that you go back to the UK and have a full psychological assessment, have a break, possibly meet up with Sarah and your friends, de-stress."

"I'm okay Bert, honest. I could do with a break and think about things. A lot happened and I'm concerned about Juan, he should be okay."

Bert reassured Steve, "I am certain Juan will be fine, no prosecution in the circumstances, it wouldn't benefit anyone. Leave it with me and my Spanish partners, they are very happy at the result, very happy."

Steve left the office and had a couple of beers in The Covent Garden with some colleagues. He bought a sim card before he took the metro towards his apartment.

Steve made a call to Leon, "Hello mate have you been into the office?"

Leon, "Yes, I went in today. No drama, the bosses are happy with the result, they're wanting me to do another job, said I've been on a jolly for a few weeks. I wish! What about you?"

Steve, "I've been in and done my report. Bert is sending me for psychological testing in the next few days. He thinks I've had a rough time, he doesn't know the half of it. There is nothing anywhere about Delgado. They are all extremely happy about the result. Have you spoken to Gabi today?"

"Not yet, I will ring later, I've not been in long."

"What are your plans, have you decided yet?"

"I want to live with her if she will give up the chase on the Colombians, or at least let it lie for a while. What about you?"

Steve paused, "I've been thinking about it today, Sarah finishes her course in four weeks. I can leave it until then and talk about things, unless the shit hits the fan first."

Leon, "If the shit hits the fan, I'm off with Gabi. We'll get out while we can, that's what I'm thinking now to be honest. We'd both be banged up, her forever."

Steve, "I'm the same. I could pack in and work with the security team, I'm getting funded by them now and doing nowt."

Leon was curious, "What would you do, security guard,

changing locks?"

"I was thinking private investigations, personal protection, rescue missions."

"Sounds good, any position for me?"

"Could be. Wait and see what develops when I meet up with Sarah. I might just stay where I am."

Later that evening Leon made a call to Gabi. They discussed their plans, living together, moving in Spain or away from Spain. Gabi told Leon that she had visited Jennifer and was now in possession of two black holdalls full of cash, that could be a help to them all. Gabi did not mention the discussion about Pantera.

CHAPTER 20

Thursday 15th June

It was mid-afternoon in Madrid. Steve was sat at his desk when Bert returned from an Operation Portcullis joint heads meeting at the Guardia headquarters. He briefly stopped at Steve's desk, "Time for a coffee and an update on Portcullis, can you get the coffee while I liaise with London?"

Steve was very interested in the update, "Yes of course Bert, ten minutes?"

"That should be good. Just come in, no secrets, you need to be aware of everything."

Steve made the coffee and waited for the call to be ended, he then entered Bert's office and took a seat.

Bert was leaning back in his chair, stretching his shoulders, "Well that was an interesting morning. As an aside, the fresh tortilla was very nice indeed, just a touch of added onion, much to my liking."

Steve couldn't give a flying fig as they say about how good the tortilla was, "I have been told they do good tortilla, anything else that was interesting by chance?"

Bert smiled, "I digress, but it was very nice. So, we had a good three hours going over the information, including your written report. They believe that they have identified some locations on the river Catatumbo from the aerial photography, these will be passed to the national Police of Colombia. The first thing you want to hear is that they will not be putting charges to your friend Juan, as you call him."

Steve, "That's excellent news, when will he be told?"

"They will be asking him to return to the headquarters tomorrow if he is available and he will be told then."

"Thank you Bert, I know you will have been persuasive in your discussions."

Bert was honest, "Do not thank me. They have completed the forensic examination; fingerprints of both men were found on the automatic weapon used and residue was found on the skippers clothing which verified what both of you had said. They believe that he had been pressured, blackmailed into going to Colombia, and after discussions with their prosecuting lawyers they decided not to proceed."

Steve was smiling, the plan had worked. "He will be relieved and able to continue with his fishing. It's all he ever wanted, the future of his family."

Bert continued, "They are really pleased, ecstatic I would say, at the outcome of the short operation. What a result Steve, you will get a lot of credit out of this. They're considering giving you an award."

Steve, "Really Bert, that's not necessary but appreciated."

"The only one part of the operation where they did not get the result they wanted, was the inclusion of Delgado and his OCG."

Steve was taken aback but reacted quick, "What about the video of him giving me the tickets at the airport?"

"Unfortunately, that is the only bit of evidence linking him to the operation. What does it prove? The only witnesses are Juan and yourself. The prosecutors decided against progression as it would possibly bring danger to Juan and yourself and it would probably result in you being identified as an undercover officer. Those facts outweighed the chances of a very unlikely successful prosecution."

"Were there no other links, or sightings, communications?"

"None. We believe all the communication was on the encrypted mobile networks. During the surveillances undertaken, Delgado was only seen once with Torres or Alvarez at the warehouse and nowhere near any drugs. The operation probably would have seen his involvement in the cargo from the iron ore carrier, but that was never completed as the diver died and he has never been found or identified. It's believed that Delgado would have been at the slaughter."

"Have they identified the main negotiator, the contact with the Colombians?"

"The Nacional, they believe that Delgado was the organiser. He had the contacts, and they had previous intelligence as did the Guardia."

"So, what happens now? Is that the end of the operation?"

Bert, "Yes. The operation that was planned is finished, it achieved its aims and excelled in terms of the quantities recovered and the results against two major OCG's. We move on now. Obviously, you will not be involved. Too close to home as they say with the participating groups in that area. They reckon that Delgado has left the country and probably gone to Colombia, there have been no new sightings of him."

"Permanently or keeping low."

"Unofficially, the word is permanently. Nacional have said, from a source, he and his team met some Colombians who arrived in a private jet near to Oviedo to discuss what had gone wrong with the cargo delivery. Bearing in mind everything had gone according to plan until the cargo was in sight of Vigo. Then the two other OCG's were involved in a gun fight of sorts. He is the only beneficiary so it is anticipated he will be blamed. So, I doubt if we will see him again."

Steve was slowly exhaling, "He will not be a miss and will be an easy target if he comes back."

"Between the Guardia and the Nacional, they're fighting over who can have the vessel if it can be salvaged. For two excellent teams that work well together, excuse the language, they fight like fucking idiots over results and mementos."

"I know the feeling, it's the same in the army. Each regiment wants the honour and prestige but, in a battle, side by side they couldn't give a toss as long as they win. Is Delgado married, is there anyone that would report him missing?"

"Nacional have been to his house and spoken to his wife, as usual, the lady was very pleasant, polite and told them nothing. She would probably be better off without him as well."

"Who were the Colombians, any ideas?"

"Put it this way, they didn't go through passport control, but they are believed to be the MMV cartel."

"Thanks for the update Bert, I'm really pleased for Juan, I'll say nothing to him about it. I've sorted out a flight for tomorrow evening back to Newcastle, I'll have a few days in the town then travel to London for the assessments on Thursday."

Bert opened his hands towards Steve, "Well done Steve, really amazing job you ended up doing. When you have finished today, don't bother coming in tomorrow unless there's something you need to do." Bert stood up and put out his hand, Steve stood and they shook hands.

"Again, thanks Bert."

Later that afternoon Steve made a call to Leon and passed on the good news.

Friday 16th June.

Jennifer had gone through the visitor process at the penitentiary. She had handed some clean clothing to the staff for her brother and was now in the queue for a glass visit.

She had just taken her seat as Lucas walked through the door, they were both smiling and obviously pleased to see each other.

Lucas, "My beautiful sister. It is good of you to visit me so soon, you look well Jennifer."

"I am Lucas, you look good yourself considering the circumstances."

"I have a comfortable existence, restricted but alive and

well. Do you have some comfort Jennifer?"

"I do, I'm very comfortable, very, and so are some of your friends. I have brought you some clean shirts and underclothes today."

"Thank you, have you spoken to Gabi?"

"Yes, Gabi sends her love and she is very grateful, she mentioned a name you might know."

"Yes, Andrés Palacio Zapata that is him; I have met him in Colombia. I went to his work place; he has a garage in Cali. He's a strong man, dark skin, very nasty man, he doesn't do work on cars in his garage. He gets answers." Lucas grimaced.

Jennifer repeated, "Andrés Palacio Zapata, I will remember his name. Gabi thinks you are a magician, making things disappear, she was very pleased."

"I am repaying a debt; it is fully paid now I think." Jennifer stayed for her allowed 60 minutes, she repeated the name several occasions.

Upon leaving the penitentiary, Jennifer made a call to Gabi.

Steve had packed a small suitcase, he didn't know how long he would be staying in England, he had more clothes in his apartment if they were needed. He had made a light lunch and was impatiently awaiting a call from Juan. He was ready to leave to head to the airport when he received the call, looking at the screen it was the one he was waiting for, he answered, "Buenos tardes Juan."

"Hello Steve, how are you?"

Steve was not giving his knowledge away, "I'm okay Juan, how are you, Veronica and your mother?"

Juan was keeping his surprise, "They are good thank you, have the Guardia been for you?"

"No, is there a problem I don't know about?"

"Yes, they took me back to the headquarters today."

"Why, what for now, what did they tell you?"

"Friend, they have dropped any prosecution. They know I was blackmailed to go on the journey."

"That's fantastic, did they mention me at all?"

"No, my friend, I asked about you but they would not give me an answer."

"Okay, I will have to wait a bit longer maybe, I'm not worried. Good news for you though, you can start fishing now."

"Yes, yes I can. You can still come with me if you want, we would work well together."

"Thank you Juan, but I'm keeping away from the sea for a while, maybe sometime in the future. Good luck mate. I will keep in touch."

"Thank you Steve, I hope everything will be good for you. You have done so much for me."

It was 8:30 that evening when Steve got out of the taxi at his apartment in Newcastle upon Tyne.

Leon had been waiting since he received a call from Gabi, he made a call to Steve, "Hi Leon, you have timed that well. I've just walked through the door of the apartment. You okay?"

"I am mate, is it good to be home?"

"I don't know yet, wait till I get to the pub! What's your news then?"

Leon passed the news, "Gabi has identified Pantera, she has his name, he has a garage in Cali and she is trying to locate the garage."

"That could be passed to the Santa Monica police, they could do something."

"She is wanting to get something done herself."

Steve was shaking his head in disbelief, "That's ridiculous, she would be identified in Colombia before she got anywhere near him"

"As usual, she has a plan."

"Leon, her plans are usually shit."

"I know, she is determined for revenge."

Steve reluctantly asked, "So, what is it this time?"

"It is simple, walk into the garage and kill him."

Steve was amazed, "Wow, how long did it take to think of

that?"

"Obviously not long, but I was thinking it could be done."

Steve was smiling, "Did you find any problems along the way? How is she going to get into the country? More importantly, how is she going to get out? Does she not think she will be identified?"

"She is not going, just me, and possibly you."

Steve started laughing, "Are you for real, really? You think it is that simple?"

"Where's the problem, Steve? We could do it"

"Leon, I know we might have forgot what we are for a while, but we are not contract killers."

"Steve, think about it, he killed Jessica."

"Look, stop there, I know what he has done and Greg Simons, we are not an execution squad, whatever you want to call it."

Leon, "We could do a Swedish job, fly in, hit, and fly out."

"Listen, I know she is desperate, if we know where he is why not inform the Santa Monica police, I'm certain they would do the necessary action."

Leon made a suggestion, "There's a flight tomorrow afternoon to Cali, we could be there Sunday, do the business and fly back on the Monday night flight."

Steve, "How do we explain our absence? Where would we get what we need when we get there, what if he isn't there?"

"I know what you are saying, but, if the cops American, Panamanian, locked him up, what kind of evidence would they have? He's not called Pantera for nothing, never seen, dressed in black, head to toe, deadly then disappears."

Steve, "He sounds familiar. I'll say it again, no more killing."

"Gabi has said if Pantera is out of the way, she would stop the revenge stuff on the other guy. We could live together, get on with life."

"Leon, it sounds like blackmail. Do you honestly think there's not another Pantera waiting to emerge from the jungle, another trained killer? Count me out on that plan, why not just get the police, they would probably end up killing him."

"Okay Steve, you're out, I just thought I'd ask. I've booked the flights, I'm going. It would have been good with you by my side. I understand mate."

"Leon, don't be stupid, you can't do it. Do you think he will be on his own, its madness, please mate?"

"Steve, it's okay, I understand how you feel, leave it there."

The call was closed.

Steve threw the mobile onto his bed, he walked to the fridge, opening the door, no beer, he slammed the door closed, "Fuck, fuck, fuck, shit." He left the apartment then took taxi to the quayside area.

CHAPTER 21

Saturday 17th June

Despite coming back to the apartment having drank far too many pints of assorted beers, topped off with a few large Laphroaig whiskeys, Steve had set the alarm that made him open his eyes. He was very tempted to roll back over but he forced himself to sit up. He felt rough, drink never helps, a thick head and a headache from over thinking, not drinking he believed. The inside of his mouth was feeling like the proverbial bottom of a budgies cage, it was so dry, sticky and dirty. In the quayside bars, amongst the vibrancy of youth with all of the continuous array of feminine distractions, the ear-splitting noise of the surround sound music and the thumping of the boosted bass that he could feel through his feet and legs, he had made a decision. He picked up the glass of water from the bedside drawers and drank the glass dry, getting off the bed he walked to the kitchen, refilled the glass and drank that one too. He put the kettle on, placed an espresso pod in the coffee machine and waited, leaning against the worktop. He knew his plan, going through it again as he waited. The coffee was in the cup but he didn't wait for the kettle to boil, just poured the heated water into his coffee. He collected his mobile, sat on the sofa and made a call.

"What time is the flight?"

Leon had been up for two hours, "Good morning mate, you're up early, you sound rough. 12:30 will you make it?"

Steve had a look at his watch, 07:12, "If I can get the flight from the town about nine I can. I'm not promising anything mate, I just don't want you getting into trouble unnecka," Steve couldn't pronounce the word, Leon was laughing, Steve continued slowly, "when you don't have to."

"Terminal 5 if you make it, stop off in New York."

"Okay."

Steve booked a British Airways flight from Newcastle to London Heathrow, leaving at 09:30 he would land at 11:00. He sent a text 'Land at 11' then walked into the shower, it was cold and what he needed.

He booked a taxi to the airport; he only had one small hand luggage case and a shoulder bag for his documents and electronic devices. He stopped off at Greggs inside the terminal and bought steak bakes, sandwiches and cookies for the two flights, buying extra rations for Leon. He had time for a take away coffee and a bacon sandwich as he waited to go to the departure gate. He sent another message to Leon confirming he was on time. He sent a message to Sarah, 'really missing you, having some quiet time away on my own, I need it. See you soon. X'

They met up in Starbucks in the departure lounge, it was a strange meeting, the shake of the hands and a fist pump.

Steve spoke first, "I don't honestly know what we are doing, but I couldn't let you go by yourself."

Leon was apologetic, "I'm sorry mate, I know I've more or less forced you into coming, I'm really glad you are here though."

Steve was sipping from his large mug of very hot, Americano coffee, "Like I tried to say earlier, I don't want you getting into any unnecessary trouble. We both have to look and assess the situation when we see it, figure it out and, well not so much as risk assess, because we wouldn't be fucking going would we," Leon was nodding his head and keeping quiet, "Try and find a method to deal with the situation without being killed by the Cartel or incarcerated by the Colombian police, that would definitely not be good."

Leon, "He is just one man, I know we could do something."

Steve, "I agree, but can we do something and get away? Do we have an address as yet?"

"Yes, she sent it to me during the night, just have to hope it's the right place."

Steve stood up, "Come on, we need books and maps on Cali. Remember, we are going on a recent history tour, we need to know where we are going, what there is to see and escape routes."

Two hours later, they are flying over the Atlantic sat next to each other in their black leather, extra leg room, premium economy side by side seats. Having finished their provided lunch, kale salad followed by slow roasted beef which was very tasty, Bert would have enjoyed it, plenty of onions, they both had a beer as they started to look through the city guides and street map.

Calle 94, in the area of Juanchito Guali was to the east of the city, inside a horseshoe of the Rio Cauco, from the limited map they had, it did not look an affluent suburb. There were only two vehicle entrances and exits, both leading to and from the route 3202A, they would need to check later with street level maps. They then both made time to catch up on their missing sleep for the rest of the journey to New York, slipping on the provided ear phones they listened to the music of their choice until they were both asleep.

After landing in New York, they had a few hours to wait for the connection flight to Cali. Steve took his tablet from his shoulder bag, when he obtained Wi-Fi, he looked on street level mapping. They both looked at the tablet which Steve placed between them on the table, their burgers and chips either side. It only took seconds for the ariel view of the area to appear on the small screen, he placed the walking man image onto the street he was looking at, near to the eastern junction of the 3202A. It was as anticipated, a poor area of the city, the road was not tarmacked, just a compressed, barren, brown, dusty uneven surface with potholes and bumps, it was thought to be about 15 metres wide. There was one row of buildings on each side of the dusty access route, the buildings on the left as the figure moved down the road, backed onto the river. The figure progressed down the road slowly, as they examined the buildings on both sides, they were poorly built with grey concrete bricks, some buildings had tiled roofs, others had wooden or corrugated iron roofs, mainly single level housing. There were not many cars evident but motorbikes were parked outside some of the buildings. The businesses that had been in the road appeared to be closed, with metal doors and shutters across the doorways and entrances, what appeared to have been an allotment area inside some wire fencing was overgrown and unattended. At the side of the fenced allotment, they believed they found what they were looking for, a two-story building with dirty, once cream coloured cladding. This was attached to a large single-story building with blue metal doors for vehicle access, an old metal sign with the paint cracking from the constant sun and heat was above the doors, 'Zapata Mecanica y Reparacion Autos'. There was waste land at the side of the garage where broken building materials, a dismantled car and other assorted rubbish had been accumulated. On the other side of the road the single-story ad-hoc built housing continued. Amazingly, 30 metres from the garage was a bar/café, with white plastic seats and tables outside, they were under an old tarpaulin sheet on scaffolding poles. Steve stopped eating his chips, "It's going to be difficult getting in there unnoticed, I make it about 250 metres from the main road."

Leon, "Agree, and possibly half a mile the other way back to the road. I didn't see any street lightening."

Steve nearly choked on his cola and laughed. "You're right, I forgot to mention that, but it would be useful possibly for any night time recce. I bet there's loads of dogs, got to be."

Leon, "Do you think the garage would be open when it was dark, what time will it get dark?"

Steve, "Not too late, sometimes 6 or 7, we can check that on the weather app." Steve did the check, "6:16, that's early, the businesses will still be open until later, they have an afternoon siesta, it's more comfortable to do anything on the cooler evenings."

Leon, "We just have to hope he's there and open."

"And no-one else there would be a big help. Anyway, how are we supposed to do it?"

Leon, "Put your coke down and I'll tell you." Steve put the coke down on the table, sat back in his chair, crossed his arms and looked at Leon and nodded. Leon continued, "This is serious, don't dismiss it straight away, it's a plan from Gabi." Steve raised his eyes but said nothing, Leon continued, "Her plan is, we buy some tribal blow pipes," Steve was struggling not to laugh, "apparently they are easy to get at the souvenir shops and we use them."

Steve interrupted, he couldn't control himself, unfolding his arms without smiling, "Are you fucking serious?" Leon went to speak, "Wait until I finish, this guy is a hitman, a fucking good hitman, who knows how many he has killed, he's probably armed to the teeth inside his buildings with automatic weapons, pistols, knives, whatever, and we are going to use a blowpipe, really Leon, that's the plan?"

Leon, "Now, you let me finish." Steve sat back in his chair and crossed his arms again. "Okay, we get close to him it will be silent, we hit him with poisoned darts, he dies and we leave quietly."

Steve, "Question one, where do we get the poison from, the local farmacia? or do you know a local tribe we can visit up the river?"

"I have what is needed with me."

Steve was shocked, "What, how," he was hit with a sudden realisation, "she hasn't, no fucking way?"

"Yes, she has." Leon was nodding his head.

Steve, "This is unreal, fucking hell, finish this meal, I need to think."

Leon, "No, you eat and listen, if you can do both," Steve glanced at him as he was taking a bite from his burger. "You were told about the frog poison, well she was given some by the natives, it was in a small plastic bottle, about the size of an old film container for a camera."

Steve, "She said she was drugged when she was taken away, so how wasn't it found."

Leon looked down towards his groin, "She put it somewhere."

"That was taking a risk, if it leaked." He paused for effect, "Why didn't she use the case for the camera instead of the film?"

Leon responded with a smile, "Bastard." They both started laughing, "I'll get a couple of beers."

"No wait, is it still in a plastic case?"

Leon, "It's been washed, if that's what you wanted to know. Anyway, no it isn't, she has put into a small travel aftershave bottle, I showed the security it at Heathrow in one of them little bags, no problem. She does think sometimes, it's called Bad." The laughter started again; Leon walked to the bar.

It was 11pm in Cali when they left Alfonso Bonilla Aragón airport, they took a taxi to the NH Hotel Cali Royal, a superior twin room had been booked for them for two nights.

CHAPTER 22

Sunday 18th June

It was an early start, 06:50, and after a coffee in the hotel breakfast bar they left the cool air of the foyer and walked into the heat and bright sunshine of a typical Cali morning. They were both wearing lightweight trousers, t-shirts, baseball caps, and sunglasses. They walked towards a waiting taxi. There was light traffic on the roads as they were driven towards the motorbike hire company which specialised in tours of Colombia. They hired two Yamaha XT 660R motorbikes which would be good on the city roads and on the rough roads where they were heading. They collected the touring maps and arranged for the bikes to be collected in a week from the hotel car park. They had paid the extra for a mobile phone holder to be attached to each bike, Leon installed the address in the sat-nav and within minutes, now wearing the open face helmets provided, they headed off towards the east of the city.

Leon led the way as they turned off the smooth surfaced route 3202A onto the uneven dirt road of Carrera 8. The speed was slow, as they both concentrated on the buildings either side of the track and the uneven rutted surface. There was no activity, two house front doors were open behind the metal gates which were closed, preventing anyone entering. They saw the house they believed to be the home and business of El Pantera, they maintained their speed as they slowly navigated the potholes and bumps in the surface. As they passed, there was no sign of life inside the house or garage, no cars or motorbikes were parked outside of either building. The two bikes were ridden slowly along the track, the bar was opening, one female was wiping the dirty chairs and table tops which had been covered in the dust from the track. She appeared to have ignored them as they continued towards the return junction of route 3202A. They had completed their first recce of his house and the area and had learnt a lot from what they had seen. Leon led the way, they parked outside a roadside café and stopped for breakfast.

Steve ordered Calentado, a dish of rice, mixed peppers, tomatoes, onions, and chorizo with a fried egg on top. Leon picked Caldo de Costilla from the menu photograph, a spicy beef and vegetable broth. They took a table outside in the early morning sun, the first early morning customers. They both had coffee delivered as they waited for their meals. Leon, "The bikes we have should manage that surface well if we need to need to get away quick."

Steve, "We know we can get out both ways, didn't look like any sign of life at his place. We would be noticed if we keep going down the track, it's a locals place."

Leon, "I probably wouldn't draw as much attention as you, if I walked through."

"You would be knackered if someone started talking to you." Leon nodded, Steve continued, "We knew it wouldn't be easy, it might take more than a couple of days. The garage he has mightn't open on Sundays, he might not be here. If he does turn up, what can we do? hopefully he will be on his own."

Leon was nodding his head, "Don't laugh again but I don't think the blow pipe idea will work. How much poison would be on the end of each dart? would it be enough to kill him in one go and would the dart things penetrate his skin through clothing?"

Steve, "Has Gabi told you about how she killed Borja."

Leon, "Of course, she poisoned him with an injection."

"There's one of the answers, there was an amount of

the toxin, more than would be on a dart, inside a syringe disguised as a pen. She injected him on the Biffins Bridge and he died very quickly within seconds."

"She told me it was in a hotel not a bridge."

Steve was smiling, "Sometime you surprise me and other times you really are thick. Biffins Bridge is the area between your balls and your arsehole that your balls bang on when you're doing the business, shagging."

"Never heard of it mate, must be a Geordie thing. How did she get the injection there?"

Steve, "You will have to ask her that. But, if we forget about the dart idea, we have the poison in a spray bottle, we could use that if we can get close enough but we would have to be careful not to spray ourselves, or better still buy some syringes from a local farmacia."

The two breakfasts were being delivered by a waitress; it stopped the conversation. As Steve picked up his cutlery, "We're going to need a couple of good knives as a secondary weapon." Leon nodded as he was eating his very hot and spicy broth which was burning the inside of his mouth.

Later that morning they returned to the hotel room; they had been shopping. Leon emptied the contents of the shopping bag onto the bed, two black belt bags with zips, a box of 10ml. insulin syringes with needles, a box of latex gloves, a pack of light blue surgical masks and two spring assisted black coloured pocket knives, with sharpened blades.

They both slipped on the latex gloves and face masks, Leon retrieved the bottle of aftershave from his case. Steve prepared four syringes by removing the red coloured safety plastic covers from the needles, they went into the bathroom. Steve, removed some tissue from the toilet roll and folding it over placed it flat on the bench next to the sink, he then stood back from the sink. Leon placed the bottle on top of the tissue, he slowly and very carefully removed the top from the small black aftershave bottle, he separated the top from the bottle and placed the top and the plastic tube onto the tissue.

Leon filled the syringes with 5ml of the toxin from inside the bottle and placed them on the tissue, the plastic safety cover was then replaced over the needles. The top of the aftershave bottle was replaced firmly, the syringes were placed inside the two belt bags, two in each. Finally, Leon picked up the clean tissue and wiped around the top of the perfume bottle to remove any toxin that may have escaped whilst being opened, then flushed the tissue down the toilet. Job done and they were still alive, Leon gave a sigh of relief then a fist pump with Steve.

They both fastened the belt bags in position for easy access, the knives were in their right trouser pocket, they had their plan, as Leon once said, "Simples." If they see him, attack if not totally outnumbered. When they returned to Carrera 8, Leon had a slow ride through the track back onto the 3202A, there was no sighting. Leon took a position near to the eastern entrance into the track, he was on the bridge overlooking the river watching someone fish, the sun was now at its highest. Steve was at the city end of the track, sat in the shade of a large advertising hoarding. They watched every vehicle, motorbike, and pushbike that entered onto the track, they were looking for a man with black skin, that's all they knew.

After more than two hours, Leon turned his attention from the fisherman when he saw a black Toyota Prado SUV slow down on the approach to his junction, there was a black man sat in the driver seat, shaven head, the rear windows of the car had been blacked out, this had to be him. He had called Steve as he saw the car, "It's him, I'm going in."

Steve didn't have a chance to say anything. As the call ended, he mounted his bike, he didn't bother with the helmet and started at speed towards the address.

Leon was following the cloud of brown dust that was being thrown up by the car, the brake lights illuminated as the car approached the properties and came to a stop outside of the metal doors of the garage, The driver got out of the car, it was him, it had to be, black skin, 1.80 tall, athletic, decision time.

The male walked towards the garage door, he was pulling it open as he heard the noise of the motorbike behind him and turned to look at the bike, Leon accelerated the short distance towards him. Pantera reacted in lightning speed and jumped to his left as the bike crashed into the blue steel gates throwing Leon onto the ground away from Pantera. Leon dropped the unfastened helmet to the ground as Pantera walked towards him, he jumped to his feet. Pantera was dressed in a dark electric blue buttoned collared shirt, dark blue jeans, there was no firearm visible. He didn't look as if he would need a gun, his face snarled as he approached Leon who held his arms out in front in a defensive position. Pantera swung a punch with his left fist towards the head of Leon, Leon blocked the blow with his right forearm, bone on bone, that hurt but he didn't flinch. Leon went to throw a retaliatory punch with his left fist as his left knee was kicked buckling his body, this was followed with a blow to the left side of the head of Leon, he stepped backwards away from his opponent who followed him, stalked him, another punch came from the left, Leon jumped inside the blow and headbutted Pantera in the right side of his face on his cheek bone, knocking him backwards. Leon was now the aggressor, a right punch into the ribs didn't appear to have an effect. Another left leg swing from Pantera into the right knee dropped Leon to his knee, Pantera followed up with a backwards right swinging elbow into his face, the nose burst, blood was flowing, he could taste it, he was dizzy, trying to focus and move, he was attempting to stand up, he felt the force of the right boot of Pantera to the left side of his head on the ear, he was falling backwards as Pantera was moving in on him. Leon fell to the floor and swung his right leg hard into the knee joint of his assailant, he could see it hurt him, Pantera was looking angry as he bent over Leon who was desperately swinging his arms to stop the assault as he lay on the ground. Pantera grabbed hold of the back of the head of Leon who was fearing the worst, he was being pulled up from the floor, a strong arm was around his neck, Leon was trying to shake his head in a desperate attempt to be released from his grip with no avail, he was lifted from the ground and dragged backwards towards the open garage door. Leon had his arms clamped in the vice like grip of Pantera who was also choking him as he was being dragged backwards inside the garage.

Steve slid the bike and jumped off as it continued along the dirt track, making more cloud dusts, he rushed the door and burst inside the garage. Pantera dropped the near unconscious Leon down onto the dirty oil-stained ground, Leon was desperately struggling to breathe and focus. Pantera faced his new opponent, he picked up a crowbar and began to swing it at head height towards Steve, who was forced to move backwards, the space was limited inside the garage, which had obviously not been used as a garage for some years, an old jeep was in the middle of the ground space with four lifting gear posts around it. The first swing hit into one of the posts with a loud crash, the second hit the pillar of the old jeep. Steve rushed between the swings hitting his shoulder into the chest of Pantera pushing him backwards and forcing him to drop the crowbar. He could feel the powerful, muscular body of his adversary as he pushed him into one of the posts, Steve was aggressively pushed backwards away from Pantera. Pantera picked up an acetylene torch and flicked it alight and started walking towards Steve with the red-hot flames licking towards his face, sweeping from side to side as Steve walked backwards, Pantera was smiling, he was winning. Steve pulled out his knife, it flicked open, Pantera grinned, looking at the small bladed knife, he pushed the flames longer towards Steve who was being cornered, he held the torch in his left hand and picked up the crowbar in his right hand. The red and green hoses were stretching across the garage floor near to Leon who was regaining his ability to breathe, he grabbed hold of the hoses and pulled them backwards forcing Pantera to turn away from Steve. He took his chance, he took the syringe out of his belt bag, flicking the safety cover from the needle with his thumb he pushed the needle into the fleshy, muscular tricep of the upper left arm and pressed the plunger into the syringe, it appeared to have no effect, Pantera walked towards Leon who was still on the ground. Steve moved quickly towards him and stabbed Pantera in the lower back, near to the kidney with the knife, he turned and looked into the face of Steve, there was pure evil in his face. Steve was believing this man is indestructible, the crowbar was directed at the head of Steve who jumped back away from the blow, Pantera followed him, the flames, the searing heat getting closer, he could feel the heat on his face. Pantera suddenly stopped, he was looking into the face of Steve, his facial expression was dropping, he collapsed onto the floor dropping the acetylene torch next to some old empty discarded cardboard boxes which started burning immediately. Steve stood over him, he could see the death in the eyes of Pantera, there was nothing in the dark brown unmoving eyes, "This is for Jessica, Greg, Gloria, the guards and many others, burn in the hell you will be in." Steve helped Leon to his feet. Leon was in pain but smiled with a grimace as he looked down on Pantera, "Fuck you, justice is done." Steve turned up the gas and watched the flames on the torch reach other combustible material that was scattered in the derelict garage, the inferno had started. They both left the garage, looking up and down the track, there was no-one to be seen, the house doors were closed, the woman came out of the bar. She looked in all directions then gave a small wave as they got onto their bikes, they rode slowly away from the quickly intensifying inferno of the funeral pyre that was developing inside the garage.

They returned to the hotel, the damaged bikes were parked in the underground secure car park, the damage would have to be paid for but that would not be a problem. They took the lift to their room; Steve didn't have any injuries but Leon was suffering. His face and head were sore and swollen, both of his knees were painful, but he felt good. Steve went to the nearby farmacia and bought pain killers while Leon lay in a cold bath.

Leon didn't think that pain killers would work, 'Jack' would help. He didn't usually drink spirits but there were two good reasons tonight, one was medicinal to alleviate the aches and pains, the second to celebrate an achievement.

Steve was quiet as he sat on the bed. He was thinking again, a few glasses of smoky Laphroaig which was available in the hotel bar would help. The thought of the smell from the whisky did a lot to cheer him up and smile, he was laughing as he said quietly to himself, "Laughing frog."

They stayed in the hotel that evening; Leon explained his injuries as having been involved in a street robbery. The hotel staff readily accepted his explanation, it was a common occurrence in the city. They had a table out of view of most of the other hotel guests. When they saw Leon's facial injuries, they kept their distance. Their evening meal consisted of large steaks, chips, Jack Daniels and Laphroaig, also known as 'the frog' by Steve.

Steve, "What are you going to do now?"

Leon, "I'm done now, no more for me. I'm packing in and moving in with Gabi, getting out while I can, that was too close, too scary mate. What about you?"

"I don't know mate, honestly. I want to stay with Sarah, see how that works out, it's good at the moment, but she doesn't really know me, I don't know me now. We have been lucky but it could still go pear shaped somewhere."

Leon was thinking, "There is a load of cash, millions I'm talking about, Gabi has loads of cash, she doesn't need any more, take some and make a new life together."

"I couldn't Leon, it's money from crime it wouldn't be right."

"You're funny, won't take money but will kill."

"The killing was in self-defence, a necessity."

"How was killing Pantera a necessity?"

Steve smiled, "I was going to arrest him, but he attacked me with a crow bar and an acetylene torch, anyway he would have killed you if I hadn't come into the garage."

Leon looked Steve in the eyes, "You're smiling, I thought I was a dead man, that choke hold, I couldn't do a thing, he would have snapped my neck, I'm sure."

They chinked their glasses of spirits together.

Steve continued, "How are you going to explain your injuries when we get back to the UK?"

"I'll not explain, I'll go to my doctors and get a sick note, depression, anxiety, stress, tell him I'm drinking too much and just disappear then send in my resignation."

They were quiet for a few seconds, Steve, "If you tie up with Gabi, I'll not see you again, I think I might miss your company."

Leon asked, "Why will we not see each other?"

"I could hardly bring Sarah to your place by the sea for the weekend, could I?"

"I see what you mean, will you two be okay, will you tell her anything?"

"I'll tell her what Bert knows, nothing more, she wouldn't like it or accept it, anything to do with Gabi would finish us, I'm sure."

They sat at the table for a few hours and savoured 'Jack' and 'The Frog'.

CHAPTER 23

Friday 14th July

He was waiting at the arrivals gate at Madrid Barajas airport. The flight had landed 25 minutes earlier, he saw the person he was looking for walk around the corner from the baggage reception area towards the exit gate. His heart was pounding, he knew he could not be seen, he was hidden behind others who were waiting, watching impatiently for their family or friends to arrive. Pushing the trolley with one large suitcase, a flight case and a shoulder bag, totally unaware of the observation, the passenger continued towards the gate. He stepped in front of the trolley and reached out his arm, he was holding a large bunch of dark red roses.

Sarah saw the roses first, then Steve, they embraced each other and kissed, in public. Steve looked into her smiling blue eyes, "I have missed you so much, so much." they hugged again.

Sarah replied, "Not as much as I've missed you."

Steve pushed the trolley, as Sarah carried her roses towards the taxi rank.

He had prepared a meal for Sarah's return, he wanted to keep the conversation for later, but Sarah had questions.

Steve poured the Rioja red wine into large glasses and handed one to Sarah, they sat on the sofa together. Sarah asked, "I don't want to do a lot of talking but what has happened to Leon? Lauren is really upset that he hasn't been in touch since he went on that job."

They had spoken before on the calls they had made; Steve knew it would be asked again and had prepared himself. "Leon had enough of the job, it was getting to him so he decided to pack it in, he wanted to travel. He should have told Lauren, no excuse."

"Have you spoke to him."

Steve continued his story, "I haven't seen him since the job finished, I'll tell you the full story about the job another time. I know he was annoyed, then when he got back to his office, they wanted him to do another job straight away, they said he had been on a holiday on the job we were doing. He gave me a call and told me he was packing in, we spoke about it, but he didn't change his mind, put his ticket in and left."

Sarah pushed, "Is there another woman, I know what he was like?"

Steve lied, "Not that I know of, but I didn't see him for the time I was away so who knows."

Sarah was curious and pushed again, "Steve, I know it was a tough job, is there anything you haven't told me?"

"I was going to tell you tomorrow, I wanted to have a nice night together, welcome home private party, will you wait until tomorrow?"

"No, Steve. If there is something I should know about I want to know now, please. Then we can continue our party."

"Okay, but I will keep it brief. You know most of it, I've already told you. When I was in the jungle with the two other men, the young lad Pepe was killed, he accidently knocked over a guard, they thought he was getting his gun. They stripped him, tortured him, then killed him and threw his body into the river. Listen, you can read all of this when you get to the office on Monday."

"That's shocking, you must have been affected somehow. Did you tell the psychiatrist about it?"

"Of course I did, it's not every day you see something like that, so cruel, vicious, the memory will last for ever, but I'll get over it."

"So just two of you to bring the submersible thing over the Atlantic? what happened then?"

"When we had unloaded the cocaine onto the boat, I pulled the plug I suppose and the thing started sinking quick. Juan, the other bloke, he had climbed onto the boat beforehand thank God."

"What do you mean, thank God. What happened?"

"As I was climbing out, they tried to kill me, shot at me as I was about to leave. The boat was leaving without me and the submersible was sinking very quickly, I thought I was gone. Then Juan got a gun off the deck of the boat and killed all of them on the boat and stopped it then pulled me on the boat."

Sarah was looking in astonishment at Steve, her mouth was open, there was a silence. "Why haven't you told me this before? I should have known."

"I couldn't, it would have interfered with your course, I even told Bert not to say anything to you."

"That Juan, he saved your life."

"He did, he definitely saved my life. Then they were going to prosecute him, Leon and I lost our rags and said he should be commended, not getting done. He had been compromised, blackmailed to do the run, he's not into drugs or any crime."

"Can we go and see him?"

"No, we cannot. Anyway, they've now dropped the proceedings against him, but he doesn't know I'm a polis."

"Holy Moly Steve, are you all right now?"

"Yeah, I'm okay now."

"But Leon wasn't involved like you were."

Steve took a sip of his wine, "Leon blames himself, because he was going to collect the drugs and we decided to change, it was my decision, he was sickened by all of the killing that's happened on this job and the last one. It was getting to him."

"But he didn't do any killing, he wasn't involved."

"We both know that," he lied "but there has been a few, I reckon about 15 or more, including the group from A Coruña who have gone missing."

"You should have told me Steve, but why not a call to Lauren?"

"I don't know, his head was done in, he just wanted to leave everything behind. He doesn't contact me now; he's changed his mobile. Can I get on and cook the meal now?"

"Before the meal, is there anything else I should know about while I've been away?"

"No, I've told you everything, you can see it in the report on Monday if you don't believe me, Bert will tell you anyway. Now can I cook the meal?"

"Yes, we can do it together."

Leon had recovered from his injuries and was living with Gabi in the villa. They had planned to move from the villa to find a new home together, leaving the past behind. Gabi had arranged with her legal advisor and accountant to place her money into an offshore account and to maintain a 'living' fund into one account for each of them. The accountant would place money into the account on a regular basis when the money had been cleaned. Gabi had given explicit instructions to the legal advisor for actions to be undertaken with other cash sums, which would benefit others known to her and Leon.

Everyone was looking ahead, as Steve once quoted, 'Don't waste time looking back, you're not going that way'.

AFTERWORD

Spanish authorities successfully recovered a narco-submarine that was captured off the coast of Galicia near to Vigo in November 2019. This was the first time any country in Europe has seized one of these smuggling vessels and it's not entirely clear how it made the thousands-of-miles-long journey from Latin America.
Spain's Guardia Civil, National Police, and Customs Service captured the vessel after it was seen by using night view equipment. The crew had attempted to scuttle it after failing to transfer the three tons of cocaine onboard to another vessel due to poor weather.

The Guardia and Nacional police went to court to determine which Department would own the rights to the vessel recovered. The court decided in favour of Nacional.

BOOKS IN THIS SERIES

No-one said it would be easy

Crime thrillers following the overseas investigations of Detective Sergeant Steve Bond. From an initial muder enquiry in latin America, Steve gets involved with further murder and large scale drug importations investigations involving the Cartels and European Organised Crime Groups. He works together with local Newcastle upon Tyne and NCS colleagues in the UK, as well as the Guardia Civil and Nacional Poliicia in Spain and officers from several other countries. A constant test of his skills physically and psychologically in dangerous and threatening situations.

Tropical Passion Killer

A chance meeting of two young men from the UK and two young latin american women on a cruise, starts a series of events, which lead to Police Departments in five countries working together on different time scales.
The start from a murder enquiry, leads onto several other murder investigations, large scale drug importation by the drug cartels and corruption.
Steve Bond is the central figure and link.

Devils Crossroads

Steve Bond enjoyed working overseas and is accepted by the NCA to work in Madrid. he is working with his colleague Sarah from the Newcastle upon Tyne office. Together they instigate the operation, Devils Crossroads, which is initially dealing with the large scale movement of drugs from Spain to the North of England. Several International OCG's are involved in the area, competing together for the large distribution sales. Steve and Sarah work with the Guardia Civil and Nacional Policia in the major investigation which uncovers so much more.

El Pantera

The past meets the present. What would you do?